For . . . ,
with love,
Jen

Changing Perspectives

Jen Silver

Changing Perspectives

Jen Silver

Affinity
eBook Press
NZ
2017

Changing Perspectives
© 2017 by Jen Silver

Affinity E-Book Press NZ LTD
Canterbury, New Zealand

1st Edition

ISBN: 978-0-947528-79-9

This is a work of fiction. Names, character, places, and
incidents are the product of the author's imagination or are
used fictitiously and any resemblance to actual persons living
or dead, businesses, companies, events, or locales is entirely
coincidental

Editor: JoSelle Vanderhooft
Proof Editor: Alexis Smith
Cover Design: Irish Dragon Designs

Acknowledgments

I have been asked, as writers often are, where do you get your ideas? For this story I could answer, the supermarket. I was walking down the BDSM aisle when this idea fell off a shelf into my basket.

The real answer is more complicated. Working in London in the late 1980s/early 1990s, I came into contact with a great mix of people and, particularly relevant to this story, advertising agency creatives and business executives from large corporations. Seeing a woman dressed completely in leather walking down the street sparked the idea. Who was she? Where did she work? Was she into SM? (Plain SM in those days; the BD was added later.) Miss Whiplash had featured in the news during that time, so this was clearly in my mind.

I started writing the story in 1993, and when I revisited it a few years ago and thought about how to expand it into a novel length, I decided that 1993 was where it should stay. It's very much of its time. The Internet was in its infancy, not everyone had mobile phones, and social media had yet to be invented.

This is my seventh novel published by Affinity Rainbow Publications. Although *Changing Perspectives* is very different to the previous six books, I am once again thankful to the Affinity team, especially their beta readers who responded so positively to the story.

Dedication

To my characters, Dani and Camila.
May they continue to enjoy their "hopeful ever after".

Table of Contents

Chapter One

London, 1993

The bar was noisy, hot, overcrowded, and smoky. Dani stood by the door; she had found a niche where she could observe the room and the comings and goings, without getting her drink jostled out of her grasp. It was a typical Friday night crowd for this particular bar. Not one of her favourite places, but Penny had convinced her she should get out a bit. And where was Penny now? She had accompanied Dani here and then said she had to go home. Well, why not? She had someone to go home to, even if it was that stuck-up cow, Astrid.

They had been working late to finalise the wording on the print media ads for the all-important Redmond pitch on Monday. Dani appreciated Penny's willingness to stay behind to work on the copy. Her two young assistants in the art department had other plans for the evening and although she could have pulled rank and insisted they work late, she let them go. She could finish up the artwork on Monday morning. The storyboards for the television ad only needed a few extra scenes.

She took another swallow of her drink. It was in danger of going flat from the heat of her hand. The beer on tap was never very good in here anyway and she wished she had ordered a bottled lager. Her eyes wandered around the room.

Six months gone and she still looked for Trish everywhere—on the street, in shops, on buses and the Tube—and sometimes thought she glimpsed that tantalising streak of gold. She couldn't explain this obsession to anyone, let alone herself. They'd had fun while it lasted, but in the end there was the usual issue. Trish did the taking, enjoying what Dani gave her, but she couldn't give Dani the satisfaction she needed. The start of the relationship was filled with constant excitement, discovering the many ways she could please her new lover. But when Dani let her know what she desired, Trish turned away, couldn't face her, and wouldn't even discuss it.

"Hey, Dani!" She looked down at the girl in front of her and smiled in recognition. It was impossible to be heard without shouting, so she didn't waste words, just pulled the smiling face towards her own and kissed it full on the mouth. Dani could feel the heat of the other woman's crotch through her jeans as she pressed her leg between willing thighs.

"So where have you been, Sal?" she breathed into her ear.

Sal pulled back and stared at Dani. Her eyes tracked down to the front of her jeans, then she looked back up at Dani, eyebrows raised questioningly. Dani shook her head. "Not tonight. Just cruising." She knew what Sal's look meant. For years she hadn't gone to any club without wearing a dildo. It had been her trademark and had gone down well with the femmes at the time. But for as many years now she hadn't bothered.

"Can I get you a drink?" she mouthed. Sal nodded and Dani started to push her way through to the bar.

Then she saw her.

Trish was leaning against the wall next to the bar, eyes unfocused, staring into space. Dani couldn't stop herself; she found herself standing in front of Trish. The six months might never have been. Trish looked tired; Dani just wanted to take her in her arms and tell her how much she loved her. That they could try again. Pure habit moved her to reach out and touch Trish, gently, on the cheek.

Trish's face relaxed into a smile briefly before she started shaking her head and saying no. Too late Dani realised she wasn't saying the word to her. A large hand on her shoulder spun her round and she found herself face-to-face with a grim-looking dyke wearing a studded leather vest. She only caught a glimpse of one of the tattoos on the large arm as it swung out and caught her on the side of the head.

Dani didn't know how many times she was hit. She heard Trish pleading with her attacker to stop before she passed out.

When she came to she was sitting on the pavement outside the bar with her head between her knees. And she was alone. With some difficulty, she stood and steadied herself on a meter. *About all a parking meter in central London is good for these days.*

Several minutes passed before a taxi appeared. With the state she was in, she was surprised when it stopped. The driver even asked which hospital she wanted to go to. She shook her head and gave him her address. During the journey across town, she closed her eyes and tried to block out the various pain points on her face and the ones spreading through her torso.

"You should get that looked at, love," he said, offering more sympathy while she eased herself out of the seat. She thanked him and said she knew a few nurses. Dani stumbled up to her door, dug her keys out of her jacket pocket, and let herself into the dark hallway.

†

Penny sat on the edge of the bed lacing up her trainers. Astrid stood by the door glaring at her. She was already dressed and ready to leave.

"Look, Pen, it's not our problem."

"Yes, it is. Mine anyway. I left her there."

"What you were doing there is what I'd like to know."

"We've been through all that. I was only keeping Dani company."

"She's old enough to go into places like that on her own."

"Yeah." Penny stood and picked her jacket off the chair where she'd abandoned it only a few hours earlier. "I'm sorry, love," she said, knowing no amount of saying sorry could make amends. "You don't have to come. I just feel responsible for Dani, having left her there," she finished lamely at the stony look on Astrid's clear, finely chiselled features.

"Right!" Astrid exploded, predictably. Penny didn't even flinch; she just stood looking down at her shoes waiting for the inevitable tirade. "She's over thirty. She makes more money in a week than you make in a year, yet you're responsible because her life's a fucking mess! I didn't realise you wanted to be a social worker."

Penny started for the door. She made her living as a copywriter, writing words for other people to use, but sometimes she couldn't find words for herself. She couldn't

4

expect Astrid to feel ecstatic about her friendship with Dani right now. They had been on the verge of drifting off to sleep when Dani phoned. At first, she thought it was a drunken prank. She could barely hear what Dani was saying. Eventually she worked out that Dani wanted her to go to the chemist for her. And she wasn't mumbling because she was drunk.

Finding a place to park on Dani's street wasn't easy. Finally, Penny decided to take a risk and park in a "permit holders only" spot. They walked along the road to Dani's house. It was mid-row in a tall terrace backing onto the river. Penny never ceased to be amazed that Dani lived in such an upmarket part of London; that she owned this expensive pile of bricks and mortar in an area where Penny couldn't have rented a studio flat, even sharing. Most people at the agency thought Dani lived in a squat or a cardboard box from the way she dressed and her general attitude to the commercial world.

Dani had left the door on the latch. Penny pushed it open and walked in, followed closely by Astrid who clutched the bag of bandages and pills.

"Dani," called Penny. A light was on in the room at the back of the house. Penny went down the hall and found Dani slumped in an armchair facing the open french windows. It was a fresh night with a breeze coming off the river. Penny shivered, in spite of her fleece-lined leather jacket. "Dani," she said again, and walked around the furniture to face her.

"Oh shit!" She dropped to her knees in front of Dani's chair.

"Might as well be at work." Astrid put down her paper bag and went into the kitchen. Penny could hear her filling the kettle, still muttering about Friday nights in A&E.

Dani opened her eyes, as far as she could, squinting at Penny. Dried blood caked her nose, lips, and chin. Astrid returned with a bowl of hot water and sent Penny off to make an ice pack with as many ice cubes as she could find.

An hour later, with Dani cleaned up as much as possible and laid out in bed asleep, Penny and Astrid sat together in the sitting room.

"I'd better stay with her."

Astrid sipped the coffee she'd made and regarded her lover thoughtfully. "Why do you always think the worst of me?"

"What do you mean?"

"I mean, you think I'm going to abandon you, go home to the comfort of my own bed, just because I don't like Dani. Do you think I'll really leave you here in this state?"

"I'm not in a state."

"No, of course not."

They sat in silence for a bit. Astrid broke it saying, "Why does she do it?"

"Do what? I don't think she wanted to get beaten to a pulp."

"She must have done something. Whoever did this to her wanted to hurt her, badly. I know she attracts fights. She might as well have 'hit me' written on her forehead. I've seen her in action, remember?"

Penny remembered. The incident Astrid had witnessed had been at a party, at another friend's house. "That was different. And it wasn't her fault."

"It never is." Astrid put her empty mug on the table. "But believe me, every time she sets foot outside the house wearing black leather gear, people will assume she's itching for a fight. Look, Pen, those bruises on her ribs, I'm surprised she hasn't got any broken ones. She was obviously kicked after she'd gone down, a number of times, savagely. Maybe she just picked a fight with the wrong person, or several people."

Penny closed her eyes. She still felt sick. She had almost got used to Dani's battered face, after Astrid had cleaned the blood off. When they undressed her to put her to bed, the bruises on her body had come as a second shock to Penny. She also had hand-shaped marks on her upper arms; Astrid suggested she'd been held while someone used her face for a punch bag. That was when Penny had rushed to the bathroom and vomited.

"But why? Who would want to do this to her? And why didn't anyone stop it happening?"

"Things like that can happen quickly. People are generally slow to react to situations where they might put themselves at risk." Astrid spoke with the confidence of an experienced paramedic. "Especially in a bar; especially, perhaps, in that particular bar. Anyway, we'll have to wait until she regains consciousness and can tell us about it. Come on. Let's go and crash in the spare bedroom. I take it there is one."

Penny slept fitfully and got up several times to check on Dani. The second time she returned to bed, Astrid was awake. She put her arms around her and they held on to each other until they both fell asleep again. But it wasn't a restful night. Astrid had to work a shift on Saturday. She left at six thirty, taking the car so she could get washed and changed. She promised to bring Penny a change of clothes when she returned.

†

Dani regained consciousness and immediately wished she hadn't. Every part of her body hurt; parts she didn't even know existed. After a few moments she established that she was in her own bed, alone.

She tried to sit, groaned and fell back. She didn't understand why her face hurt, along with her upper arms and ribs. Her left eye wouldn't open and the right one hardly at all. Just enough to know it was daylight. Then she heard a voice above her.

"Dani? Can you hear me?"

It was, she realised with relief, Penny.

"Yes." At least that was the sound she tried to make. Her lips felt swollen and she wasn't sure if she moved them.

"It's okay. Don't try to say anything. You don't look as bad as you did last night. The swelling's gone down a lot. And Astrid says that by tomorrow you'll look almost normal." Dani could hear the catch in Penny's throat. "Except for the black eyes and a few other bruises. She says you're lucky not to have broken anything. Your ribs are pretty badly bruised, but I suppose you can feel that."

Dani digested this information with her right eye closed. She tried again to open it; she could just make out Penny's shape against the light from the window.

"I'm sorry, Dani. I shouldn't have left you there."

"Where?" she managed to croak.

"At that bar."

Images flashed through her mind: Sal in heat; seeing the face that had haunted her dreams. "Trish!"

"Trish? You saw Trish? Is that what this is all about?"

"Mm."

"Did you talk to her?"

"No."

"So what happened?"

"Reached out. Only…wanted…hold…" Her whole body convulsed. Christ, the pain! Penny held her hand. She could feel her own tears, but she didn't really know who she was crying for.

Dani sent Penny home telling her it would be all right; she wasn't going anywhere. Penny made her promise to call if she needed anything. After a shower and change into a loose-fitting tracksuit, Dani knew she could cope on her own. She would need to make it up to Penny and Astrid, having dragged them out in the middle of the night.

Most of the rest of the weekend passed in a blur of lying in bed, dozing, and drinking gallons of water, as per Astrid's instructions. She tried walking about occasionally to keep from stiffening up, but she could only take the pain in short bursts. She could handle pain usually; she even enjoyed it. But this wasn't a good-feeling pain. Several hours passed as she stared at the river. It was the quietest weekend she could remember spending in a long time. Since Trish left. Somehow, alone with only her thoughts for company—and she didn't want to keep company with most of these, as a lot of them centred around Trish. Thinking about the relationship they'd had, or tried to have, it had been doomed from the start she realised now—although for a time she did think they could get past their differences.

Watching the muddy water flow past the end of her garden, she wondered why it was people never appreciated what they had until it was gone. Irretrievable. Like the flowing river, there was no turning back.

Trish had wanted her, in the beginning. They'd made love everywhere that year. And not often in bed. Dani had finally suspected Trish of being an exhibitionist; she enjoyed the danger of "doing it" in public places. She would take Dani's hand and ask her to kiss her; on the street, in the shops, on the Tube. And it didn't stop with a kiss.

Dani had loved every minute of it; she wanted the world to know this was her woman. She wanted the world to know she fucked her and made her happier than any man could, or any other dyke. And through all this, Dani knew it couldn't last. There wasn't going to be a fairytale ending. Trish was never going to take Dani the way she wanted, fulfilling her deepest cravings. At thirty-six years old, Dani thought it unlikely she would meet anyone who could, other than on a part-time, pay-for-the-pleasure, basis.

The phone rang. Dani thought the caller would give up in the time it took her to reach it.

"Dani?" Gordon's voice brought her sharply into the present moment. "Glad I caught you in. You're not sitting at home reading a book, are you?"

"No, just a little yoga and meditation." At least her voice sounded normal.

He continued as if she hadn't spoken. "As I didn't see you before I left on Friday, I thought I'd better check that you remembered the client meeting tomorrow."

"Would I forget?"

"I see you haven't lost your sense of humour, unfortunately. Look, pea-brain, do me a favour. Ten o'clock at Redmond's sharp. Oh, and best behaviour. I've been warned they're bringing in their finance director, Callaghan."

"Why?"

"To make sure we don't overextend ourselves on the budget."

"I thought you and Robert had that sorted."

"They've got a new brand manager and the top brass are probably a bit nervous about it. This is a big project, so I guess they're just being careful. Oh, and no jeans, please!"

"Wearing jeans to a client meeting, I wouldn't dream of it."

Gordon didn't rise to the mock outrage in her tone. "I'm serious."

"So am I. Hope they don't mind the panda look, though."

"Fine. Come dressed as a bear if you think it will help with the account." He rang off before she could explain. Dani started laughing and couldn't stop, even though her ribs hurt like hell.

†

She was in the office at seven. Gordon's call had not only reminded her of the client meeting she'd totally forgotten, but more importantly of the artwork left unfinished on Friday evening. Dani shut herself in her office with a large cup of black coffee. Declan and Gary arrived at nine but knew better than to walk in on the boss on a Monday morning until she emerged and greeted them.

At nine thirty she packed the storyboards into her portfolio and walked out to meet Gordon. The boys looked up at her and stared, open-mouthed. She willed them to silence with her eyes and continued through to Reception. Gordon had, she discovered, already left. She took a taxi to Redmond's offices. It wasn't far, but she didn't feel up to walking.

The receptionist repeated her name several times, as if the incantation could make her disappear. It was a shame, she thought, she had made an effort with her attire. She liked wearing leather, liked the smell, the sexy feel of it between her legs, the jangle of chains against her thighs. She was even wearing a clean T-shirt under her black leather jacket; no holes and a reasonably polite, if faded, message.

The girl stood finally and said, "I will take you up to the boardroom."

"Thanks." Dani picked up her portfolio case and followed her. Nice tight bottom in a short black skirt—the London secretary's uniform.

"Uh, this is it. I will leave you to it, then."

Dani attempted a smile, but it hurt too much, so she settled for a friendly lip curl. The girl fled back to the safety of her reception desk.

Gordon was standing by the coffee urn and talking to another suit when she entered the room. Dani put her case flat on the table and went over to join them. "I'll have a coffee, thanks, Gordon."

He turned round. "Jesus Christ!"

Dani turned to look back at the doorway. "Oh, is he coming too. I thought it was just the FD."

"Not even remotely funny." He handed her a cup of black coffee and hissed in her ear. "I'll kill you later."

Chapter Two

Camila Callaghan finally felt she had achieved success in her career. It was still a struggle to make sure she maintained her standing, but she felt it always would be, regardless of her gender. Five foot four inches in her stockings, she added a few inches in her best heels and managed to make her presence felt in the company with an always-immaculate and stern demeanour.

Making the move to the Redmond conglomerate five years ago had been a big step up, but she had met all the challenges head-on. The family business being carried forward effectively by the two brothers, Eric and Carl, continued its expansion into new markets, not only domestically but globally.

Eric asked her to attend the advertising meeting to make sure the marketing department didn't get carried away on budget. The agency, having got the contract, would now be pushing for juicy extras— posters, direct mail, brochures, T-shirts, mugs, pens. The million-pound budget on the TV, radio, and newspaper adverts alone wasn't adequate to cover these essentials, so they would have their client believe. Josh Soper, the brand manager on this particular project, was barely out of nappies, and the brothers felt he needed babysitting.

Camila was the last to arrive in the boardroom. They were all seated with cups of coffee and notepads in front of them; all rose like a flock of seagulls from the rubbish tip when she walked in.

"This is Ms Callaghan, our director of finance." Robert's introduction was unnecessary. They all knew who she was and why she was there. Robert's young assistant, James, quickly got her a cup of coffee and placed it delicately in front of her as she sat and took time to arrange her own paperwork. She gave the boy a smile of encouragement. It couldn't be easy working for that creep, Robert. She looked around at the rest of the assembly.

Gordon McKenzie she had met before at some PR event; maybe it had been Ascot. It was, she recalled, his agency. He was very successful—typifying the yuppie of the late '80s and early '90s; his desk-size Filofax lay open in front of him, and the face of an imitation Cartier watch glinted from the edge of his spotless white cuffs adorned with gold cufflinks, initialled no doubt.

The leather-clad creature beside him had to be the creative one. At least they hadn't come mob-handed; a sign they weren't planning to push for too much too soon. McKenzie was no fool. Camila was probably going to find she was surplus to requirements at this meeting. Robert wasn't going to want her opinion on the artwork.

Gordon cleared his throat. "As I was saying before you arrived, Ms Callaghan, we are just going to have a look at the storyboards that have been worked up from the promotion statement Josh provided us with. Our art director, Dani Barker, will present them to you." They all turned towards

Dani, who was looking down at the table, and waited expectantly.

It continued to amaze Camila that, just by virtue of being able to draw, these people could wear what they liked, be rude to everyone, clients included—some would say, especially clients—and the more outrageous their behaviour, the more talented they were perceived to be. At least this one didn't have a ponytail and earrings in one ear. Dani looked up and caught Camila staring.

Camila was shocked, and she was sure it showed. Two black eyes and some other purplish-yellow bruises around the mouth; not a pretty sight. But she couldn't keep her eyes off Dani's face. She continued to watch, fascinated, not hearing a word of the presentation. Only when Dani sat down and Robert and James passed the boards over for closer inspection did Camila realise, with another jolt, that Dani was a woman. She suppressed a shudder of revulsion. How could a woman get herself into that state? Camila gave the storyboards a quick glance and passed them to Josh. They made no impression on her; she didn't make artistic decisions.

Robert jumped in with the question that must have been hovering in the air above her head. "How much is this going to cost?"

Gordon smiled. Thankfully, with Robert's prewarning that the high-powered bitch was attending the meeting, he was prepared. "Production costs will be much lower than we predicted initially because of the use of animated graphics." He looked at Dani for agreement but she was slumped in her chair with her eyes closed. He kicked her ankle viciously under the table and carried on smoothly. "And our media buyer got a good deal on airtime for prime-time radio and TV slots."

"When can we see the schedules?" asked Robert.

"As soon as we get them, we will pass them on to you."

"How much of a saving are we talking about?" Camila's question cut through the cosy camaraderie between him and Robert. He sensed she was aware they'd cooked this little act up between them. From the look on Josh Soper's face, he didn't have a clue what was going on.

Gordon shot his cuffs, straightened his already much-straightened tie, looked her in the eye and said, "About two fifty."

"About?" She looked through him.

"Definitely no less than two fifty."

"And what were you planning to do with this money?"

"Robert and I haven't discussed details yet, but we thought a poster campaign in carefully targeted areas in the South East would—"

"So you're saying you can do this advertising campaign, production, airtime and print media, all in for £750K?"

"Yes, but—"

"No hidden extras—like charging for dupes or changes to artwork?"

"Of course not."

"Good. That settles that nicely. Well done, Josh, Robert." She gathered up her papers and stood. They all rose with her, except Dani.

Gordon attempted another gambit. "But the campaign will be more effective with a few posters—"

"And some brochures, point of sale, yes, I agree. But you didn't pitch for that. If we want you to do anything other than the ads we have agreed on, we will let you know, but quite frankly I think you will be too expensive." She left the room.

†

No one said anything for several minutes. Dani collected the boards and put them back in her case. She was aching all over and thought a drink would go down well, but it didn't look like anyone was going to offer.

"I'll send you the production schedule," Gordon said listlessly, closing his Filofax. "What are you grinning at?" he said suddenly, catching sight of Dani's face. Dani had merely grimaced in pain.

"She's got you lot by the balls, hasn't she? Look, I'll leave you these roughs I've mocked up for some poster ideas. You can run them by her some other time. Okay? Coming, Gordon? I've got other things to do today, even if you haven't."

"Yeah, like running into doors."

Robert laughed. Dani turned her blank panda stare on him and he stopped. She stalked out of the room ahead of Gordon, knowing he would take a few minutes commiserating with Robert before saying goodbye.

Dani put her case down, leaning it up against the reception desk. She perched on the edge to make a call to the office using the already scandalised receptionist's phone. "Declan? Have you finished the Bentley job? Good. Get the copy from Penny and bike it over to them. You've got the contact name." She paused to listen. "None of your fucking business!" Dani slammed the receiver down. The receptionist had moved her chair back and was staring at her, no doubt wondering if asking her to get off her desk would be safe. She was saved from finding out by Gordon's arrival.

†

Camila reached the sanctity of her office and sat down shakily in her chair. She had managed to keep it together as she walked away from the meeting room. Those eyes. They had drawn her in despite the bruising. The woman handled herself with confidence, as if she didn't care how others viewed her.

Talking down the agency's expectations had helped her regain her equilibrium. But try as she might to concentrate only on the numbers, she was aware of Dani's presence throughout. It was ridiculous to think she was remotely attracted to such a woman. Camila took a deep breath. Her interest was merely fascination. The art director was a curiosity.

She looked at her diary and noted the next meeting in Eric Redmond's office was in half an hour. He would want to talk about the upcoming conference costs, and she thought she would likely be making a trip to Berlin soon. She turned to her computer screen, opened the relevant spreadsheet and slowly regained the composure she would need to get through the rest of the day.

†

"Do you think she could be bribed?" Gordon asked bitterly as he waited for the receipt from the taxi driver.

"Nah. Too classy. How about coming across the road?" Their local, the Rising Sun, was just opening its doors.

Gordon looked at his watch, then looked up at the sky as if it held the answer. "Okay. Just the one. As you're buying."

"How do you figure that?" Dani asked as they walked to the pub.

"You fell asleep!"

"I was only resting my eyes. Thanks to you, I've now got another bruise to add to all the others."

"Are you going to tell me what happened?"

"No."

"Why didn't you say something when I rang yesterday?"

"What difference would that have made? Were you going to come over and nurse me?"

"Dani! I do care about you."

"Yeah, sure. Only when it affects your bank balance." She handed him a fiver and went to sit down.

Gordon got the drinks and brought them over to their regular corner seat near the fireplace. "So what did you think of the Callaghan woman?"

"Not bad-looking, if you like that kind of thing. Does she have a first name?"

"Robert always refers to her as 'that fucking bitch'. But her name is Camila."

Dani mimicked his pronunciation. "Ca...meee...la. What kind of name is that?"

"Spanish, I think."

"Hm. I suppose." Dani pictured the dark-haired woman. "Maybe her mother's Spanish."

"What do you reckon?" Gordon sipped his gin and tonic. "Flowers, theatre, racing? I'm sure I saw her at Ascot last year."

"That doesn't mean anything. Everyone gets tickets to Ascot."

"Except you."

"I've been...on Ladies Day too. Don't you remember?"

"Oh shit, I'd forgotten that."

"I thought I looked rather good in the morning suit, didn't you?"

"Too good. How was I supposed to explain to Lord and Lady Whatsit that my partner is a transvestite?"

"Too cruel, darling. Just a harmless bit of cross-dressing."

"I don't care what you call it."

Dani could tell he was worried; his insults weren't up to his usual standard. She touched his arm. "Look, it isn't a problem. She was just throwing her weight around—what there was of it. You know we're going to do an amazing ad and they will think the sun shines out of your arse. And then they will give you whatever you ask for."

"I wish I had your confidence."

"Confidence, bollocks. I know I'm brilliant. It hurts me that you don't know it too."

"Oh, fuck off, Dani."

"That's better. Are you having another?"

"No. I've got a lunch appointment in Mayfair."

He went out to catch a taxi while Dani sank back into the comfortable seat and hoped no one would disturb her for a few hours. The pain in her ribs made itself known when she leaned back. Reminded of the Friday night beating, Dani thought the difference between her and Gordon could be summed up easily. While she was sucking up stale beer in a grotty bar looking for action, he was hosting a civilised soiree at home with his wife, whose ambitions had them on track for entertaining the rich and the famous. Melissa McKenzie was everything Dani wasn't and could play the charming hostess to perfection.

Sometimes Dani wondered how their partnership had lasted so long. But fifteen years ago he had been a hippie with the requisite long hair and guitar, happy to mingle with her art college crowd. He had changed after making his first million and marrying the socialite-wannabe. Dani hadn't changed at all.

A touch on her arm brought her back to consciousness just after she had closed her eyes. "Another pint? No thanks, I need to get back to work." But as her eyes focused she realised it wasn't the landlord who had placed two full glasses on the table.

Penny slid into the seat Gordon had vacated. "Oh, so you do remember there's work to be done. No one saw you come back from Redmond, so I thought you were probably over here." She took a sip of her beer. "Astrid said to thank you for the flowers. You really didn't need to send any. But the chocolates were a nice touch."

Dani sat up. "Yes, I did. Need to send something. To thank you both for your help. You didn't have to do it. I'm sure I wasn't a pretty sight on Friday evening."

"Not much improvement now."

"Well, anyway, I'm sorry. I ruined your weekend."

"Not as much as you might think." Penny smirked at Dani over the rim of her glass.

"Oh, really. I might have been mostly out of it when you came round, but I know Astrid was pissed off. At both of us."

"Yes, but now she appreciates having a normal girlfriend. Not a freak like you. Her words, not mine."

Dani took a large gulp of beer. "Thanks. I've been called worse."

"She wanted me to ask if you enjoyed it. Being beaten up, that is."

"I didn't enjoy it on Friday night. That was an extreme reaction from whoever it was who didn't want me to talk to Trish. If they had asked nicely, or even just given me a slap and a few pushes, I would have walked away. Sometimes, however, I do want it, crave it even."

"'Freak' about covers it then."

Dani eyed the rest of her drink and decided she better not finish it if she was going to get anything done that afternoon. "Yeah, well, this freak has work to do. I better go and see what the boys have been up to in my absence." She got to her feet slowly, making an effort not to wince in front of Penny.

"Dani?"

"Yes."

"Did we get the Redmond job?"

"Of course. Never any doubt."

"Gordon seemed worried about it."

"He always worries too much. Are you going to drink that?"

Penny gulped the rest of her beer and followed Dani out of the bar. They parted ways in the reception area as Penny returned to her office and Dani made her way up the stairs to the studio.

Chapter Three

The last two weeks had been busy. The Redmond TV ads were in the final production stage, pretty much out of Dani's hands now.

She had started work on the furniture store account. Mundane stuff, she could draft the storyboard in her sleep. But when she looked down at her drawing table, a face was looking up at her. A dark curl drooped over one eye, just begging to be moved gently to one side. Camila. The name was starting to haunt her waking hours as well as her dreams.

Dani stared at the phone on her desk for another minute. The old saying *faint heart never won fair lady* came to mind. She strode over and dialled Redmond's number before she lost the impetus. The receptionist was helpful when Dani gave Gordon's name; she was put through after only a short wait.

"Hello, Gordon. What can I do for you?"

The perfectly modulated voice sent a shiver through her. Dani gripped the handset tightly. "It's not Gordon. It's Dani. Dani Barker."

"Ah yes. The art director."

She sensed more than a hint of sarcasm. Dani moved the receiver to her left hand and wiped the moist palm of the other on her shirt. "I was wondering if we could meet."

"I really don't get involved in creative decisions. You want to talk to Robert, or perhaps, James."

"I don't think they could be of much help. I have, uh, I have a business proposition."

"That's a bit vague."

"I can't tell you more, on the phone."

"It's not illegal, is it?"

"No, of course not." *Thanks to Queen Victoria.* "How about this evening, at say, seven?"

"All right. But it will have to be brief. I have another appointment at eight."

"Would Flounders suit you?"

"Yes, fine. I'll see you there. At seven." Camila put the phone down, mildly amused at herself for agreeing to meet this stranger on such a flimsy pretext. But Dani was hardly a stranger to her dreams. More than once in the last few weeks, she had woken to a memory of those eyes haunting her.

Camila picked out a folder from one of the piles on her desk and went in search of James. He was in the marketing office, alone. The poor fellow jumped when she put her head around the door.

"Hello. Just came to see how the other half live," she said with a smile, trying to put him at ease. "How is the ad coming?"

"Oh, it's looking good. I've got a rough cut here if you want to see it."

"Yes, I might as well see how they have spent our money."

24

He put the cassette in the player and they watched the sixty-second ad together in silence.

"Could you run it again?" she asked.

He complied eagerly. After the second time, he waited for her to comment.

"I like it," she said finally. "Yes, it's much better than I expected it would be after that meeting. This Dani Barker, she's pretty good, is she?"

"Yes. She's absolutely the best in the business."

"So, why has she stuck with a small outfit like MBE?"

"She's a partner. They started the agency together. McKenzie Barker Enterprises."

"Ah. I see." That would explain why a man like Gordon McKenzie tolerated her turning up for an important client meeting looking like she'd been brawling in the street. "Have we got a media schedule yet?"

"Yes. I'm just running them off. You will have a copy this afternoon. There are thirty and fifteen-second versions."

"Too much information, James, but thank you. Tell Robert I'm pleased with the ad. It should go down well at the conference."

†

James sat staring at the door after she left. Slowly, he dialled the number now ingrained in his memory. Declan put him through to Dani, and he told her what had just happened. "Maybe she has some artistic feelings after all," he whispered, looking over his shoulder.

"I'm sure of it," Dani said calmly, before hanging up.

†

Camila entered the bar, looking around for a leather-clad creature with puffy black eyes. With some relief she realised no one of that description was in the room. However, she wouldn't mind being cruised by the good-looking dyke at the bar. Camila ordered a gin and tonic. She was getting out her purse when she found her wish had come true.

"Put your money away, this one is on me. After all, I invited you."

Camila took another look. The voice was certainly familiar. The woman still had some faint bruising around her eyes, which were green, she noticed. "I'm sorry," she said, regaining her composure. "I didn't recognise you. You were in disguise last time we met."

"Actually this is my disguise."

†

Dani had taken a long time deciding what to wear. She had registered the look of disgust on Camila's face at the meeting and she wanted to get it right this time. She wouldn't likely get another chance. So she had gone for classic butch with clean white shirt—the creases still evident from the packaging—and new black jeans. One of the boys had been sent out midafternoon to buy them. Word had quickly got round the building that Dani had a "new" pair of jeans. Penny had come to her studio and asked point-blank if this was a sign—who was the new woman? Dani had told her, politely, that she just needed a new pair of jeans and she was busy. Penny took the hint and left, but Dani didn't think she had been fooled for a minute. Luckily she had actually been busy; she hadn't had much time to worry about the evening. Now that the time had come, she was still unsure what to say. Camila seemed to be calmly appraising her in the cool, assessing way she did everything.

Dani led the way to a table overlooking the river. They sipped their drinks and looked at the view. Camila broke the silence, saying, "So what is this business proposition?"

"It's a bit of a crazy idea. You may not think much of it."

"Now you've got me here, you may as well tell me."

"Yes. Okay." Dani put her hands on the table. Camila noticed the long, tapered fingers, clean fingernails; expressive, creative hands. "I've done a T-shirt design."

"T-shirt! You don't seriously think I'm interested in T-shirts, do you?"

"No. Of course not. But this would tie in with the ad."

"Right. I was wondering how long it would take Gordon to get around to the add-ons. I thought it was going to be posters. Did he put you up to this?"

"No. He doesn't know anything about it. Look, it won't cost you anything, initially."

Camila looked at her. Dani seemed nervous. "Go on."

"Right. So once people see the ad, they will want something. I mean posters are ideal; they're easy to mail. Robert has my designs for those. But the T-shirts can be sold for a decent profit. They don't cost much to make and you could sell them for, say, £12.99."

"You think the ad is going to be this popular?"

"Yes. No question."

"Modest too." Camila sipped at her G and T. She wanted to knock it back but she didn't want Dani to know she was nervous. "Why haven't you told Gordon about this?"

"He would have a fit. He doesn't let me talk to clients on my own."

27

"Why? Do you bite?" Their eyes met. Camila was startled by the direct look that met hers. There was no mistaking the message. She was also startled because she wasn't unaffected. She hadn't felt this way since...since the last time, and that had been a long time ago. Since before Chris, before Allison even. She pressed her knees together. She didn't need this; she couldn't afford to lose control. Not with this woman, who was clearly dangerous. "I have to go," she said. "We will have to discuss this further, in the office." She stood abruptly.

Dani got up too. "You haven't finished your drink."

"No. I'm sorry. I have got another appointment."

"Okay." Dani pulled a business card out of her shirt pocket. "Call me," she said, handing the card to her.

†

Camila didn't look at the card until she got home. When Dani gave it to her, she just shoved it in her briefcase and made her exit as quickly as possible. She had the MBE number at the office on one of Gordon's business cards, so she knew Dani would have written something on hers. She had. On the back, she'd scrawled a phone number.

Surprised to find that she was trembling, Camila collapsed onto the sofa. Had it been so long? It had been three years almost exactly. Was she so desperate for a good fuck? She knew that was what the men in the office said behind her back. What they didn't know, and wouldn't have believed, was how keenly she did want a good fuck, with a woman. It had taken her a long time to come to terms with Allison's death. They had lived together for ten years and had expected to go on together for years to come. They had lived quietly, discreetly, happy in each other's company and that of a few select friends. Camila had never "come out" to anyone, not even her parents. She put forward the front of an all-consuming passion for her career. Perhaps that was why Dani frightened her. She was so obviously "out" and not afraid to take whatever abuse came her way.

†

Dani sat for a time after Camila left the bar, nursing her drink. She considered whether there was anywhere she could go, dressed as she was. She had been keeping a low profile for the last few weeks, letting her face and body heal.

Eventually she decided on something totally out of character. It went with the costume, she thought. She bought two bottles of chilled champagne and took a taxi to Penny's flat.

Penny opened the door. "Oh, hi. Come in. We're just watching TV."

Dani followed her into the living room. Astrid was slumped on the sofa and looked up, alarmed. "Pen!" She was wearing a short dressing gown that gaped where it failed to adequately cover her ample breasts. Dani got a full-frontal view as Astrid jumped to her feet and rushed into the bedroom.

"Hope I haven't interrupted anything," Dani said, feigning innocence. "What were you watching?"

Penny glanced at the television as if noticing it for the first time. "Uh, I don't know. It doesn't matter." She switched it off.

"Well, come on. Haven't you got any glasses? I'm thirsty."

"Sure, make yourself at home," Penny said sarcastically, heading for the kitchen. She brought out three glasses as Dani popped the cork on one of the bottles.

Astrid re-emerged, fully dressed in jeans and sweatshirt. She had even put a bra on. "Oh, it's you," she said as Dani handed her a full glass of champagne.

"What does that mean?" asked Dani. "If you had realised it was me, you wouldn't have bothered to get dressed? I'm flattered."

Astrid blushed and gave Penny a searing look, but Penny wasn't looking at her. She was observing Dani over the rim of her glass. "So what's the occasion? Are we drinking to anything in particular? Christening the new pair of jeans? Or is it commiseration? Did she stand you up?"

Astrid smiled and joined in. "I guess that's why I didn't recognise you right away, Dani. You haven't got two black eyes and you're wearing normal clothes."

"If you can call going around looking like some sort of throwback from the fifties normal...."

"Shit. Have a good laugh, girls. This is the last time I'll waste decent champers on either of you."

"I don't know why you're wasting it on us in the first place," said Astrid. "Unless Penny's right about your date."

"I would have gone home and changed if I'd known you two were going to take the piss. I only wanted to say thanks again, you know, for patching me up last time."

"I hope it is the last time," said Astrid heatedly.

Before Astrid could launch into a lengthy tirade on Dani's lifestyle, Penny jumped in. "So tell us about this mystery woman."

"Who said there was any mystery woman?"

"Oh come on. Everything you are wearing is new, right down to your boxer shorts."

Dani looked down to see if her flies were open. "How did you know?"

"I saw the wrapper in the loo before I left. So come on, who is she?"

"I'm not going to tell you."

"I won't tell anyone else."

Dani sat back in the chair, crossed her legs, and took another gulp from her glass. "Hm, not bad shampoo, if I say so myself."

"Did she stand you up?"

"No."

"It must have been a real quickie. You left the office at ten to seven and arrived here at eight having stopped off to buy two bottles of champagne. So, assuming she was probably a few minutes late, that means you spent, say twenty minutes with her, at the most—"

"Penny! Lay off. Dani obviously doesn't want to talk about it."

"Thank you, Astrid. I don't know how you can live with her."

"That's rich, coming from you," retorted Penny.

"Who stepped on your corns? Did you have a bad day at the office?"

"You could at least tell us her name."

"That would be telling, wouldn't it? Look, one day I will confess all, but right now, as Astrid rightly said, I don't want to talk about it."

Penny refilled their glasses, which took care of one bottle. "All right," she said, sitting down next to Astrid on the sofa. "Let's go back to the night of—"

"I'd rather not."

"What time did we arrive? We had been working late on the Redmond print ads, left the office about nine thirty. You suggested we go to this bar. Only you didn't tell me it was a leather night."

"I didn't know."

"Luckily, or unluckily as it turned out, we were both wearing leather jackets, so they let us in. We ordered drinks.

You had a pint. I had a half which I finished quickly because I wanted to get home."

"A likely story," said Astrid with a smile, putting her hand on Penny's thigh. "I didn't believe it at the time, either."

"I left you with most of your pint left to drink, leaning against the wall. What happened then?"

"Nothing."

The champagne was obviously having a strong aphrodisiacal effect on Astrid. She was leaning into Penny now, one hand playing with the buttons on her shirt. Penny wasn't immune to this attention either but she continued. "It didn't look like nothing."

"Look, I told you what happened. I don't remember much about it."

"At least you know how to find Trish now. She must be into leather."

Dani looked at her; Penny was clearly drunk. Astrid had undone the top two buttons of her shirt and was going for gold. Dani could see Penny's erect nipple from where she was sitting.

"I knew that," she said quietly. "Enjoy the other bottle."

They didn't say goodbye as she let herself out.

The thing was she didn't want to find Trish now. Trish had disappeared from her head, from her dreams both sleeping and waking. It was a lousy way to let go, but she had. She was free of Trish now.

Now she was obsessing about Camila Callaghan instead. Funny, it was Penny who had told her that *obsess* was now commonly used as a verb, in America anyway. And who was she to argue? Penny knew about words.

Dani didn't know what specifically about Camila obsessed her. Perhaps it was the overwhelming desire to rip her clothes off and make her sweat. Dani was willing to bet that underneath her cool composure, Camila was hot stuff. But what would turn her on? Did she want to have her clothes ripped off? Or would she prefer a subtler approach? Dani had just about reached her limit on subtlety.

Watching Astrid and Penny had made her feel incredibly horny. Too bad they hadn't invited her to make a threesome. It may have been the drink, but she had been on the verge of finding Astrid attractive. Definitely time she got herself sorted out.

So far she hadn't made any progress. She had given Camila her home phone number on the back of the business card. And Camila had given her nothing. Dani had no idea where she lived, or who she lived with. She didn't even know for sure if she was gay. There had only been that fleeting second when their eyes met in the bar. Nothing definite; only a feeling. And her intuition of late wasn't on top form; it had failed her a few times recently.

She could send flowers. That was subtle, sort of. At least Camila would know what Dani had in mind and could decide what to do about it.

Here she was, however, sitting at home at nine thirty on a Friday evening waiting for someone to call; knowing she wouldn't. Camila had said she had an appointment. Not a date, an appointment. That could mean something or nothing. It could just mean she hadn't wanted Dani to know she was going home to an empty flat.

Dani started drawing. At first it was an aimless doodle, then the pattern began to take shape, a face. She looked at it critically; she really was obsessed, obsessing.

Friday night was long. She masturbated until her arm felt like it would fall off and she still wasn't satisfied.

Saturday she was restless; she couldn't settle down to anything. Saturday evening, unable to bear the thought of another night alone, she went to *the* club; dressing carefully for the occasion in tight leather trousers, no underwear, and leather vest; likewise studded collar with matching belt and wristbands.

It was an exclusive club; so private that only a select number of women knew of its existence. Dani had tried a mixed venue once. Once was enough. If she was going to let herself be tied up and whipped, she wanted the added pleasure of knowing that a woman was getting off on doing it to her. Some would say, if you put yourself in that situation, what's the difference? There was a difference. She was getting wet just thinking about it.

†

Dani didn't get home until six on Sunday morning, elated by the sensations coursing through her as she stripped off her leather gear and turned the shower on.

Walking home had been slow and painful; she wasn't going to be able to sit down properly for at least a week. But it felt so good. She didn't know how she had managed to go so long without. The last time had been three months ago. She had promised herself, once the euphoria passed and she was left with just the yellowing bruises, that she would give it up. Now she wondered why she had ever thought she could.

Somehow she didn't think it would be Camila's thing, although she had been imagining her wielding the cane, watching angry red stripes form on her lover's—well, it was a fantasy—buttocks. She had called Camila's name out, twice. And been given extra strokes for it.

"Who is Camila?" Lisa had asked her afterwards.

"No one you know," Dani had mumbled.

"Someone I should know."

"I don't think so."

After the whipping, strapping on the dildo and fucking Lisa had been extremely painful. Lisa knew this and made her work hard to bring her to orgasm. She did come, eventually, several times. Dani knew that fucking Lisa like that wasn't a turn-on in itself. All the other stuff was what made her feel high, stimulated, and somehow, weird as she knew it would seem to anyone else, at peace with herself.

She slept most of the day, waking at last around five, ravenously hungry, in pain. She stayed in bed a little longer, aroused by the memories of the night's experiences. Ecstasy took over her body again as she came. She heard herself crying out and hugged her pillow tightly. If it had been a warm body, it would have been suffocated in the crushing embrace.

Dani got out of bed carefully and shrugged on a short cotton robe. She called the Chinese takeaway and ran a bath. The food arrived before she could get in the tub, but it didn't matter. She bathed slowly, savouring the feel of the soothing water on her battered body.

She was still wet when she dressed, pulling on a pair of loose-fitting jeans and a baggy sweatshirt. None of it mattered. Rippling sensations from the cuts across her butt brought a smile to her face. The residual pain and memory of each stroke as it landed would stay with her for days; she just felt so good. Ripping open the cartons of food and emptying them onto a plate, she recalled Lisa's parting words that morning. She had just managed to put her jacket on over her vest and was standing by the door ready to leave when Lisa came over to her. She was naked except for the black leather harness that outlined her generous pelvis and breasts.

"Hey, babe," she said, leaning against Dani and slipping her small hands under her jacket. Dani had leaned down and kissed her gently on the lips.

35

Lisa pulled back and looked at her, "You know…I could fall in love with you."

"But…?"

"But that would spoil the fun, wouldn't it?"

"Yeah."

"Don't leave it so long next time. I missed you." Lisa pushed Dani out onto the street and closed the door firmly.

Sad but true, Dani thought as she scooped up some egg-fried rice with her fork. Her relationship with Lisa was the longest she'd ever had. An introduction to the then-trainee dominatrix twenty years ago had been the beginning of her love affair with the cane. She didn't love Lisa, and she knew Lisa's words were just an extension of the pleasure she had given her. Their shared history had forged an unbreakable bond that, perhaps, was the closest to a real love either of them would ever find.

Chapter Four

Camila's weekend had been sedate. She had taken some work home, as she often did, and spent most of the evening tweaking spreadsheets for her monthly financial report.

Saturday she went grocery shopping, washed her clothes, took a suit to the dry cleaners, did some more work on her report, and made a list of things to do on Monday.

In the evening she went to a dinner party at Chris and Deborah's place in Grove Park. She didn't go out much, as it only reminded her of happier times. Allison was the sociable one; Camila preferred to stay in the background. She would have liked to duck out of this event, but it was Chris's birthday and she knew it was an honour to be amongst the select few invited to dinner on the day itself. They were having a bigger party in a few weeks' time hoping, if the weather was good, to have a barbecue.

Camila arrived just after seven thirty carrying a bottle of wine and a present for Chris. Deborah greeted her at the door. From inside came the welcoming aroma of a mixture of cooking smells. She was the first guest. It always embarrassed her, but she couldn't bear to be late for anything.

"Who else is coming?" she asked, following Deborah into the kitchen.

"Oh, I thought Chris would have told you." Deborah tossed her head to get the long dark hair out of her eyes. "There are eight of us altogether."

"That's quite a crowd…to cook for, I mean." Camila always felt uncomfortable with Deborah. Residual guilt from having slept with her partner, but she generally managed to convince herself that it hadn't really meant anything. Chris had only been trying to comfort her, and Camila was the one who ended it. She couldn't handle the emotional turmoil; it was too soon for her after Allison, and it was easier to live celibately and keep it all at a distance.

Deborah's smile didn't reach her eyes. "I enjoy cooking. And Chris has helped, mainly by staying out of the way."

Camila took the hint. "Where is she now?"

"In the garden. Why don't you join her? I need to check the potatoes." She bent to look in the oven door.

†

Chris turned from her study of the wisteria vine drooping elegantly on the trellis against the wall of the house when Camila walked out onto the terrace. They hugged in greeting. Chris pulled back and looked at her critically, "What's this? Someone new in your life?"

"No!"

"Not even a suggestion of romance?"

Camila could feel herself blushing.

"You can't lie to me, Cam."

"It's just, I don't know. It may be nothing."

"Someone has caught your eye. Anyone we know?"

"No. It's nothing, really."

"So you say. Is she interested in you?"

"Yes." Camila recalled the look in Dani's eyes the night before. She found herself blinking back tears.

"Hey, come on, Cam." Chris put her arms around her. "What is this?"

"I don't know. I just, you know…I haven't felt attracted to anyone for so long, I'm not sure what I feel."

†

Deborah watched them from the window. She couldn't hear what they were saying, but Camila was crying and Chris was comforting her. They thought she didn't know about their affair. She would have had to be deaf, blind, and indifferent not to have been aware of another one of her partner's infidelities. Chris tried to pass it off as a chance encounter, but Deborah had known immediately. Camila was the last person she would have suspected, had Chris been smart enough to shower before coming home that time. When she saw them together now, even in larger groups, she couldn't help feeling twinges of jealousy. Chris had other affairs, ones they talked about, and Deborah knew that Chris would always come back to her.

But Chris had never told her about Camila. Perhaps they still saw each other; she couldn't be sure. It certainly seemed strange to her that even after all this time, three years, an attractive woman like Camila hadn't dated anyone seriously. Still, maybe tonight? Deborah turned away from the window. There was no harm in a little matchmaking in self-defense. Camila obviously liked tall, dark-haired butch types, and Sandy fit the bill. Looks were important to Camila with her expensive clothes, flashy jewellery, and perfect hairstyle.

The doorbell rang and Deborah went to answer it.

†

In the garden, Camila dabbed at her eyes with her monogrammed linen handkerchief. She hated to show any signs of weakness, especially in front of Chris. "It's a bit awkward," she said, trying to explain. "We met through work."

"Oh. She doesn't work for you, does she?"

Camila knew that Chris didn't have much idea of what she did. As a primary school teacher, the business world was something of a mystery to her.

"Not directly. She's the art director at the agency that's done a new TV ad for us."

"How did you meet?"

Camila told her about the marketing meeting—leaving out the bit about Dani's black eyes—and the meeting in the bar the night before. "That's when I realised she was interested in me. She had this crazy story about a T-shirt design relating to the TV ad. I mean, that's not something I would normally deal with, and she knew it."

"It was just something she could talk to you about? Did she ask you if you're gay?"

Camila shook her head. "No. I didn't give her the chance. I left saying I had another appointment. She gave me her business card with a number written on the back; obviously prepared in advance."

"Her home number?"

"I guess."

"So are you going to call her?"

Camila shook her head again. "I don't think so."

"Why not? Aren't you curious? It wouldn't hurt you to meet her, you know, go on a date."

"I don't think she's the romantic type."

"Sounds romantic to me. She's given you her number. The next move is up to you."

"I don't know, Chris. I'm happy as I am."

"No, you're not."

"Chris!"

"But you're not, are you? You bury yourself in your work, and by keeping your mind occupied you think you can ignore your body. It's a great body; it shouldn't be ignored."

"Chris!" shouted someone from the house, saving Camila from having to respond. "Happy Birthday! What is it now? I've lost count."

"So have I," said Chris, smiling at the newcomer.

The dinner party was not a success from Camila's point of view. She was never comfortable in a group situation and sat back watching the others, particularly when they got into a heated discussion of feminist issues. At one point, Chris tried to draw her into the conversation when they were talking about the introduction of hiring quotas designed to give women a fairer chance of promotion in the workplace. Camila's statement that she would prefer to be promoted on merit didn't go down well. So she decided not to voice her opinion that she found men easier to work with, as they were generally more straightforward and less emotional.

Eventually the talk veered away from contentious issues and deteriorated into unfavourable comments about the other people they knew who weren't there. Camila was bored by nine o'clock, but leaving would have been rude. And she had to resist the unwelcome attention of a rather loud woman whose name she had forgotten as soon as they were introduced. She did learn, however, that she was a PE teacher and played rugby in her spare time. Camila knew nothing about the game and wasn't particularly interested in learning.

It was eleven thirty by the time she took her leave, and she was relieved to get home and into her bed, alone.

Chapter Five

Penny noticed it as soon as she saw Dani on Monday morning. Declan and Gary had been nudging each other and giggling like a couple of schoolkids when she went over to the art department to check on a copy for an ad. When she asked if Dani was in, Declan said, "Yeah, but you'll have to peel her off the ceiling," and started laughing again.

Dani was standing at the drawing table, working. It wasn't unusual for her to draw standing up, but her outfit drew Penny's attention. She was wearing one of her grottier pairs of jeans and a grubby white T-shirt with the faded message: *I can't even think straight.* The red bandana round her neck and ancient cardigan with enough moth holes to match the number of tears in her jeans, completed the ensemble.

She acknowledged Penny's presence and finished what she was doing before speaking. "Hi. So you've come up for air."

Penny glared at her. "Dani!"

"What? Spit it out, Pen. I left my crystal ball at home."

"Dani." Penny could feel tears starting. "You said you wouldn't...."

Dani looked at her. "Oh for Christ's sake, you're not my mother. And don't tell me you believe everything I say."

"Why, Dani? Just tell me why?"

"Because it makes me feel good." Dani carefully enunciated each word.

"But it's not good for you."

"Who says? What the fuck do you know about what's good for me? You should talk. You'll wear your tongue out licking pussy. And who knows what chemicals you're sucking on the cling film. You do use that or a dental dam, don't you, seeing as we're on the subject of what's good for you?"

Penny stormed out and slammed the studio door behind her. She managed to hold it together until she got back to her desk, then she let the tears fall.

Why should she care what Dani did to herself, or rather, what she let someone else do to her? As Astrid was fond of reminding her, Dani was a grown woman.

Her computer screen looked as blue as she felt. Penny envied the art department's latest acquisition, an Apple Mac. The word-processing programme Declan had shown her looked so much more user-friendly than the old version of WordPerfect on all the other office computers. She was sure her copywriting would benefit from being able to type black letters onto a white screen.

She blew her nose and studied the brief she had found sitting on top of her In Tray that morning. Why did account managers think that writing *Urgent* in red ink on the paper would bring it to the top of her to-do pile? She checked the transmission date and shuffled it into its proper place with the other jobs urgently awaiting her attention.

†

Dani chewed on the end of her pencil; she wondered if Camila had received the flowers yet. She glanced at the drawing board, and the outline of a face stared up at her. She had been pencilling in the dark eyebrows when Penny arrived.

Obsessing again. What was it about this woman that had her appearing nightly in her dreams? The air of complete control. Perhaps that was the draw. That was something Dani craved. A woman who would offer her a safe space to come home to. As satisfying as sessions with Lisa were, Dani knew they were only temporary, necessary interludes to stave off the overwhelming need. A psychiatrist would no doubt have enough material from her thought processes to fill several books. *Tell me about your childhood. Let's start with your relationship with your mother.*

Dani had difficulty remembering any meaningful interactions with her mother. She hadn't been a dominant factor in her early years. Was that what she was searching for? A dominant female figure in her life?

Camila's dark eyes captured her from the face emerging under her pencil strokes. This woman could dominate her like no other. She was sure of that.

Smiling to herself, she covered the compelling eyes with a clean sheet of paper and started work on the mailer for the satellite TV company. There were deadlines to meet, and obsessing about a woman who probably wasn't interested in any kind of relationship with her wasn't going to get the job done.

†

Gordon sat back in his swivel chair and contemplated the facts of life. One of the facts was that he could afford to buy Dani out. But did he want to? Melissa was pushing for it, but one of the other facts was that she didn't like Dani. Another fact was that in spite of, or maybe because of, their differences, he did like Dani. She was good at her job. Getting another art director with her talent would be difficult. And he would have no guarantee they would stay with him. He felt a loyalty to Dani, and he knew that in her own way, she was loyal to him. In their business loyalty was a rare commodity. It wasn't something you could buy. He decided to go talk to her.

Declan was at his desk gazing wistfully at his computer screen. Gordon hadn't been convinced that computers were necessary in the graphics department, but Dani had overruled him, and they had paid off. There was no sign of the other lad, Gary.

"Is she in?" he asked.

Declan looked up, startled to see the other boss. He didn't often make an appearance in the creative department. "Yes," he said seriously, "but I don't think she should be disturbed."

"Oh?" said Gordon, waiting for an explanation. *What is she doing, masturbating?*

"I mean, this might not be a good time to see her." Declan was starting to stammer and go red.

"Oh, I see. Well, it's never usually a good time, is it?" He walked past Declan and went into Dani's lair without knocking.

"Hello, Gordon," she said calmly.

So this was what Declan was trying to protect him from. Did he think Gordon and Dani had just met? "Young Declan's coming along all right," he said.

"Oh, do you think so?"

46

"Yes, quite promising."

"Fine. But I don't suppose you've come in here to discuss my staff."

"No, not really." He walked over to the window and looked out. The pavement was wet, but the rain had stopped.

"So what is this? A board meeting?"

"Yes. I suppose so."

"Spit it out, Gordon. I'm a grown-up now."

"Melissa wants me to buy you out."

"Oh." She put her pencil down. "What do you want, Gordon?"

"I don't want to. I think we're a good team."

"But your wife doesn't think so."

"No."

"She wouldn't." Dani moved over to stand at the window next to Gordon. "I mean she doesn't approve of me, does she?"

"No, but—"

"But what? She's right. Times have changed. People will look back on this as the neo-puritan era. Back to basics, back to family values—that's what the government's preaching now. Which doesn't include people like me. So, yes, you should ditch me and get a respectable family person instead, only that doesn't include single mothers, either."

"Dani, shut up!" Gordon sighed and shoved his hands deeper into his pockets. "I'm not such a good family man anyway."

"Are you kidding? You've got a wife, the kids, two mortgages, three cars, and a timeshare in Portugal; you can't get much more 'family' than that. The Prime Minister should be giving you an OBE. Maybe I'll write in and recommend you for the next New Year Honours list."

"Sometimes, I wish...."

"What?"

"I wish I could just chuck it all, walk away."

"Do a Reggie Perrin, you mean? Shed your clothes on the beach and disappear."

"Yeah."

"What would you do?"

"I don't know. Contemplate my navel."

"Ah, back to the 'summer of love'. When was it for you?"

"Nineteen seventy-three—I was seventeen. Hitched to the south of France. Spent six glorious weeks busking on the seafront by day, fucking in the woods by night."

"And you never dreamt that twenty years later you would be stuck, caught in the same old money-go-round as your parents."

"What happened, Dani? It used to be fun. I used to enjoy coming to work."

"Yeah. You used to be fun. I blame the yuppies myself. Five years ago it was cool to wear three-piece suits, drive Porsches, be vegetarian, and drink lager. Only now you're stuck with the image, but not the atmosphere. The party is over, but you're still dressed for it."

"What are you dressed for?" It seemed safe to ask now.

"The morning after."

The phone rang. Gordon picked it up automatically. "Yes."

"Dani?" the voice on the other end asked tentatively. Gordon handed the phone over.

"Hello."

"I just wanted to thank you for the flowers."

Dani grinned, turning away from Gordon. "Do you like them?"

"Yes, they're lovely. Look, I'm sorry I had to rush off on Friday. I was wondering if we could meet for lunch this week."

"Sure. Let me check my diary." Dani looked out the window. "Uh, I'm busy today and tomorrow, but Wednesday would be okay."

"Wednesday? Yes, I can do that. Do you know the Trattoria on Dean Street? One o'clock?"

"Great. See you there." Dani put the phone down.

Gordon was looking at her thoughtfully. "Wasn't that...?"

"No, no one you know. Now get out. I've got work to do."

After he left, she stood at her drawing board and thought about their interrupted conversation. She could see Gordon as a longhaired youth strumming his guitar at a seaside café. Getting in touch with his inner Peter Sarstedt, singing ballad-like songs, attracting nubile young women caught up in the romantic idea of free love.

She had endured the hippy-dippy era through her school days, the touchy-feely, love-is-all-around crowd. The main benefit for her was that girls were willing to experiment and give in to her advances, even if they told her they were only doing it as practice for the real thing. Liberated through the invention of "the pill", promiscuity was rife.

The punk style in the '70s had been much more to her liking, although she had never wanted to stick safety pins through any part of her body. However, the punks' penchant for leather gear with studded belts meant she could fit in with the fashionably weird, instead of being just weird. Gordon, though, had moved on to idolising Richard Branson with the burning desire to emulate his success in business. Sometimes she wished they had come up with a name like *Virgin* for the agency, but they were stuck with boring initials.

†

Camila sat looking at the phone, smiling to herself. The flowers really were lovely. Perhaps Chris was right; she should give herself the chance to feel something, anything, even if it did turn out wrong. But meeting for lunch was safe enough. They would soon know whether or not they had anything in common. If they got through lunch.

Several people in the office had already asked her who sent the flowers. "An admirer," she replied, knowing they were desperate for more information. But she was used to keeping her private life private, so they would just have to be satisfied knowing she had a love interest.

It was after nine when she got home that Monday evening following a board meeting and further discussion about the upcoming conference. She would have to give her presentation about budgets, which she knew bored everyone rigid. But she found the subject interesting. She had drafted her slides on Sunday and given them to James first thing that morning to get produced, along with her handout. The conference was only two weeks away and they would be having the first speaker rehearsals later in the week.

She put the flowers, a dozen long-stemmed red roses, in a vase. They looked a bit lost on her otherwise bare mantelpiece, but she decided they could stay there while she had a bath.

The hot water was soothing; Camila lay back and tried to empty her mind of the day's events. The bubbles from the herbal bath foam had all but disappeared, and the water had cooled to lukewarm as her hand idly fondled her pubic hair. She rarely touched herself, only performing necessary ablutions and inserting or removing tampons. When she had tried masturbating after Allison's death, it only brought back memories and the aching void that nothing could fill…not even the recommended ten-inch silicone vibrator—a present from a well-meaning friend—which she now sometimes used to massage the soles of her feet…without a condom.

She had almost nothing left of Allison now—a few holiday snaps, a poem she had written after they met. They hadn't made wills and Allison's family took full advantage, removing all traces of their life together. Camila had given up the fight before it started, fearing the publicity. Only she would have liked to arrange the funeral in the way she knew Allison would have wanted it. They excluded her from that too.

Chris and Deborah had tried to help by organising a commemorative service with a few other close friends. And what had been the result of that? She had gone to bed with Chris, twice. She thought Chris might feel guilty about cheating on Deborah, but not half as guilty as she felt. It was a betrayal of Allison and her memory.

Now she wasn't so sure—about the betrayal. Closing her eyes, she saw Dani's face close to her own. Her hand, unhampered by her usual stiff control, found its own rhythm. She cried out when she came and found that tears were flowing as well. Was this the release she had sought, and fought, for so long?

†

Dani checked her bruises in the mirror before pulling on a clean pair of boxer shorts. They had passed from the livid purple-and-green stage and were yellowing out nicely. A few more days and her butt would just look vaguely striped. God knows how long it would take to get Camila into bed, but it wasn't likely to be two o'clock today. Still, one could always hope.

All morning she was on tenterhooks, jumping whenever the phone rang, in case it was Camila crying off. She left the studio at 12:45, telling Declan she would be out for a few hours. He just said, "Yeah, boss," but she could tell he was puzzled. Dani didn't "do" lunch. A few hours in a pub maybe, but that was likely to be midafternoon when she thought they needed to lubricate their thought processes for a "creative" meeting.

Penny was on her way out as well; they walked as far as Soho Square together. She was meeting Astrid for a sandwich. "And a grope in the grass," Dani said with a leer.

"I might ask where you're going, dressed to kill," Penny countered primly.

Dani could tell she still hadn't been forgiven for her transgression, as Penny saw it. But she didn't feel the need to explain herself. If Penny couldn't handle it, or rather, the idea of it, that was her problem. "Just meeting an old friend."

"Not Trish?"

"No, not Trish. I'm finished with Trish."

"She finished with you, if I remember rightly."

"You know what I mean."

"Oh, so getting your head kicked in finally helped you get over her, is that it?"

"Yeah, I suppose so." Dani really didn't want to discuss it, but it was less dangerous ground than the present.

"You're seriously weird, you know, Dani. I worry about you."

"Get the jargon right, Pen. Well weird, okay. Go and have a nice lunch with your sweetheart. See you later." Dani strode off towards Dean Street.

†

Penny found Astrid right away on a bench near the gate of the square. "I'll be right back. I promise you it will be worth it." And she set off again, keeping Dani's tall figure in sight.

She watched her go into the Trattoria and debated whether she could get a look in without being spotted by her quarry. Just as she was deciding it wasn't a good idea, a taxi pulled up and a smartly dressed businesswoman emerged. She didn't stop to pay the driver; company expense account, thought Penny, watching her go into the restaurant—a real looker, every hair in place.

Penny seized the moment and followed her inside. The woman in front didn't wait to be seated; she headed directly to a table in the corner. Holding a menu up to her face, Penny observed the meeting. She needn't have worried about being seen; they only had eyes for each other. Mumbling an excuse to the approaching maître d', she replaced the menu on the desk and hurried back to Astrid.

So there was a new woman! But who was she? Penny knew she had seen her before somewhere. But where? And what was she doing with Dani? She hardly looked her type.

†

"Have you been here long?" asked Camila as she sat down on the chair the waiter pulled out for her.

"No, I've just arrived." Dani hadn't expected to feel nervous, but seeing Camila again was overwhelming. Her fantasies had been good, but the real thing was infinitely better. She took a deep breath; Camila was still arranging herself. "What do you want to drink—wine, champagne?" She hoped the answer wouldn't be water. The three-hour-long business lunches of the '80s were giving way to the

53

American-style of sandwiches eaten at the desk with a bottle of Perrier.

Camila's dark eyes met hers. "The house red is very good here."

"Okay. A litre of house red," Dani said to the waiter. It was incredible. She had been having conversations in her mind for days and now she couldn't think of a thing to say. They both studied the menu in silence, and when the waiter came with the wine, they ordered separately. Dani wasn't sure she would be able to eat anything.

"I've been thinking about your T-shirt idea," said Camila, fiddling with the cutlery.

"Oh." As an opening gambit, it wasn't what Dani had expected.

"In fact, looking at the figures, I think it would be a good idea to get some produced."

Dani sipped her wine. If she wanted to talk shop it was, at least, a start. So she outlined her design ideas for the T-shirts and said she could have them ready by Friday as long as she had no other distractions.

When they had exhausted that topic, Dani asked what it was like working for Redmond. Camila seemed more relaxed talking about her work. She liked the variety and the opportunities for travel, which she wouldn't have if she had stayed with an accounting firm. They talked about some of the countries she'd visited, and the time passed more quickly than Dani could have anticipated.

Camila left the restaurant at exactly 2:15, having asked the waiter to order a taxi five minutes earlier. They had, briefly, haggled over the bill and Dani won. She settled up after Camila left and walked slowly back towards the office, not noticing anything about the fine spring day and the bustle of people, buses, cars, and bicycles. Even through the haze of more than a half bottle of wine, her senses were on fire.

She couldn't get Camila out of her head. Everything about her—the way she sat, talked, used her hands—Dani was totally smitten, like a teenager after a first date. Should she have kissed her? Did she want to be kissed? And if she had kissed her, would she have been able to stop there? Unanswerable questions.

And the worst thing was she really had no idea how Camila felt. The cool mask had been firmly in place. Was she wasting her time? She gave no indication of her sexual preference, as it were. Perhaps she should have given her a form to fill in. Please tick the boxes, yes-or-no answers only: a) are you a lesbian? b) do you have a lover? c) do you have a cat? Very likely, if the answer to a) was yes.

She couldn't remember what they had talked about, apart from the T-shirts at the start and her promise to have the artwork ready for Friday.

Soho Square looked inviting in the sunlight. The office workers had returned to their dreary desks and the grass—which half an hour earlier had been covered with office workers consuming their sandwiches and enjoying the sun during their all too brief lunch break—was now left to the pigeons and the homeless. Dani sat on a bench and closed her eyes.

She was going to have to work late to do the T-shirts, and what was she going to tell Gordon? "Oh, by the way, Redmond's financial director rang me and ordered three T-shirt designs." Best not to tell him anything. Eventually, he would think it had been his idea.

Melissa McKenzie was coming through Reception as Dani walked in. "Hello, Dani," she said, smiling.

Must have been sharpening her claws, thought Dani, "Melissa, darling. What brings you here?" she asked, with what she hoped looked like genuine, wide-eyed candour.

"Just checking to make sure you're not corrupting my husband."

"I've stopped trying. He just won't wear the frocks, you know."

Melissa gave her the kind of look she probably reserved for those less fortunate than herself. "You must come to dinner soon. We haven't seen you for simply ages."

"Yes, doesn't time fly?" The last time she'd had dinner with the McKenzies was before either of their kids were born. Melissa probably thought her mere presence would have a corrupting influence, even when they were in her womb.

"Must be off. Bye. Don't work too hard."

Dani looked at Amanda, the receptionist, who had been watching the encounter avidly. "Exit Lady Macbeth," said Dani calmly. "Any messages?"

Amanda giggled and shook her head.

†

It was eleven o'clock before Dani left the office. Working seemed the best way to shut out thoughts of Camila. And she succeeded until she got home and into bed. She had hoped for oblivion as soon as her head hit the pillow; instead, she was awake until after two with some very vivid fantasies and a lot of hand work.

She didn't get into the office until after ten the next day, Thursday. And then she waited until five to tell Gordon about the T-shirt designs. He had been, predictably, negative.

"I'm having trouble selling them posters and you want to do T-shirts!"

"It's worth a try. I think they might go for it."

"Look, Dani, you stick to drawing pretty pictures, I'll stick to the business."

"I can do some brilliant designs." He didn't need to know she'd already created a few images that only needed light finishing touches.

"Jesus, Dani. If you want to get into T-shirts, book a market stall in Rupert Street. And while you're at it, buy yourself a new one." He was referring to her faded and ripped Bay City Rollers shirt. She was quite fond of it.

"All right. But don't blame me when you find out you've missed the marketing opportunity of the century."

"What do you mean?"

"If you're afraid to approach them, I'll do it myself."

"Now wait a minute. I worked my butt off to get this account. I don't want you destroying all my hard work. Dani!"

She had picked up the phone and dialled the number. "May I speak to Camila Callaghan, please? Yes, I'll hold."

Gordon sat back in his chair and linked his hands behind his head. "This is a windup. I'm not going to buy it."

"Gordon McKenzie wants to speak to her. Yes, she knows him. MD of MBE—we did your recent TV ad. Yes, it is good, isn't it?" She winked at Gordon. "Oh, hello, Miss Callaghan. It's Dani Barker here, of MBE. Yes. I just wanted to let you know we've done some T-shirt designs, you know, to tie in with the ad, and Gordon would like to arrange a time to come and talk to you about them." Pause. "Yes, he's here." She passed the phone over. "She wants to speak to you."

"Dani, I'm going to kill you," he hissed, taking the phone from her. A look of total amazement crossed his face as he listened to the voice on the other end and realised it wasn't Declan in the next room. "Yes. I see. Tomorrow at ten. No problem. We will be there. Thank you, goodbye." He stared at the phone before glancing across at Dani, who was grinning broadly at him. "That's amazing. The bitch has hardly even acknowledged my presence before and suddenly she wants to order ten thousand T-shirts."

"See, I knew it was a good idea."

"What are we going to show her tomorrow?"

"Oh, don't worry. I'll knock something into shape."

†

After he'd gone, she slipped the pages of designs she had created the night before out from under the furniture company's storyboard. Giving them a critical once-over, she selected four that just needed a little tweaking. Only two were likely to be chosen, and she could have presented just the ones she knew they would pick, but it was always good to give clients more than they expected.

The finishing touches didn't take long. She pasted the pages onto presentation boards and propped them up in a line on her windowsill. All this to impress a woman who possibly wasn't even interested in her. There had been a hint of warmth in her tone when she said she liked the flowers and invited Dani to lunch. But in the restaurant, Camila reverted to the cool tone of a meeting with a business colleague.

A knock on the door brought her out of her reverie. "Come in." Not many staff members would still be in the office, so she expected to see either Gordon or Penny when the door opened.

"Hiya, boss. I was in the neighbourhood, so thought I'd pop in." Jan's grin gave away what she was going to say next. "Did they work?"

Dani smiled at the young courier's enthusiasm. "Not sure yet. We did go out for lunch yesterday, but...."

"What! She didn't instantly fall at your feet? Mind you, she is one classy chick."

"You met her?"

"Yeah. I told the receptionist my instructions were to deliver the flowers in person."

"I didn't say that."

"Hey, I improvised. You've never sent flowers to a love interest before. I had to see who the lucky lady was. Anyway, while I was waiting for her to appear, the receptionist asked who they were from. I could tell she was dead curious. But she didn't get any joy from me. And your Ms Callaghan, well, you'd think she got sent a dozen red roses every day. Just took them, thanked me, and walked back to wherever her ivory-tower office is located. Although how she can walk anywhere in those heels is beyond me."

Dani sighed. Maybe sending flowers had been a mistake. "I'll be seeing her again tomorrow. What do you think of these?" She indicated the boards leaning against the window.

Jan put her helmet on Dani's desk and moved closer to look at the images. "What are they meant to be?"

"For T-shirts. A tie-in with the new Redmond ad."

Jan gave the boards a closer look.

"I mean, would you wear any of them?" Dani watched her face closely. At twenty-one, Jan was closer in age to the target audience, so her opinion could count as market research.

"Yeah. That one, and possibly that one. But what does drinking coffee while sitting on a beach watching the sunset have to do with Redmond? I thought they were mostly into electronic gadgets."

"An old marketing ploy. Selling the sizzle, not the steak."

"Hm. Sneaky."

"It's the subliminal message that gets through to people. The subjective versus the objective."

"Too deep for me, boss. I know what I like, that's all. So you want to go for a drink?"

Dani smiled. Jan had nailed it perfectly. "Yes. I'll just put these in a case ready for the morning."

"Woo her with flowers and art. It's a done deal."

"We'll see." Dani set the portfolio case next to her desk. "Come on. I'll buy the first round and you can tell me about your love life."

"That will hardly get us through the first pint."

As they crossed the road to the Rising Sun, Dani wondered if her designs would make any impact on Camila, either consciously or subconsciously.

Chapter Six

Dani let Declan carry her art portfolio to the Friday morning meeting. Gary had pretended to be upset about being left to "hold the fort", but Dani had no doubt he was straight into the next level of *Prince of Persia* by the time they got into their taxi.

Declan clutched the case and looked out the window, evidently not sure how to behave with both bosses in such close proximity. Dani had told him that if the deal came off, she would want him to liaise with James—that was why she wanted him at the meeting.

Gordon was, of course, immaculately turned out, whereas Declan and Dani looked like they had tumbled out of the same cardboard box that morning. Declan had flattened his normally spiky hair, but that only served to make him look like a fourteen-year-old on his way to a remand centre. However, his T-shirt and jeans were acceptable compared to Dani's outfit. She looked like she was dressed for a convention of SM dykes on bikes with a leather vest over a white T-shirt, and leather trousers complete with metal-studded belt. Gordon hadn't commented. He was aware that clients expected creatives to look weird; he was just thankful neither of them had any visible bruises this time.

James was waiting for them in reception. He could hardly contain his excitement; he and Declan were soon chattering to each other like long-lost twins. The scene in the boardroom for Dani was reminiscent of the meeting six weeks earlier. Robert was there to greet them, but there was no sign of Camila. She sat down at the table while the boys gathered around the coffee urn. Declan brought her a cup; she didn't want it but thanked him anyway—he was trying, after all.

Camila made her entrance on the hour and everyone quickly took their places at the table. She and Dani exchanged the briefest of glances during the shuffle of chairs and rattle of cups on saucers. Dani looked away first; they would have to stop meeting like this. She couldn't handle the feelings the sight of Camila stirred up. She was looking exceptionally beautiful this morning. Was it the natural effect of good genes, or was there an oil painting in her attic?

They passed around the mock-ups of the designs she had produced on Wednesday evening. After much discussion they picked the two Jan liked best. Costs were discussed, along with the marketing and the pricing of the shirts. Once these had been agreed, Camila left. Dani signalled to Declan so he followed her out with the portfolio.

"We're leaving. Gordon wants to talk to Robert about some other things. I'm just going to the loo; meet me in Reception. Ask them to order a taxi."

"Right, boss." He set off towards the lift.

Dani took a deep breath and turned the other way. She pushed through the double doors at the end of the corridor and was in luck. Camila's office was the first one she came to, and the door was open. Camila was at her desk, writing.

Camila looked up, startled. "Dani...what...?"

"Nice office." Dani had quickly taken in the quality of the carpet, designer furniture—complete with state-of-the-art PC—and tasteful vertical blinds. She walked over to these and expertly twiddled the stick to close them. This movement brought her close to Camila, who was now standing as well. "How about dinner tonight?"

"Dani! This is outrageous. You can't just walk in here—"

"Well, I have. Saved a phone call. A simple yes-or-no answer will do." It wasn't what she had planned while sitting through the meeting but now, with Camila's face so close to hers, she had to do it. She leaned forward and kissed Camila on the mouth. She had expected Camila to pull back, protesting. But, after only a fleeting hesitation, she responded.

They broke apart. It had only been a few seconds, but to Dani it felt like a lifetime. "Yes or no?" she whispered.

"Yes. I...where?"

This was new; Camila wasn't taking charge. "Faze," she said firmly. "On Compton Street. Eight o'clock."

†

Declan was waiting patiently in Reception. Dani walked straight past him and he had to hustle to make it into the taxi with her.

"Tell him to stop at Oxford Circus," she muttered.

Declan did as he was told. "Are you okay?" he ventured as the taxi crawled slowly up Regent Street. "You look a bit green. I just wondered if you had been sick."

Dani looked at him and smiled. "Don't tell anyone in the office, will you? I don't want anyone to know—you know." She patted her belly, which was as flat as a pancake.

"You mean, you're pregnant?" he squeaked.

The taxi came to a stop at traffic lights on Oxford Street. Dani jumped out. "Just popping along to Mothercare. See you later." She slammed the door shut and joined the crowd crossing the road.

She found the shop she was looking for, off Wigmore Street.

Charles greeted her effusively, as he did all his regular customers. "Darling, it's been so long. Anything special this time?" He had fitted her for a white tux for a fundraising ball the previous year.

"Sorry to disappoint you, Chuck. Just a casual outfit for this evening."

"So, we will have to see what we have got in stock for you." He looked her up and down critically. "You've lost some weight, I'd say."

"A bit."

"What is it tonight? A new woman?"

Dani winced. "Yes, but…."

"Yes?" he probed, gently.

"I haven't felt this nervous about a date since I was a kid."

He sighed, and moved around behind her to measure across her shoulders. "You dykes, when will you learn? A fuck is a fuck is a fuck. Now come on. I'll get you a drink and we will talk about what you need."

She followed him into his office. He pulled out a bottle of whisky and poured her a shot. "Just to steady your nerves. Now tell me, what is she like, this woman who has rattled your libido?"

Dani swallowed the whisky in one gulp and shuddered as it burned its way through her torso. She grinned at Charles. "Thanks, I guess I needed that."

"So come on, Dani…give."

"She's just special, that's all."

"That's not all! How am I to know how to dress you if you don't tell me more?"

"She's not like me."

"Ah. But she is a lesbian?"

Dani sat back in the leather chair and closed her eyes; she could taste Camila's lips, responding to hers, warm, inviting. "Yes."

"She's really got you hooked, hasn't she? Let me guess. She's not like you. Not into leather, although she would probably look good in it. Stop me if I'm wrong. So she's probably very feminine, a stylish dresser, in business perhaps, a high-flyer. Passes as straight. Am I close?"

Dani nodded. "Spot on. I'd say you had been following me around."

"No. Just describing the opposite of you. Where are you taking her?"

"Faze."

"Good choice. Now, let's see what I've got that will fit you." Charles whisked the measuring tape off from around his neck and indicated where she should stand.

Dani put her glass on his desk and stood. She held her arms out and let him take the measurements he needed…chest, hips, arms, legs. She felt a pang of nostalgia.

"I still miss her, you know."

"Of course. She was a one-off. Times are changing, though. Mistress Bea wouldn't like all the rules and regs we have now."

"I think she would have just ignored them and carried on."

"That she would." Charles replaced the tape around his neck and looked her up and down again. "You're in luck. I have something in just the right size. Perfect for a summer evening's seduction."

"I'm not sure I'll get that lucky."

"Chin up. Confidence, sweetie, is what makes the difference between win or lose."

"Don't take up fortune-cookie writing."

He shook his head and walked through to the shop. "Come along. Have faith in your tailor and all will be well."

Chapter Seven

After a long bath, Dani sat out in the garden in the sun for a while, finding it difficult to keep her mind still. She would have liked to have a drink, but she was determined not to give in to the desire. A change of habit, indeed!

At 6:45 she ordered a taxi. She dressed carefully. Charles had chosen well; she just hoped it wasn't too over the top for Camila's tastes. But then, what did she know about Camila's tastes?

Dani arrived at the restaurant at five minutes to eight. Camila wasn't there, but she didn't expect her to be. She sat in the bar area and declined the offer of a drink, but asked that they have a bottle of champagne ready to open when her guest arrived.

Ten minutes later Camila entered looking flushed and out of breath, a sight Dani would like to savour in more intimate surroundings.

"Sorry I'm late. I was halfway over Battersea Bridge before an empty taxi came along."

"You can open the champagne now," Dani said to the waiter as Camila settled into the seat next to her.

"You're full of surprises, aren't you?" Camila gave her an appraising look that seared right through to Dani's groin. She was certain she'd stopped breathing, so she was relieved when Camila looked away to accept the glass of champagne.

"Have you been here before?" asked Camila, glancing around. The décor was very art deco, with lots of naked but visually attractive imagery of both sexes. Faze was a renowned openly-gay-and-lesbian restaurant. Dani wondered if she'd made a mistake with her choice of venue.

"Once or twice, yes."

"I don't go out much, apart from business occasions."

"I guess that's why I haven't seen you around, on the scene." Still cautious, testing the water, Dani hoped she didn't look as nervous as she felt. Camila looked stunning in a simple cotton sheath-style dress; if she were wearing makeup, it didn't show, and the only jewellery on display were small ear studs and a gold chain necklace. "So, uh, here's to the T-shirts." Dani raised her glass.

"Dani, if you mention T-shirts to me ever again, I will pour this straight over your head."

"What should we drink to?"

"How about to a perfect evening?"

"We might have different ideas about what is perfect," said Dani, looking at her over the rim of her glass.

"We might."

They drank, both sipping slowly.

"Your name, Camila." Dani drew out the middle syllable slowly. "It's Spanish, right?"

"Yes. But my mother's from Manchester and the only connection with Spain is the holiday they took while she was pregnant with me. That's where they heard the name and liked it."

"But you look Spanish." Dani hoped that didn't sound too personal.

"My father's side. I just hope I don't inherit the male-pattern baldness from him too."

Looking at the head of luxurious dark hair, Dani didn't think there was any danger of that. "Any siblings?"

"No. I'm an only child."

"Do you see your parents much?"

"Not that often nowadays. They moved to France two years ago, having fallen in love with Brittany. That's where we always went for summer holidays. What about you?"

"I haven't seen my parents since I left when I was sixteen. My brother works in town, so I see him occasionally." She didn't add that their meetings usually took place outside a police cell.

Dani found relaxing difficult. She was thankful, once again, for the rituals of eating out—reading the menu, deciding what to eat, what to drink. They had finished the main course and made inroads on the second bottle of champagne when Camila said, "Do you bring all your prospective girlfriends here?"

"Of course," said Dani lightly. "If I spend enough money on them, they'll feel obliged to go to bed with me."

"I would have settled for a cheeseburger."

"Does that mean...you don't want to feel obligated?"

Camila just gave her a Mona Lisa smile. Dani realised she was probably drunk; she decided they could forego the pudding course and asked for the bill.

"Where to now?" asked Camila when they were on the street.

Dani was sorely tempted to take her straight home to bed, but she wasn't about to take advantage of a drunken woman. She had been that route before, and the aftermath wasn't generally pleasant. So she took her to a club instead, where they danced and drank water.

Camila was a good dancer and seemed to enjoy herself. Dani only hoped she wouldn't see anyone she knew. It wasn't a place she would normally be seen dead in—full of weekend lesbians. The bouncer had questioned her gender when they arrived and Dani had to remove her jacket and tie before they could go in. She wasn't going to make a scene in front of Camila, otherwise she would have been tempted to take her trousers down to make a point.

"Have you been here before?" Dani asked when there was a pause in the music. It would, she thought, be Camila's type of place. Very civilised; the kind of clientele whose adverts in the personal columns would say they liked walking and going to the theatre, and of course, had a GSOH. No mention of what they really wanted, or why would they be advertising in the first place?

"No. Never. I only went to a club once. The Gateways. That's where I met Allison."

Oh shit, thought Dani. *Who is Allison?* She had to ask. "Who's Allison?"

"She was my lover for ten years. She's dead."

"I'm sorry." Dani tried to look sympathetic.

"It's three years ago now, since she died."

"Have you had any lovers since then?"

"No, not really."

Dani decided that probably meant yes, but not anyone who mattered. They had another dance before leaving. When the taxi stopped outside Camila's flat, in one of the mansion blocks facing Battersea Park, Dani asked, "Do you want me to come in?"

"Yes, please." Camila fumbled in her bag for her keys while Dani paid off the driver.

The flat was, in a way, what Dani expected. Very tidy, lots of books all neatly ordered on shelves. A vase holding a dozen red roses dominated the uncluttered mantelpiece. Her flowers, she realised, with a jolt.

"I'll make some coffee," Camila said, slipping her shoes off.

"No. I mean, it's okay. I don't want any coffee."

"It's been a great evening, Dani."

"Better than you expected?"

"No, I didn't mean that. I didn't know what to expect. You're so…different."

"Yeah, I know. That's why it won't work, will it?" she said quietly.

"What do you mean?" Camila was alert now; she had been half-asleep in the taxi, resting her head on Dani's shoulder. It had felt very comfortable.

"Well, we could go to bed, have a good fuck, but that's as far as it goes, right? I can't see you wanting to introduce me to any of your friends."

Camila stared at her. Dani's eyes were fixated on the carpet. "So what is important to you? Taking me to bed or meeting my friends? Shall I call a few of them now?"

"You know what I mean. We're too different."

"We're not that different. Or we wouldn't have got this far." Dani still wasn't looking at her. The silence lengthened between them. Finally, Camila said, "I'm going to bed now. You can join me, or not. Because, believe it or not, I'm not interested in your mind. I just want a good fuck." She went into her bedroom, leaving the door ajar. Camila didn't realise she was shaking until she sat on her bed. What on earth had made her say that when all she had wanted to do was have Dani kiss her again and hold her?

71

†

Dani let herself out of the flat and walked down the stairs out onto the street. Of all the different scenarios that had played through her mind during the afternoon, this one hadn't even occurred to her. She must be going soft in the head. Any other time, any other woman, she would have been in bed with her right now, fucking her brains out. Why was this different? What did she care what Camila thought about her? Not Camila's friends; Camila herself?

The Albert Bridge, lit up like a wedding cake decoration, passed under her feet; she turned left automatically along Cheyne Walk and on to Fulham. It was Friday night, after midnight, and the streets were busy. Some people were just emerging to go to the clubs, a mingling of lifestyles: the clubbers, the aimless, the homeless, and the workers. Dani was cruised twice by working girls; she just shook her head and walked on through the night.

She was footsore by the time Hammersmith Bridge came into view. Once on the Mall, Dani stopped to look at the river. Seeing the river, her river, always lifted her spirits. The walk was easy now. Past The Dove, past the rowing club, past The Old Ship. She slowed down as she neared The Black Lion and sat for a while on the wall under the weeping willow tree. It was a beautiful night, calm, clear. And she felt calm herself, at last; emotionally drained.

With a sigh, she managed the next few yards to her front door and oblivion.

†

After tossing and turning for an hour, Camila gave up and stumbled into the bathroom. She found the sleeping pills in the cabinet and checked the expiry date. For a long time after Allison's death, she had been dependent on the pills to get a good night's sleep. But she'd managed to wean herself off them over a year ago.

Two months out of date. Well, the pills didn't know that, so she swallowed two and washed them down with a glass of water.

Sleep didn't come immediately after she lay back down, and she thought maybe the pills wouldn't work after all. She should have trusted the label. The nearest all-night pharmacy was probably somewhere in the West End. Or would she have to go to a hospital? Which was closest, the Royal Brompton or St Thomas's? That was her last conscious thought until she turned over and the bedside clock showed it was after nine.

Saturday morning and she had no particular reason to get up and start the day, but lounging about in bed wasn't her style. She had always been an early riser. Sometimes at the start of her relationship with Allison, they had lingered in bed on the weekend.

Camila stood in her kitchen and gazed out over the park. The trees were in full leaf now, but from her third-floor vantage point, she could see the green expanse of grass beyond already crowded with people determined to take advantage of a warm day in June, a hopeful start to summer.

While the kettle boiled she spooned coffee into the cafetière, or french press, as her father insisted it was called.

She retrieved the paper that had been delivered to her door and settled down in the living room with her coffee and toast. Ignoring the news section, she went straight to the business pages to check out the state of the markets. But even this normally absorbing pastime failed to block out memories of the night before.

What had gone wrong? Whatever their differences may be, she couldn't deny her attraction to Dani. The champagne at dinner had gone to her head. However, by the time they had danced for a while, she was clear-headed enough to know she wanted Dani to stay the night.

Conversation at dinner had been stilted to begin with when Dani started asking about her family. It had got easier when they moved on to general topics and she found Dani was as knowledgeable about current affairs as she was the arts.

When she mentioned Allison at the club, perhaps that was when Dani's interest in her had waned. Maybe she'd thought it wasn't worth competing with a dead lover.

Or was her closeted lifestyle that had put Dani off? Would she only ever feel comfortable going out with someone who dressed like a man, continuing to fool people into thinking she was straight?

She couldn't even contemplate coming out at work. The thought of telling either of the Redmond brothers she was a lesbian made her feel sick. Although sometimes she had caught looks passing between them in meetings that made her think they suspected the truth.

Living with Allison had been so easy. She couldn't recall now who had told her about the Gateways Club. In a way, finding it had been a relief, but she didn't feel comfortable watching women openly dancing closely together, bodies touching, kissing. She had decided to have one drink and leave.

A young woman stood next to her at the bar, also sipping a drink tentatively. She was taller than Camila, but then most people were, and had wavy dark hair that fell over one eye. The eye she could see was a deep blue. The woman brushed at her hair self-consciously when she caught Camila looking.

"Is this your first time?" she'd asked with a smile.

"Yes. And probably my last," Camila had replied. "Not really my scene."

"Hm. I know what you mean. I thought I should try it, but now that I'm here...." She left the sentence trailing.

The next song from the jukebox was one Camila recognised and she started tapping her foot in time with the music.

"Do you want to dance to this one?"

Camila hesitated briefly before nodding and allowing herself to be led onto the dance floor. She found her body moving fluidly against the other woman's and it felt good.

When she said she was going to leave after they'd shared a few dances, the woman offered to go with her. Once out on the street, they started walking down the King's Road in search of taxis. Allison then introduced herself and suggested, as it was still early, that they find a quiet pub for another drink before parting ways.

That had been the beginning. They started to see each other, meeting for dinner once a week at first.

Her coffee had gone cold and she went back into the kitchen to reheat it. The sky had clouded over and it looked like it might rain. She sighed and wondered how she was going to fill the day. There was probably a spreadsheet that needed tweaking. Losing herself in numbers was the only way she was going to get both Allison and Dani out of her thoughts.

†

Dani put the finishing touches to the storyboard. The positive outcome of having a free weekend was catching up on her freelance work. The client had been waiting a few weeks for this one but hadn't put any pressure on her, so she was pleased to have completed it before that happened.

She picked up the phone to call Jan, then put it down again. The idea of making the delivery herself took hold. It would help stave off the loneliness of a Saturday night on her own.

The afternoon rain had eased and the two-mile walk was pleasantly refreshing with the scents of flowering shrubs and well-tended gardens of the houses she passed. Reaching the corner of Grove Park Terrace, Dani looked at the imposing structure and hoped the boys were in. If they were hosting a dinner party, it wouldn't be starting until much later and they rarely went out for a meal before ten o'clock. It was only six thirty now.

She pushed the doorbell and smiled as a gothic-sounding gong reverberated in the hallway. The man who opened the door was wearing a dressing gown and nothing else if the amount of chest hair showing was anything to go by. He gave her a wide smile.

"Hello, darling. Do come in."

"I'm not interrupting anything, am I?"

"Not at all, sweetie. Just trying to decide what to wear for an evening of fun and frolics later."

A disembodied voice called out, "Who is it?"

"DBS delivering in person," he called over his shoulder before turning back to Dani. "Come on in. I want to see what you've brought us. The maid is mixing drinks as we speak."

She followed him into their living room, where his partner was indeed standing by the cocktail cabinet dressed in a maid's outfit; complete with a little white hat perched on his blond hair. He grinned at her.

"Can I tempt you to a small cocktail, or would you prefer a beer?"

"Beer, please."

He sniffed. "Such a pleb. You will be getting it in a glass, though."

She laughed as she sat on one of the leather sofas. "I know. What would the neighbours think if they saw me drinking out of a can?"

Several glasses of beer later, she left the house, content with their approval of the artwork. Despite the ease of their companionship, she hadn't felt able to ask for information on the subject that was still foremost in her mind. But the woman was so self-contained, particularly in her work persona, that it was possible they didn't know that much about their employee anyway.

†

Her Sunday routine of reading the papers, going for a walk in the park, and cleaning the kitchen and the bathroom only took half the morning. Camila thought about going out for brunch just to have some human interaction.

There had been a message from Chris on her answerphone when she got back from her walk. She deleted it. Chris might still be entertaining thoughts of going to bed with her again, but Camila knew that wasn't what she wanted. She wasn't going to play the other woman in that relationship. Although she'd never had much rapport with Deborah, she didn't want to cause her any distress. Starting anything long-term with Chris wasn't something she was going to pursue. Chris might be comfortable with having an open relationship, but Camila thought that only worked if the other partner was also playing the game. She was pretty sure Deborah wasn't really into it.

Allison had experienced no difficulty talking to Deborah. But she'd always been more outgoing than Camila.

With her job as a mental health nurse, she had a broad understanding of the human psyche and often teased Camila for her occasional lack of insight. Particularly when someone was flirting with her and Camila failed to pick up on the cues.

It was a different matter when it came to business. Sitting around a boardroom table, she had no trouble recognising the games being played. Her male counterparts often underestimated her ability to read a situation, mistakenly thinking they could intimidate her with a barrage of facts and figures.

Rain started lashing the windows, so she decided against going out again. Instead, she retrieved the small photo album from her desk drawer and sat in her chair, cradling it in her arms. These were the only photos she had of Allison, taken during their last holiday together. Allison's family had taken the rest, mementos of their ten years. No doubt, cutting her out of the photos as completely as they had cut her out of Allison's life…and death.

She only had these photos because the film was being developed and Camila had the receipt in her bag to be able to retrieve them. As well as denying their relationship, Allison's family had denied her a focus for her grief. There was no grave for her to visit. Her lover's body had been cremated and the ashes given to her family. Allison hadn't made a will. Neither of them had, but you didn't consider your mortality in your twenties and thirties. You didn't expect to go to work in the morning and not return that evening.

Scanning newspaper reports for information after Allison's death, she had only managed to find out that a patient, not named, had stopped taking their medication and was somehow able to obtain a knife. The hospital was absolved of any negligence.

Sighing, she put the album back in the drawer, unopened. Wallowing in self-pity was no way to spend a wet Sunday afternoon. She reached for the newspaper sections spread out on the coffee table and selected the TV guide. Maybe there was a film she could lose herself in, for a few hours at least.

†

Dani loaded the washing machine and started the wash cycle. Her clothes may be faded and worn-looking, but despite what Gordon thought, they were clean.

The Sunday paper hadn't held much of interest. Glancing through the Arts pages, she thought of popping into the Royal Academy to check out the Summer Exhibition. But summoning the energy to go into the West End was proving difficult. She considered taking her bike out for a ride, but when the rain started pelting down, that idea went out the window too.

She wondered what Camila was doing. Had she been wrong to walk out on her on Friday? Were their differences irreconcilable, or was her insecurity just taking hold?
Sending flowers might not work a second time. Would Camila be willing to give her another chance? It didn't seem likely after her dramatic exit. Best to forget the whole thing.

Chapter Eight

It was 11:00 p.m. by the bedside clock—11:03 to be precise. Dani was spreadeagled face down across the bed, handcuffed to the headboard. Lisa was somewhere in the room, preparing to give her the thrashing she desired. Or so she had thought.

Something was wrong. By now she should be wetter than a summer's day in Edinburgh. When Lisa had called earlier, she had jumped on the phone, thinking it might be Camila. And she had likewise jumped at the chance to come over to Lisa's and take her mind off Camila for a few hours.

"Lisa," she called.

"Don't be impatient." Lisa stroked the riding crop gently across Dani's buttocks.

"I'm not impatient. Take the cuffs off."

"You haven't said the word."

"Fuck that, Lisa. I'm not in the mood for games."

"You should have thought of that earlier."

Dani pulled at her restraints, but it was no use. She was well and truly secured. "Lisa!"

Lisa sighed. Then her tits brushed across Dani's back as she leant over to unlock the cuffs. Dani crawled off the bed and rubbed her wrists. "Sorry, babe." She started pulling on her clothes. "I just can't do it tonight."

Lisa stood in front of her when she was fully dressed and looked up into her face. "What's the matter, Dani?"

Dani shrugged. She couldn't meet Lisa's gaze.

"It's her, isn't it? This Camila woman."

"Maybe. I don't know."

"Jesus, Dani. You're not going vanilla on me, are you?"

"No, I...."

"Are you thinking about her now? Look at me, Dani."

Reluctantly Dani met her eyes. Lisa stepped back. Without warning she struck Dani hard across the face with the crop and ran out of the room.

Dani grabbed her jacket and left.

†

Dani didn't know the time exactly, she thought it was after one o'clock in the morning; her watch was next to the digital clock on Lisa's bedside table. And that seemed like an eternity away.

The cash she'd had when she left Lisa's was gone too; on the drinks she had bought at the second club she'd visited. The first one hadn't let her in. However, the second having a mixed leather/rubber fetish night. She had been cruised by both men and women, attracted no doubt by the macho-looking welt across her cheek.

Lisa had hit her hard; hit her in anger to hurt her. She couldn't have stayed after that, anyway. Anger had no part in it. That Lisa was genuinely upset, Dani was sorry about. But

81

there wasn't anything she could do. Lisa would get over it, eventually. She might even forgive her, sometime.

And now, it was sometime between one and two in the morning. She was standing outside Camila's building gazing up at the dark facade. Windows gaping, no lights on anywhere. Camila's flat had been on the second—or was it the third?—floor. It faced onto the park, she was sure of that. She wasn't sure of anything else.

The police car slowed and stopped. It had been past before. Two policemen got out; they put their hats on.

"So," said the taller one, "haven't you got a home to go to?"

Dani didn't reply. She continued to stare at the building, as if it held the answer.

"You can't stay here," said the other one. It was a woman.

"Why not?"

"It's the middle of the night. You can't just stand around on street corners."

"Why not?" Dani repeated. "It's a free country, isn't it?"

"Have you got any money?"

"What is this? A mugging?"

He spoke to his partner. "What do you think? Drunk? Vagrant? Escaped loony?" His partner shrugged. "Well," he continued, "if you won't move along of your own accord, you had better come with us." He put a hand on her arm.

Dani looked at the hand. "You've got to be kidding." She shook him off and started running. He caught her easily and after a brief struggle managed to snap handcuffs on her wrists and drag her over to the car. She spat in his face as he bent to shove her into the back seat. She had seen that in a film once. It wouldn't do any good, but it made her feel better.

At the station she refused to give her name. They put her in a cell to think about it. A little later she was strip-searched and given a once-over by a doctor. When she was returned to her cell, she was amused to see she was designated "unknown vg"...*vegetarian, very good, vagina?* A little while later, a WPC came in with a cup of sweetened tea.

"Where did you get the cut?" she asked, looking at Dani's face.

Dani just smiled. "Thanks for the tea." The woman shrugged and left.

More time passed, slowly.

Apparently they weren't going to allow her to make a phone call. Who would she call, anyway? Gordon would be horrified at the thought of setting foot in a police station. Lisa wasn't speaking to her. She had few other people she could call on to bail her out. Invoking her brother's name wouldn't improve the situation. Best to just sit it out and see what happened. They would let her go eventually.

She settled down on the hard mattress, resting with her hands behind her head. It wasn't the best accommodation, but she'd been in pub toilets that smelt worse.

Dani was sorry she had upset Lisa. They went back a long way. Back to Dani's first year living in London. Sometimes, looking back, Dani couldn't believe her luck that night, her third one on the streets and down to the last of the money she'd stolen from her dad, after she'd kicked him in the groin, leaving him writhing on the floor of her bedroom in pain.

Leaving home had been on the cards for some time. Neither of her parents really cared for her. She was their first born, unplanned, so her mother blamed Dani for her being stuck in a loveless marriage. Her father, initially disappointed she wasn't a boy, was then aggrieved when she didn't behave like a little girl. When she reached her teens and hit puberty, he couldn't grasp why she didn't have a boyfriend. After putting up with his inept fumblings, escalating to squeezing her breasts or grabbing at her crotch whenever he could, she'd finally told him she was only interested in girls. That tipped him over the edge. After a week of screaming abuse at her, calling her names she didn't fully understand, he came to her room that last night, with one aim in mind...to give her a taste of what she was missing.

The walls of the cell and the previous occupant's stench faded out as her memory of the fateful encounter that changed her life formed clearly in front of her closed eyelids.

...A tall, well-dressed woman stepped out of a black cab and walked towards the steps of the building where Dani was sheltering.

"I'm sorry, but you can't stay here."

Dani's teeth were chattering as she tried to form words. "Nowhere else to go."

"Come with me." The tone was commanding, and without thinking Dani obeyed.

She followed the woman into the ancient lift. As the gate shut with a clang and the contraption started to rise, creaking its way up two floors, the only thought that came into her head was that they were the same height.

Revived after a bath, a hot meal, and a tumbler of whisky, in that order, Dani started to take in the luxurious nature of her surroundings. She was wearing a borrowed bathrobe, and only when her benefactor sat down next to her, did she wonder what would be required of her in return.

"What's your name, honey?"

"Dani."

"Is that short for anything?"

"No, just Dani. My parents were hoping for a boy."

The woman gave her an appraising look. "Well, I think they did better than that." She reached out and stroked Dani's cheek. "A good-looking baby butch."

Dani's experience with girls had only reached the kissing and breast-fondling stage. Hurried glances at her father's stash of porn gave her an idea of what could be done, but she hadn't been able to put any of it into practice. She wondered if this is what would be expected of her now.

"My name's Bea, sweetie. Well, to my clients I'm Mistress Bea. I know you're wondering if I want you to have sex with me. The answer is no. However, instead of sexual favours, I would like a companion to go out to dinner with, see plays, enjoy the delights of the city without complications. A handsome young butch like yourself fits the bill nicely. Tomorrow we will go and see Charles. He will outfit you properly. That is, if you agree to this arrangement."

Dani didn't hesitate to say yes. What other option did she have? A few days on the streets had shown her that the world wasn't kind to homeless beggars, particularly young ones.

Bea's patronage allowed Dani to explore the part of herself she'd kept hidden for so many years, knowing it wasn't normal. Learning from Bea how to pass as a man on the street satisfied one of her cravings. The other was taken care of a month or so into their "arrangement" when Bea introduced Dani to her young protege, Lisa....

†

After what felt like days, she was taken out of the cell and put into an interview room. Two men followed her in

85

and identified themselves as detectives. One of them turned the tape on. The other started to question her.

"What's your name?"

"What are you holding me for?"

"We will ask the questions."

"What do you suspect me of?"

"We will get on to the difficult questions later. Right now we just want to know who you are."

"I don't have to say anything. Your colleagues picked me off the street. For no reason at all. I was just minding my own business."

"You resisted arrest."

"What was I being arrested for? No one gave me the speech. You know the one...about what you say may be given in evidence—"

"We have reason to believe that illegal acts—"

"What acts? I was on my own. Oh, I get it. Because I'm dressed like this; because I have this cut on my face? Is that it? Have I been asleep and woken up twenty years later into a police state?"

The two men looked uncomfortable. They were saved from answering by a knock on the door. One went out into the hall; the other switched the tape off. His mate returned almost immediately. "You're free to go," he said without looking at Dani.

"Oh, great. You pick me off the street for no good reason. You hold me here for hours, strip-search me, give me one lousy cup of tea, and now you're not even going to charge me with anything. You'll be hearing from my solicitor."

The cop shrugged and held the door open for her. He obviously didn't think she had either the means or the wherewithal to hire a solicitor.

†

It was 9:23 by the station clock when she walked out onto the street after collecting her belt and studded collar from the desk sergeant. She hadn't been paying attention when they brought her in. She looked around for a sign. Poland Street. How convenient—only three minutes' away from the office.

Gordon's secretary, Maria, had put the coffee on. Dani walked in and helped herself to a cup. Maria stared at her in horror.

"I don't suppose you could be a sweetie and get me a bacon roll?" Dani asked.

"No, I could not. You're a disgrace. How dare you come in here looking like that," she screeched.

Gordon appeared in the doorway of his office. "Maria!" He looked at Dani. "Maria, It's okay. I'll deal with this." He took a tenner out of his wallet. "I'd like a bacon roll too, and get whatever you want for yourself. Okay?"

She pulled herself together, took the money, and left.

Gordon looked at Dani again. "You better come in and tell me all about it."

She drained her cup and followed him into his office. "I've spent the night at the Poland Street nick," she announced.

"I guessed it was either that or a cardboard box. So what is that cut on your cheek and the marks on your wrists? Police brutality?"

Dani looked at her wrists. She had forgotten about them; must have happened at Lisa's. "I should have been so lucky. Brutality would have been interesting. It was just so fucking boring. Eight hours in a cell, one cup of tea, three offers of a smoke, a strip-search, and no explanation at the end of it. Just piss off, you can go now."

"So how did you get those injuries?"

"I didn't tell them, so why should I tell you?"

"Because I'm buying you breakfast."

"Okay." She looked him straight in the eyes. He looked away first. "I upset my lover. She was holding a whip at the time. Not a good move."

Gordon sat silent, staring at her. He was shocked, she could tell. He knew about her preferences, but he didn't like being confronted with the evidence. He shifted uncomfortably in his well-padded chair. "Look, Dani. You agreed you wouldn't bring your private life to the office. The black eyes the other week were bad enough, but this...you saw how Maria reacted."

"Maria's a tight-arsed little bitch."

"Maybe. But she's only paid to type letters and make coffee."

"Yeah. She makes good coffee. Could you get me another cup? I'd go myself but I don't want to frighten anyone else."

She stared at the picture on the wall behind his desk, glad of the peace and quiet, until Gordon returned with the coffee and the bacon rolls. They ate in silence. Dani spoke first. "I don't have any money. That's why I came here," she said after she had finished eating.

Gordon was still brooding. "Most people stay at home on Sunday evenings, have a bath, watch telly. What the hell were you doing?"

"I'm sure you don't really want the details. Just relaxing, in my own way."

"You're a fucking pervert."

"Thanks. If you'll lend me the taxi fare, I will go home and make myself presentable."

He shook his head. "A bath isn't going to make you any more presentable." Gordon threw two twenties across the desk. "Melissa was right. I'll get my solicitor to sort it out. I don't ever want to see you on these premises again."

Dani picked up the money. "I have one word for you. Redmond."

"Fuck you!"

"No, thanks." She stood and threw the money back at him. "I'll walk instead."

Maria was studying something fascinating on her desk as Dani went past. Amanda called to her as she walked through Reception. She stopped and looked at her. The receptionist stared at her face but didn't comment. "Message for you." She handed her a telephone slip.

"Thanks." Dani stuffed it in her pocket and stalked out, setting off in the direction of Oxford Street. She didn't really fancy the walk back to Chiswick, so she wandered aimlessly along, looking in shop windows. How long would it take to get the fare if she begged? Several days judging by the coins in the busker's hat. Mugging? People were giving her as wide a berth as possible on the crowded pavement. She would have to go back to Lisa's, collect her watch and pawn it.

Lisa lived near Regent's Park; it didn't take her long to get there. The walk along Marylebone High Street was pleasant enough. She banged on the door; the lazy bitch was probably still in bed, she thought. But Lisa opened the door before Dani could knock again. She was dressed in street clothes and looked like she was on her way out.

"What are you doing here?" she said coldly, her eyes flicking briefly over Dani's bruised face.

"I left my watch behind."

"Oh?"

"Yeah. I need it. For the taxi fare home."

"You had better come in and get it, then." She stayed in the doorway; Dani brushed past her and headed straight to the bedroom. Her watch was where she had left it. She snapped it onto her wrist.

"So who did you spend the night with?" Lisa asked.

"Do you care?"

"Sandy saw you at a club. Said you seemed to be popular."

"Yeah. But I left alone. In fact, the cops picked me up and I spent the night at the nick. So unless you count the WPC who strip-searched me, I have been utterly faithful to you, my darling."

Their eyes met. With her high heels on, the top of Lisa's head still only reached Dani's shoulders. "Don't you 'darling' me, you bastard!" she hissed.

Dani grinned at her. "Does that mean you still love me?"

"Damned right it does," Lisa said calmly, then slapped her hard across the cheek, clocking a bullseye on the cut. Dani's eyes watered. Apparently, there was no rush to get home after all.

†

Camila watched the presentation intro again. It wasn't her job to comment on creative decisions, but she did think opening the conference with Tina Turner belting out "Simply the Best" was a bit over the top. At least Eric had vetoed the first suggestion from the marketing department—Yazz singing, "The Only Way is Up".

Her slides were all set for the event. She had supervised the insertion of the 35mm transparencies into the carousel and asked James to run through them on the projector to make sure they were all placed correctly in the tray.

Carl Redmond had laughed at her, saying she needed to use the latest technology. James could have produced her slides on the computer using their recently installed PowerPoint software.

"Belts and braces," she'd told him. "Remember last year, when the laptop crashed in the middle of Eric's opening speech."

"We're prepared for that this year. Three laptops and all the handouts printed. Who were the flowers from?"

She'd given him a small smile. "Nice try, Carl."

He had left her office none the wiser, and she planned to keep it that way. She was determined to keep thoughts of Dani at a distance. Over the weekend, that hadn't worked out as planned. Images from Friday evening kept intruding— Dani looking incredibly handsome in the tailored suit, raising a glass of champagne to her in the restaurant with a smile that promised more than the sharing of food and drink.

When the preconference meeting finished, she returned to her office intending to finish the Berlin proposal, but after half an hour she hadn't made any progress, staring at a blank page on the screen.

All weekend she had been wrestling with conflicting thoughts on whether or not she wanted to see Dani again. Her mind was telling her to forget it, write it off as an interesting interlude and move on. Her body had other ideas. There was no mistaking the response in her lower regions to Dani's closeness and touch while they were dancing.

Giving up on Berlin, she dialled MBE's number. She had left a message in the morning, telling the girl it was an urgent matter. She hadn't received a call back before the meeting or any messages afterwards. The agency's receptionist sounded subdued when she answered the phone and when Camila asked to be put through to Dani, she lowered her voice further.

91

"Um. She's gone."

"What do you mean? When will she be back?"

"She won't. She's left the company."

"Oh, that's very sudden. Why?"

"I'm afraid I can't say. Would you like to speak to someone else in the art department?"

"Not at the moment. Thank you." Camila put the receiver down and stared at her blank screen again. What on earth was going on?

Her phone rang and she snatched it up eagerly before registering that it was an internal call—Eric, asking when he could expect to see a draft of the Berlin proposal. Promising to have it done before she went home for the day, Camila pushed aside thoughts of Dani and concentrated on working through the figures she would need to present when negotiating with the Germans.

She didn't get back to her flat until after seven. She kicked off her heels, poured herself a glass of wine, and collapsed onto the sofa. Camila closed her eyes, expecting to see the numbers that had been dancing through her brain for the last few hours, but Dani's face appeared instead. That nervous smile she'd caught a few times. What was she worried about? Had she been planning to leave MBE even before they'd met to talk about the T-shirts?

Camila opened her eyes and sat up with a start. Dani had given her a card at that brief meeting in Flounders. A card with her phone number on the back. She leapt to her feet and retrieved her briefcase from the hallway. After searching through all the pockets, she resorted to emptying everything out. The card wasn't there.

What had she been wearing that evening? Most of her work clothes didn't have pockets. And she only carried a handbag when going out. Her briefcase held everything she needed for work.

She had taken the card out when she got home. Camila recalled looking at the scrawled phone number on the back. But she hadn't looked long enough to commit the numbers to memory. Where had she put the card if not back in her briefcase?

After looking in all the obvious places—her address book by the phone, the drawer in the kitchen filled with odds and ends, her desk drawers and the one in her bedside table—she found no sign of the elusive card.

Well, she thought, sitting down with a second glass of wine, it obviously wasn't meant to be. Short of grabbing Gordon McKenzie by the throat and demanding Dani's personnel file, that was the end of it. A brief fantasy fling. She needed to forget Dani. And she had more than enough things to concentrate on this week—the conference, a trip to Berlin, and producing a definitive financial forecast on the Far East markets Eric and Carl wanted to break into in the near future. She certainly didn't have time to be worrying about a relationship that would never have worked anyway.

Chapter Nine

On Wednesday afternoon, Dani was lying face down on the living room floor flicking through one of her art books that featured the work of French impressionists. She stopped at one of Manet's popular paintings depicting a picnic scene with two nude women, one in the foreground sharing a blanket with two clothed men. While these three seemed to be having a conversation, oblivious to the fact the woman had no clothes on, Dani had always wondered what the other woman was doing, a little ways apart from the group, bent over. Maybe she was picking mushrooms.

She was so engrossed in the picture that it took her some minutes to realise her doorbell was being leaned on. Whoever it was, they weren't going away. She stumbled to her feet and steadied herself before going to answer it.

Penny stood outside with her finger on the bell. "Hi, can I come in?"

"Yeah, sure, why not?" Dani followed her slowly back into her front room.

"I tried to phone yesterday."

"Oh. I didn't hear it. I was a bit out of it."

"Looks like you still are!"

Dani picked at one of the holes in her T-shirt. "So what's the social visit for?"

"The rumour at the factory is that Gordon's buying you out—that you two have had a big bust-up."

"Yeah. The stupid bastard's only just discovered that he doesn't like having a 'fucking pervert' as a partner. His expression, not mine."

"According to Maria—"

"Yes, I would really like to know what Maria has to say."

Penny ignored the sarcasm. "According to Maria, you came in on Monday with a big cut on your face looking and smelling like you had spent the night under Waterloo Bridge."

"The girl has no imagination."

"And Gordon told you to get out. That he never wants to see you again."

"Yeah, well she got that right."

"So what are you going to do?"

"Me? I'm not going to do anything. Before I doped myself up for the big sleep yesterday, I called my solicitor. He's going to do something."

"Like what?"

"Like take Gordon fucking McKenzie to the cleaners."

"I don't understand. I thought you and Gordon were mates. I mean, it's not as though he doesn't know about you, is it?"

"No. It's been coming for a while. The party's over. And Melissa isn't one of my fans."

"What has she got to do with it?"

"Everything, I'd say. She's got him by the balls and she's never been able to understand why he stuck with me."

"Why did he?"

"We were a good team. In the early days. We needed each other."

"Is this really it? There's no chance he will change his mind?"

"Penny, this isn't a lover's tiff. We're not going to kiss and make up. It's definitely over."

"Shit! What are we going to do?"

"You mean, what are you going to do? That's what's bugging you, isn't it? That's why you're here."

Penny looked uncomfortable.

Dani relented. "Do you want a beer?"

"Yeah, okay." Penny followed her into the kitchen. Dani pulled two cans out of the fridge and handed one to her. "Can I have a glass?"

"Above the sink."

Penny poured her beer into a pint glass. They drank in silence.

"Have a seat. Don't mind me, I prefer to stand."

"Jesus, Dani!" Penny took a big gulp of beer. "I bet it wasn't that woman in the restaurant."

"What woman?"

"I followed you…to the Trattoria the other day. She looked pretty classy, not your type at all, I'd say."

Dani put her can down so that Penny wouldn't notice her hands shaking. Damn, she had managed to keep Camila out of her thoughts for a few days. Since Monday, anyway. "No."

Penny changed the subject. "What do I do? About my job, I mean?"

"Just carry on doing it. Probably get bought out by a bigger agency."

"Is there anything you want from the studio?"

"No. Thanks."

"Declan and Gary are pretty upset."

"Yeah, well there's not much I can do about that."

"Declan thinks you're pregnant."

Dani smiled. "And he probably thinks babies are delivered by storks as well."

"Dani? Are you really all right?"

"Never been better."

"I just can't believe it. I mean, Gordon will come round, won't he?"

"He can try."

"You're really serious, aren't you? What are you going to do?"

"I don't know. Sell T-shirts maybe."

"Look, I'll call again Friday. To make sure you're okay." Penny placed her empty glass by the sink.

"Don't feel you have to." Dani walked her to the door and watched her walk away, shaking her head. As mystified as when she arrived, no doubt.

Penny's visit had achieved an objective, though. Dani knew she had to do something soon. Although she had lied to Penny, she had only told her what she planned to do as soon as she could face it—see a solicitor.

Thinking about her abrupt departure from the office reminded her that Amanda had given her a message. She had shoved it in a pocket. Remembering what she had been wearing took some time. Her leather trousers were in a heap on the bedroom floor. She rummaged through the pockets, hoping Lisa hadn't got there first.

It was there, a crumpled yellow telephone Post-it note. She stared at the words—unbelieving. Camila Callaghan from Redmond had rung. Could she ring back? *Urgent* was circled. Time: 9:45. Day: Monday.

Dani stood by the phone. Breathing out to calm her nerves, she dialled the Redmond number. The secretary told her Ms Callaghan was in a meeting. Dani said, politely, that she would wait while the secretary went and got Ms Callaghan out of her meeting. No, she didn't want to call back. After much hesitation, the girl decided to go and do as Dani suggested.

When Camila came on the line, she didn't waste time with pleasantries. "Where the hell have you been? I heard you've left the company. Is that true?"

"Yes and no. Do you know any good solicitors?"

"Perhaps we should meet and discuss this." Camila sounded extremely businesslike.

"Yes, I think we should."

"Today. Four o'clock. Where?"

"Uh, here, I guess." It was already after three and Dani didn't feel like traipsing across London.

"Where is here?"

Dani gave her the address and ended the call. She looked around the room. *Christ!* She started picking things up in a half-hearted attempt to tidy it, then gave up and went upstairs to shower and change.

†

Camila was on time, immaculately dressed as always. Dani had opted for a clean, loose-fitting shirt and jeans without holes.

"Come in." She ushered her into the front room. "Tea or coffee? I'm afraid it's the maid's day off."

Camila looked around, taking in the litter of drawings and papers, as if she believed this. "No thanks." She found a place to sit. Dani stood by the fireplace, leaning on the mantel as Camila opened her briefcase and took out a neatly typed piece of paper. "A list of solicitors. They're all good, but expensive."

"Fine. I want the best." Dani put the paper on the mantel.

"You realise this jeopardises the whole T-shirt deal."

"You could deal directly with me."

"With you?" Camila gave her a look that suggested she might have the business sense of a cat.

"Why not? They're my designs."

"Not according to McKenzie. You created them while you were employed by MBE."

"I wasn't an employee. I was a partner. I still am a partner; he can't fire me. And it's going to cost him a lot to get rid of me."

"What is this all about, Dani? You two have been together a long time."

"Everything, and nothing. His wife. My lifestyle. Male menopause."

"Don't you think you should try to talk to him before going to a solicitor?"

"No. Not after what he said to me on Monday."

"Look, you don't have to take my advice, but if you're going through with it, I think you should contact a solicitor straightaway. Gordon needs to have a better reason for getting rid of you than that his wife doesn't like you. And I don't suppose it's news to him that you're a lesbian."

"Uh, no, but—"

"If you're partners, he doesn't have the right to throw you off the premises. If you are serious about wanting our business, then you need to be in a position of strength. Which you won't be if you let him sideline you like this."

"Sounds like you know a bit about the law yourself."

"I've studied corporate law. And I read the papers. By all means, split from Gordon if that's what you want, but set up your own agency first. Take some of the staff with you. He's just the front man. It will hurt him like hell if he has to replace you and other key staff to try and hold on to his client base."

"Yeah. Right. I'll think about it. Do you want a drink?" Camila looked at her watch. "All right. Just one."

"G and T?"

"Yes, with lots of ice."

"Yes, ma'am!" Dani grinned at her and went into the kitchen.

†

Camila sat back and took in her surroundings. When Dani gave her the address, she hadn't realised she was coming to her house. If she had known, she wouldn't have expected anywhere like this. There was a large framed print on the wall above the fireplace, a café scene. It looked familiar, one of the French impressionists, she thought. Her father had several treasured prints like this one on the walls of their house in Brittany.

There were no family photos anywhere. If Dani had parents or siblings, their images didn't merit pride of place on the mantelpiece. Her own apartment, she thought, also gave nothing away in that respect. One photo of a holiday with her parents fifteen years ago sat in an ornate frame on the bookshelf in her living room. A cherished photo of herself with Allison lived on her bedside table.

She wandered up the two steps into the seating area with its windows overlooking the narrow strip of lawn stretching down towards the river. As she watched, a scull went past at a fair clip towards Putney.

Dani came up behind her. Camila turned and took the glass from her. "A fine view."

"Yeah, always different." They sipped in silence, watching the movement outside. "Look...." Dani hesitated.

"I'm sorry about the other night. I didn't expect it to turn out like that."

"Neither did I." Camila gulped down a large portion of her drink. "I was going to call you on Monday evening. But I'd lost the card you gave me."

Dani was staring at the river and seemed to be having difficulty swallowing. Finally she said, softly, "Did you want to go to bed with me?"

"Yes."

"And now?"

"Now, I don't have time. I'm driving down to Brighton for our staff conference. I won't be back until Friday night."

"But if you weren't...going to the conference?"

"Yes. Dani, would you please look at me?"

Dani turned towards her. Camila took her head in her hands and kissed her on the mouth. After a few minutes, she drew back. "I'll call you on Friday. Write your number down for me."

Dani scribbled it on the corner of one of her drawing pads and tore off the piece of paper. Camila tucked it carefully into the side pocket in her briefcase and let herself out, leaving Dani still standing by the window, seemingly entranced by the play of sun on the moving water flowing past the end of the garden.

†

Gordon glanced around the studio. It was as Dani had left it on the Friday before the fateful Monday morning. The half-finished storyboard for the satellite TV account lay on her drawing board. As expected, the detail was impeccably depicted. He turned the page over to see what else she was working on. A partly drawn face looked up at him. Something about the eyes looked familiar.

The door opened and he turned, half hoping to see Dani walk in. Unfortunately it was his wife.

"Amanda said you were in here."

"Yes. I'm going to have to find a replacement creative director, pronto. Just seeing what needs doing." He placed the incomplete storyboard back on the table.

"Good. About time you ditched that freak."

"Dani's very talented."

"She's a liability. How you ever thought a partnership with her could work, I'll never know."

"Oh, come on, Mel. Without Dani's creativity, I doubt we would have got this far." Gordon was already wishing he hadn't reacted so strongly to Dani's appearance on Monday morning. It had mainly been an act to placate his secretary. Maybe he should have fired Maria instead. That would solve another problem.

"Anyway, I just came in to make sure you've got the theatre tickets for Saturday."

"Yes. All booked." He wasn't looking forward to sitting through *The Phantom of the Opera* yet again. But it was Melissa's favourite and she insisted on taking visitors to see it, this time one of her university friends and her husband who were staying with them for the weekend.

Melissa carried on talking and Gordon only caught bits of it—she was taking Theo somewhere that evening and wondered whether or not they should let Tessa quit her ballet lessons. With only half an ear on what his wife was saying, Gordon's mind kept wandering back to the drawing. He knew that face from somewhere, he was sure of it.

Chapter Ten

Dani arrived at the office just after nine on Thursday morning. Amanda was at her desk. "Any messages?" she asked.

Amanda smiled at her. "Just a few. I saved them for you."

"So you didn't believe the rumours."

"Not for a minute."

"Thanks." Dani moved quickly past the reception desk, and took the stairs two at a time. Her studio was in the same state as she had left it. The boys weren't in. Declan's jacket was thrown across a chair; he was probably getting a coffee, chatting up one of the girls from Accounts. She looked at the message slips Amanda had given her. All from clients probably looking for progress on their artwork, but there was one unfamiliar name. As she started to dial the number, the phone on Gary's desk rang, so she pressed the button to connect the line. "Hello."

"Uh, hello, is Gary there?"

"Sorry, he's not in yet. Can I help?"

"Yes, I hope so. This is James. We need some slides changed. Gary was working on them. Would he be able to do them and get them down to us by this evening...in Brighton?"

"No problem. You have to pay extra for rush jobs, though."

"That's okay. This is an emergency."

"All right. Fax them through. He will do it as soon as he comes in. What time do you need them by?" Dani took down the details and rang off. She looked up to find Declan standing in the doorway staring at her.

"Hi, I thought—"

"Hey. I hear you've been spreading rumours that I'm pregnant."

"Well, I—"

"Not true. False alarm. So what have you been doing while I've been away? Reached the seventh level yet?"

He shook his head. "It's good to have you back. Coffee?"

"Yeah, thanks. And tell Gary he's got some slides to do for Redmond. They need them delivered to Brighton this evening. James is sending a fax."

"Okay. Great." He grinned sheepishly and disappeared.

He came back a few minutes later with her coffee and a pile of mail. "You would make someone a wonderful secretary," she said.

"I put it in a drawer, in case someone else tried to open it."

"Oh, right. Thanks. Good thinking, Batman." So Camila had been right. Maybe Gordon wasn't as popular as he would like to think. She drank her coffee and flicked through the letters, and rang the client whose name she hadn't recognised. They wanted to discuss a new campaign, so she made an appointment for Monday. She could always take someone else to do the sales pitch.

At nine thirty she went over to Gordon's office. Maria was typing a letter, slowly. Dani walked past her and went in without knocking. If Maria was going to say something, she thought better of it and turned back to her screen.

Gordon looked up. "So how's it going, Gordon? Lost any big clients this week? I wouldn't like to see my share of the business diminishing in any way."

"What do you think you're doing here?"

"I'm talking to you. Letting you know there's no change in the creative department."

"I told you I didn't want to see you here and I meant it."

"What are you going to do, Gordon? Phone the police? Phone your wife? I am still your partner, like it or not. I don't much like it myself. But I suppose I'll just need to look for another business manager. Someone who won't go around upsetting major clients like Redmond. And then you'll be free to go and play house with your wife and two-point-four children. Spend more time with your family. A lot of prominent politicians seem to be doing it. 'Back to basics', they call it."

"I want you off these premises."

"Yes. Or what? Anyway, I didn't come in here to exchange pleasantries, I just wanted to give you a personal invitation to the staff meeting."

"What staff meeting?"

"The one in the boardroom in five minutes. I will explain what is happening. It's not fair to keep them in the dark, wondering what's going on—whether they will have jobs in a few weeks' time."

"What are you going to say?"

"You better come and find out."

"Dani!"

†

The boardroom was full. Dani entered with Gordon close on her heels. She made her way to the front of the room and looked at Amanda. "Is everyone here?" Amanda nodded. "Right. I'm sure a lot of you are confused with rumours you may have heard. So, to set the record straight, I am not leaving. I am not being pushed out. Gordon and I are partners. We built this business from scratch, and some of you have played a large part in that over the years. MBE is well respected in the industry and we have an excellent client base. I know it may surprise some of you that I am even aware of this—but I have to be. My name and my reputation are the cornerstone of this business. And will continue to be. As it seems that Gordon and I can no longer sustain our partnership on a friendly basis, I will be setting up my own agency and I would invite any of you who are interested in joining me to do so. I'm not asking you to take sides or to jump ship. As far as I'm concerned, as far as our clients are concerned, it's business as usual. Whatever Gordon decides to do is his business." Dani looked around the room; everyone looked stunned. "Any questions?" She waited. "Okay. I'll be in the studio if anyone wants to talk to me."

She had to brush past Gordon to get out of the door. "You can't do this," he hissed.

"What is your problem, Gordon? Excuse me, I have some calls to make—damage limitation calls—to our clients."

"You can't do this," he repeated, red-faced by now.

"If you want it explained to you in simple terms, call my solicitor."

"You don't have a solicitor."

"I do now." She returned to the studio, followed closely by Declan and Gary. "What's the word on the street?" she asked.

"They're all a bit confused," said Gary. "So are we. We heard you weren't coming back."

"I never left. Did that fax come through from James?"

"Yeah. It's only three slides."

"Okay, so get on to it. They need to be processed this afternoon. Order a bike for five o'clock. Is there anything else outstanding?"

"The security mailer's due tomorrow," said Declan.

"Have you drafted anything?"

"Yes."

"Right. I'll take a look at that. Well, don't stand there like a couple of geeks. I'm here. And, like I said, it's business as usual."

†

Camila pressed the receiver to her ear; it was difficult to hear with all the noise around her. "Sunday night, yes. Book the flight. I'll collect the tickets at the desk. Tell Berlin to fax the details here."

She returned to the conference room; the next session was just starting. She had already done her presentation but she would have to be on the panel after this to answer questions. Finding her place in the front row, she arranged herself, legs crossed, to listen to the technical director's speech. They were bound to lose a few at this one; it was the last session of the afternoon and everyone had endured a long day of listening. Most would now be thinking about getting to the bar and downing as many free drinks as possible before dinner. She had trouble concentrating herself, having tried hard to keep thoughts of Dani at bay. At the previous night's rehearsals there had been a few last-minute panics, and she had stayed in the bar longer than she normally would in an effort to numb her emotions. But Dani kept drifting in. She had put herself on the line; it thrilled and scared her at the same time. She wanted Dani, but having made the first move, she wasn't sure she was going to be able to handle it.

All the time she had been with Dani the day before, each movement Dani made, came back to her. She had, desperately, wanted to touch Dani's face, to ask her about the cut, the bruising on her wrists. What did she do to get these marks? She didn't look like a fighter. Was she into something weird? Dani was probably right; they were very different. But one thing was clear: they wanted each other just as badly. Camila recrossed her legs, aware of her arousal. With a great deal of effort, she brought herself back to the present and concentrated on Carl's words, even though she knew his presentation as well as her own, having rehearsed with him a number of times.

She went up to her room for a shower and change of clothes before dinner. Her knickers were soaked through, but luckily it hadn't shown on the back of her skirt. When she came down again, getting near the bar was impossible. Understaffed, as usual. The hotel should have known better; they made more on drinks than on the accommodation at events like this. She was tempted to go back to her room and raid the minibar.

"Hi, I've got you a drink." She looked round to find Robert at her side. *What did he want?* she wondered. However, she smiled graciously and accepted the glass of gin and tonic. He must have had it for a while; the ice had melted. Still, it had gin in it, so she drank some. And smiled at him again. Encouraged, he said, "We had a small panic, but it's solved now."

"Oh?" This meant he had spent some money.

"Um. Yes. We needed some extra slides. And then we found we were six videos short. But MBE was able to sort it for us. They're sending someone down with them tonight. I said we would get them a room. Is that okay?"

"Yes. Fine. So, there weren't any problems with MBE?"

"No. James said he spoke to Barker this morning. Everything seems to be back to normal."

"Good." She smiled again. *Normal* wasn't a word she would ever associate with Dani. "Thanks for the drink." She finished it and gave him the glass. "Have you seen Eric or Carl?"

"They're over by the window." If Robert was shocked by the swiftness of her downing the G and T, his face didn't show it.

She walked quickly across the room to join the Redmonds. Although the hours were long and involved so much travel, working for their company was her dream job. Unlike other places she had worked, the brothers treated her with respect. When they asked for her opinion, they listened and more often than not acted on her advice.

Although she knew they had interviewed many candidates, she wasn't surprised when they offered her the job. During the interviews, she was drawn in to their infectious excitement about their product and the expansion into new markets, and her confidence grew with each question she was able to answer with a matching tone of enthusiasm. After she had signed the contract of employment, Eric asked if she would like to hire her own PA. Camila assured him that she didn't need a personal assistant, as she preferred to keep a firm hand on producing financial reports. Carl joked that she had already saved them money and hadn't even started the job. It had worked out well. Eric's PA made all travel arrangements and hotel bookings and she had proved over the years that she could keep up with the workload.

They also cared about their employees in a way she hadn't experienced in other corporations. The days immediately after Allison's death, Eric had called her into his office.

"You don't seem yourself. Is anything wrong?"

Camila hesitated, not sure what to tell him. Although she saw the brothers every day when she was in the office, they only ever talked business. She decided on the safe route, just saying a close friend had died.

"Would you like to take some time off?"

That question caught her off guard. Most employers only granted unplanned leave for the death of close relatives—parents, grandparents, siblings.

"Oh no. Work helps." She hoped her attempt at a smile was convincing.

"Well, you'll want to go to the funeral, won't you?"

I would if I knew where and when it was. Instead of burdening him with the whole sad story, she just nodded. A few weeks later he stopped her in the corridor to ask when she would need the day off. Unable to meet his eyes on that occasion, Camila told him it had taken place a week before, on Saturday.

Now, as she reached them, they stopped talking and looked at her in that uncanny way they had, almost like twins communicating telepathically. *Had they been talking about me?*

"I thought my speech went well." Carl beamed.

"Yes. But I was worried when you went off autocue to tell that joke."

"No one noticed. I had to do something to perk things up. At that point, you were the only one in the audience still awake."

"I was," Eric interjected indignantly.

"Your eyes were closed and you were doing that nodding, jerking thing you do when you're bored at dinner parties about to fall head first into the soup."

"I was not. I was thinking."

"Couldn't have been very interesting as you were nodding off."

"I was not nodding off." Eric turned to Camila. "Would you like a drink? I'm sure Carl would go to the bar for you."

Camila smiled at their banter and nodded. "A gin and tonic, please."

Sticking his tongue out at his brother, Carl walked away, head held high.

"I think you were...nodding off," Camila ventured as soon as Carl was out of hearing range.

"I know. The technical details bore me rigid, as he well knows. But thank you for not agreeing with him. I need to maintain the upper hand." He glanced around the room. "Is it worth it, do you think?"

She looked at him, puzzled. "Is what worth it?"

"This." Eric waved his arm at the crowd by the bar. "Spending our profits on letting the staff drink at our expense. And, boy, can they drink! We could get the same message across with a few Friday afternoon department meetings in the office."

"Yes, it is worth it. Good for morale."

He smiled as Carl returned from the bar. "I suppose so. Have to tell Robert to start planning the Christmas party next."

"Oh, please." Carl took a sip from the glass of white wine he was holding. "It's only June."

†

James met her at the front desk and Dani handed him the slides and the videocassettes. He gave her a key. "We booked you a room."

"You didn't need to do that."

"Least we could do. I didn't expect you to be delivering them personally, though."

"No problem. Our courier let us down. Luckily my bike was in tune." Not strictly true. Jan would have jumped at the chance to do a longer-distance delivery. "Are you going to check those? I might have to go back if they're not right."

"Oh, yeah," he laughed nervously. She followed him into the conference room. It felt good to stretch her legs after ninety minutes on the bike. The rest of the crew was there, rehearsing lighting sequences and sound levels. Dani watched as they checked the new slides and ran a few minutes on each video. Then she excused herself. They would all be up for a few hours more. She took the lift to her designated room; it had been a long day, but she had unfinished business to deal with.

†

Camila sat on the bed looking at the phone, wondering if she should ring Dani or would it seem too forward? Maybe she had pushed too far with yesterday's performance at Dani's house.

There was a knock on the door. "Yes," she called, hoping it wasn't one of the sound crew playing a drunken prank.

"Room service."

She hadn't ordered anything, but she opened the door anyway. A biker, clad in leather complete with helmet and gloves stood there. He handed her a bottle of champagne. "Special delivery."

"I didn't order this. There must be some mistake."

"You're a Miss..." He consulted a piece of paper. "...Callaghan?"

"Yes. That's right."

"Then it's for you. Aren't you going to invite me in to share it?"

She was just framing an indignant retort when the biker removed the helmet and she saw it was Dani grinning widely.

"Dani!" She stood aside to let her into the room. "What are you doing here?"

"I brought some stuff down for the conference."

"Oh. So you'll have your own room."

"Do you want me to leave?"

"No...I...."

"If I'm staying, we had better open this. Got any glasses?" Dani removed her gloves and threw them on the bed with her helmet. Camila found what was needed on the tray on top of the minibar. She was just in time to hold one of them under the foaming liquid as Dani popped the cork.

"So," said Dani, when the glasses were full and they were each holding one. "Here's to us."

"All right. I'll drink to that."

They sipped slowly, watching each other swallowing the bubbly drink.

"How did your speech go?" asked Dani.

"Fine. Do you care?"

"No, I was just trying to be polite."

"Well don't. It doesn't suit you." She stood awkwardly, holding her dressing gown together with one hand, the glass in the other.

"What does suit me?"

Camila put her glass down. With the two gin and tonics plus wine at dinner, she didn't really want more to drink. She moved in close to Dani, reaching up to trace the line of the barely healed cut on her cheek with one finger. "Who did this to you?"

Dani looked her in the face, aware of Camila's breasts pressing against her. "I don't have to answer that."

"Yes, you do. It's recent. This week. Who was it? I want to know."

"It doesn't matter."

"It matters to me."

"It doesn't mean anything." Dani shrugged uncomfortably. "Just someone I met at a club."

"I'd say you know her quite intimately."

"Okay. We fuck sometimes. Like I said, it doesn't mean anything."

"You know her well enough to let her hit you across the face. Were you arguing about something?"

Dani licked her lips. She could feel the heat from Camila's body through her leather jacket. Her thighs were hot, pressing into Dani's leather-clad legs. "I didn't want to do...what she wanted me to do. She guessed it was because I was thinking of you."

"You were thinking of me?"

"Yes."

"In what way were you thinking of me?

"Camila, I—" She put her arms around Camila and kissed her. They kissed passionately for several minutes before breaking off for air. Dani removed her jacket and they moved onto the bed.

†

Dani made it back to London on Friday morning by nine. It had been a wrench to leave Camila's bed at seven. She smiled at the memory, thinking she couldn't actually say she had "slept" with Camila; sleep hadn't come into it. Amanda had just arrived when Dani walked in. She smiled at her and went upstairs to change out of her leather gear.

At nine thirty on the dot, Declan brought her a cup of coffee, putting it down carefully on her desk. He stood there, fidgeting.

"What is it, Declan?"

"Uh, Maria asked me to ask you for the name of your solicitor. She said Gordon wants to call him."

"Her. And unless you're fucking Maria, you don't have to run messages for her. She can come and ask me herself. I don't play stupid office games."

"Right." He relaxed. "Was everything okay in Brighton?"

"Fine. Have you got anything to do?"

"Yeah." He took the hint and left her in peace.

Penny arrived a few minutes later. They hadn't had the chance to talk the day before, so Dani was pleased to see her.

"What happened?" Penny asked as soon as she shut the door. "You didn't seem to know which way was up on Wednesday."

"Yeah, well, after you'd gone, I realised I had to do something."

115

"You look shattered and Declan says you're a bit prickly this morning."

"Prickly? Good grief...he'll be after your job next."

"Look, you know, I'm with you all the way. And a lot of other people are too."

Dani handed her two lists of names. "How does this look?"

Penny read through them. "Fairly accurate. Although you can add Sharon and Jane to your side."

"Really? They've never given me the time of day."

"Yeah, but Gordon's always treated them like shit."

"Good. I'm not asking you to grass up any of your mates, but is there a possibility any of the account managers would come in with us?"

"I wouldn't call any of them mates. At the moment I'd say they're sitting on the fence. I mean, they've grown up idolising people like Gordon, but a few years in the real world has shown them that to be successful, they have to have something to sell, which means, however much they hate it, that they're dependent on people like you and me."

"All right. Suppose you were to let it be known that I've asked you to put ads in *Marketing* and *PR Week* for two account managers with proven track records, blah, blah, blah...you know, draft an ad, leave it lying around."

Penny smiled. "Okay. No problem."

"And I would like a list of any clients you think we can take with us."

Penny nodded. "So what happened?"

"What do you mean?"

"You know what I mean. When I saw you on Wednesday, you were away with the fairies. Then on Thursday morning you breeze in here and take charge. Like you'd had a personality change."

"Maybe I did. Can we just leave it at that?"

"Yeah." Penny clearly wasn't convinced but knew when to stop pushing. "Okay, I'll go and do those ads."

†

Camila got up slowly after taking her time with a long bath. She studied her face carefully in the mirror. Did it show, she wondered? Would everyone know how she had spent the night? She had to be awake for the presentations this morning, and she wasn't sure she could even make it through breakfast. And she needed to meet with Eric Redmond to discuss the Berlin business; she was amazed she even remembered. All she wanted to remember was the feel of Dani's hands and mouth on her, inside her, everywhere.

The breakfast room wasn't full when she arrived at half eight. The first session was at nine fifteen, and the marketing team would have wanted the crew to do a thorough run-through before their multimedia extravaganza. Luckily Eric was still sitting at a table, reading the *Financial Times*. She helped herself to orange juice from the buffet, asked a passing waitress for coffee and toast, and sat down opposite him.

He looked across and raised his eyebrows. "Late night? I didn't see you in the bar after dinner."

"Thanks, Eric. I will refrain from making personal comments about your appearance, at least until I've had some coffee."

He laughed good-naturedly, "Fair enough. You taking Josh on this trip?"

"Yes. I thought it would be good for his development. He wasn't too keen on setting off on Sunday evening, though."

"Of course not. It cuts into his football-and-bonking time. He'll survive."

117

Camila smiled. With any luck it might be cutting into my bonking time too. Her coffee and toast arrived.

"They're trying to get us to agree to price cuts."

"Don't worry. They think I'm a pushover because I'm a woman. What they don't know is I speak German."

"You do?"

"And French. I can get by in Spanish and Italian too."

"I didn't know you're a linguist."

"There's a lot you don't know about me, Eric." *And a lot I don't want you to know, either.*

"No doubt. Look, there are a few details I need to talk to you about. I'm sure Josh has got the demographics of the region covered, but I don't think he is too clued-up on the pricing and the margins we expect to make on this project. Could we meet later?"

"Yes. I'll find you during the break." Camila drank the coffee and left the toast. She didn't feel like eating and was glad Eric had finished his full English before she sat down.

Chapter Eleven

Dani checked her bruises in front of the full-length mirror on the back of the wardrobe door in her bedroom. The beating Lisa had given her on Monday hadn't been very severe. The stripes were already making the transition from purple to yellowish-green. In another day or two, the marks would fade to almost nothing. She was sure Camila hadn't noticed anything the night before, but if they were to make love during the day, hiding them from her would be difficult.

She pulled on her shorts and sat on the bed. Camila hadn't said anything more about the cut on her face, but neither of them had said much of anything; their mouths were otherwise engaged. It was too early to tell how things between them might work out. One night that had been a lifetime of joyful lovemaking, but she knew better than to let herself dwell on the future. One night at a time, take it as she comes. She smiled at that thought, Camila coming again, and again. It had been a long time since she had made love to a woman like that. She hadn't been sure she would be able to get into it, but she had. And she was getting horny again just thinking about the delights of Camila's body.

How long would it last? A novelty for a few nights, maybe, and then she would want another whipping. But she didn't think Camila would understand, somehow. A few nights of a vanilla diet and Dani would be back round at Lisa's knocking on the door.

She glanced at the clock; just after nine thirty. Camila had said she would be late back from Brighton. Dani stood and looked around the room. It was tidier than it had been for a while. She finished dressing and went downstairs; the living room needed a bit of work. By the time she managed to make it look presentable, it was after ten. She washed her hands, took a can of Pride from the fridge, and went out to the patio to watch the lights on the river.

The doorbell rang just after she'd opened her second can. Nervously, she ran her fingers through her hair as she walked to the front door. Camila stood there holding her suit bag and overnight case, looking like she had just stepped off the front page of a fashion magazine.

"Are you going to let me in?" she asked.

Dani stood aside to let her pass. She took the bags from her and put them down by the stairs. "Do you want a drink?"

"If the bar's still open, I'll have a gin and tonic, please."

Dani led the way into the living room; Camila made a beeline for the open patio doors and stood in the spot Dani had recently vacated.

She was still standing there when Dani returned with her drink. "Did you come straight here?"

"No. I went home, changed, and packed clean underwear. I'm going to Berlin on Sunday. I thought I might as well go from here; you're closer to the airport. That is, if you want me for the weekend."

120

Dani swallowed. "Yes." They both drank in silence for a few minutes.

Camila looked around the room. "Your maid has been in." Dani nodded, not trusting herself to speak. "Is something wrong?"

"No. Not really."

Camila stood and faced her. "There is something. Is it about last night? Am I rushing you? I'll go, if you want."

Dani bit her lip. She felt about sixteen years old, on her first date with an older woman, not knowing what to do. "No. I mean, I just can't believe you're here." *God, I even sound fucking sixteen.*

"Dani, put the beer down. Put your arms around me."

Dani did as she was told. Then they were kissing and she didn't have any problem figuring out what to do next.

†

Camila stood by the window watching the play of morning light on the water. The tide was in and there were little waves. She watched several rowers going past; it was the start of a bright, breezy day.

She turned back to look at Dani, asleep. The bedclothes were a tangled mess and Dani was sprawled inelegantly amongst the heap. Camila could see the unmistakable outline of welts across Dani's buttocks. They would have to talk about it, but she didn't know how to start. It wasn't something she had any experience with and it was easy to react negatively—shocked, revolted—but what did she really feel? What did Dani really feel?

She had a choice, of course—leave now and never see Dani again. It had been fun, two nights of the best sex she had ever had. Keep the memory intact. Before anything went wrong. Before they found out what they didn't like about each other.

But she couldn't, not right away. She felt tears starting; Dani had somehow unlocked the floodgates, emotions she didn't know she had. Looking at Dani, remembering her touch, she was getting wet. Camila wanted her to touch her again now. She was sure it had never been like this with Allison, even in their early days together.

"Dani." She shook her shoulder gently. Dani rolled over and opened her eyes. Camila couldn't read her expression. Was she just sleepy, or was she wondering where she was and why? Camila bent over and kissed her. Dani seemed awake enough to immediately find and grasp one of her breasts. Dani knew exactly what she wanted; her touch was firm and accurate. Camila heard herself crying out her pleasure, her desire for more. She had never been a "screamer". She had never thought of herself as being very sensual at all. She had been wrong.

†

Later in the day, much later, they managed to get out of bed, get dressed, and go for a walk. Dani's buoyant mood was infectious, and Camila enjoyed the feeling of freedom that enveloped her as she held hands with her lover out in the open. When they reached the end of the road where it turned by the church, Dani led the way into the graveyard. She found a secluded spot and pulled Camila close to her. They kissed again.

"Dani, we can't do this here," protested Camila as they broke apart for air.

"Why not? No complaints from the clients."

"No, but...."

"You've never done it in a cemetery?"

122

"No!"

"Do you want to?"

"Dani, I...."

It didn't matter what she thought; her body was responding again to Dani's touch. A little while later, she found herself sitting in the pub around the corner. Dani brought her drink over and grinned at her. She grinned back. They were like two kids with a secret. The world of Redmond and the imminent trip to Berlin were light years away.

"So what would your friends think, if they could see you now?" Dani asked, looking at her over the rim of her pint glass.

"You're really hung up on my friends, aren't you? Why should they be so different from your friends?"

Dani shrugged and traced a pattern with some spilt beer on the table.

Camila took a deep breath and spoke to the top of her head. "If you really want to know what my friends would think, you could meet some of them. I've been invited to a birthday barbecue. It's the week after next."

Dani looked at her then. "You wouldn't be embarrassed?"

"No."

Dani's eyes locked on to hers. It was a direct challenge. "What would I wear?"

"Whatever you like. It's not that formal."

Dani drank some more beer and changed the subject. They talked about other things and eventually got back to their previous lighthearted mood.

It wasn't until they returned to the house that Dani mentioned the subject again. "About this party."

"Yes."

"Where is it?"

Camila wrote the address on the telephone pad. "Starts at eight. You'll have to make your own way there. I might be late as I have a board meeting."

"Don't you need to ring and let them know you're bringing someone?"

"Yes."

"So you could do it now. You might forget tomorrow."

"I don't forget things."

"You might."

"All right." Camila picked up the phone handset and dialled. She wasn't sure what Dani's game was, but she was willing to go along with it. "Hi, it's Camila. I'm off on a business trip tomorrow, so I just wanted to let you know in advance that I'll be bringing a guest to the party. Hope that's okay. Leave a message on my machine if it's not. See you then." She put the receiver down. "Answerphone. Satisfied?"

"Yeah."

"You had better be there. Don't let me down."

"I won't. Thanks."

"Now come here and kiss me." Camila was aware of a surge of power. And she knew Dani liked it. They made love on the living room floor before making it upstairs to the bedroom.

†

The river passed by in swirls of grey, the sunshine of the day before a distant memory. Camila sipped her black coffee. It wasn't her normal Sunday routine. She wouldn't still be sitting around undressed at midday, not having looked at a single line in a Sunday paper, not having spent a few hours on her laptop. But she didn't think anything would seem normal again. She heard the front door open and Dani appeared carrying a box of cornflakes, a pint of milk, and the *Sunday Times*.

"This was all they had. If you want anything more substantial, we'll have to go to The Black Lion."

"This will be fine." Camila found herself looking into Dani's green eyes again. This was ridiculous, she told herself sternly. She was like a teenager in heat.

"What time's your taxi?" Dani asked, breaking the spell.

"Two fifteen." By her standards, that was cutting it fine. She followed Dani into the kitchen watching her open the box of cereal and pour flakes into two bowls. Then she handed Camila the milk.

"You'd better pour your own. Do you want sugar?"

"Have you given the maid the weekend off as well?"

"Yeah. Good help is so hard to find."

Camila put the milk down on the counter and pulled Dani close. "The flakes can wait. I want you, now," she whispered in her ear.

†

Snapping open her laptop as soon as the flight attendant had finished her welcome routine, Camila tried to concentrate on the figures on the screen. It was the best way of fending off conversation with her young colleague. She couldn't fault his enthusiasm. As a recently promoted brand manager, he was keen to make a good impression. He had hardly stopped talking since they'd met at the Departures desk. But this afternoon she couldn't focus. It was no use. She stowed the machine under the seat, giving in to the desire to sleep. When she woke, the plane was just coming in to land.

After Passport Control, she left Josh to wait for the luggage and slipped into the ladies' room. As she feared, she looked like she hadn't slept in a few days. Camila splashed her face with cold water. She didn't have time to do her eyes, but at least a touch of lipstick made her look less dead. She combed her hair and straightened her outfit.

The memory of Dani watching her dress flooded back. Dani had been half teasing, half trying to tempt her back into bed. "Pull yourself together, Camila," she told her reflection. "Helmut won't be amused." The thought of the next two days with the Germans was enough to banish thoughts of Dani, for a while at least.

Helmut was waiting for them in the Arrivals hall. He took Camila's case from her, leaving Josh to fend for himself and shepherded her out of the building and into the company car. With any luck, she thought, she would be able to have a bath before having to attend the corporate dinner. Taking this trip this straight after the conference had been bad planning, but she had fully expected to have a quiet weekend in her flat to rest and prepare.

In the bath, at last, she found herself thinking about Dani again; the bruising—no disguising the fact they had been caused by a whip or a cane. Dani hadn't said anything and Camila hadn't asked. It raised a lot of questions in her mind, though. And the main question was if Dani were into something kinky, how long would she be satisfied having ordinary vanilla sex with her? Camila couldn't quite see herself in the role of dominatrix, but if that's what turned Dani on, if that's what this woman did for her, the one who had hit her on the face....

Camila pulled the plug and got out of the bath. She took her time dressing and applying her makeup. The bath and the short nap on the plane had restored some of her strength. She would be sticking to mineral water at dinner, as she hadn't eaten anything all day, not even the snack on the plane. Giving herself one last check in the mirror, she decided she would pass muster, but it was going to be a long two days and nights.

†

It was three in the morning. Camila was in her hotel room in Berlin, staring at her laptop. Helmut had provided her with a modem when she asked, saying she needed to email her report to Eric. The dial-up time was even slower than the one in her office, but she was rewarded with an Internet connection eventually. Finding specialty topic bulletin boards hadn't been difficult, and the flow of information was seemingly endless.

She read on, unaware of the passing of time. Finally, she'd had enough. She disconnected the modem, switched off the laptop, and lay down on the bed. *This is ridiculous,* she thought. *I'm an executive. I have an important meeting in the morning, I should not be thinking about this.*

Finally, she reached for the phone and dialled Dani's number. It rang for a while, but she knew Dani would answer if she hadn't gone out. Her hand was shaking.

"Dani," she said, "did I wake you?"

"No."

"You're lying."

"Yes. I'm lying down."

"I was thinking about you. I have to ask you something."

"Okay."

"I mean, we should have talked about this before, but—"

"What is it?" Dani sounded more awake now.

"Dani, what really turns you on?"

"I…Jesus, Camila, it's four o'clock in the morning."

"Would you like me to give you a good whipping?"

"Christ! Have I dialled a sex line in my sleep?"

"Well? Dani, are you still there?"

"Yes."

"Is that an answer?"

"Yes."

"What do you like to be whipped with?"

"A cane," Dani answered without hesitation. "They're difficult to get hold of. Anything would do, really. A riding crop is okay. But a cane is the best. It really hurts, can't sit down for days. That really turns me on, since you asked."

"Thanks. I'll let you go back to sleep now. Sweet dreams."

"Camila!"

"Goodnight. See you on Tuesday."

†

Dani put the receiver down slowly, wide-awake now. She turned on the light. Had she really just had that conversation with Camila? Or had she been dreaming?

Camila must have seen the evidence of Lisa's handiwork during the last two mornings they had spent in bed. Her question reminded Dani of the time Bea had caught her handling one of the canes in the room the mistress jokingly called her "tart's boudoir". When Bea entertained her clients, Dani usually went out and roamed around museums and art galleries. But this day her curiosity had got the better of her and she had gone into the room for the first time while Bea was out shopping.

Bea looked at the cane Dani had been idly swishing back and forth. "Does that interest you?"

Dani could only nod, her face flushing at being caught red-handed in the room. Bea had never specifically told her it was out of bounds but she felt guilty all the same.

Instead of berating her, Bea asked, "Giving or receiving?"

Dani's blush heated up as she whispered, "Receiving."

Bea took the cane from her and replaced it on the wall with the other tools of her trade. Dani hadn't been able to disguise her disappointment, but Bea met her pleading gaze calmly, shaking her head and saying, "No. I like our arrangement as it is. But if you think you want this experience, I have a young friend, not much older than you. She's just starting out and she wants to service women rather than men. I've told her there's more money with men. She'll be lucky to scrape a living."

Lisa's career had made a slow start with Dani being one of her first regular paying clients. For the first ten years, Lisa's day job had paid the bills and it seemed Bea would be proved right. But by the mid-1980s, Lisa's reputation had grown to the extent that she could devote herself full-time to satisfying mainly women's desires.

Thinking about Lisa and Camila's phone call wasn't helping her get back to sleep. Dani stumbled out of bed, showered, dressed, made coffee, and sat out in the back garden watching the river come alive in the dawn. The whole weekend had seemed unreal and now this. It wasn't as if she didn't have other things to think about. In a few hours' time, she would be making decisions that affected other people's livelihoods. She thought of Penny. Perhaps she hadn't really appreciated before just how loyal Penny was. And Declan and Gary. She was fortunate to have people she could depend on. Gordon really didn't have a clue. Dani could go it alone with their one corporate client. She had connections he wouldn't dream of in a million years.

What could she call the new agency? She went inside and spent some time locating her drawing pad from where she'd tidied it on Friday evening. Doodling on a clean page, she quickly discarded her own name; DBS was already registered, after all. But she was bored with initials, a meaningless acronym. She would have to stay away from frivolous names too. In a matter of minutes she discarded Uranus, Creative Hands, Media Mania, The Design Factory, and half a dozen others. She rather liked Amazon, but dismissed it as being too feminist. And she wasn't going to go down the road of Aardvark or Acme just to make sure the name was first in the Yellow Pages listings. Penny would be good at this, she thought and started to dial her number, then realised it was still only five thirty.

Chapter Twelve

Dani came face-to-face with her solicitor, Annette Harmon, on Tuesday morning, ten minutes before their meeting with Gordon and his brief.

"So is there anything I should know?" Ms Harmon asked, taking out her yellow legal pad.

"You'll have to ask him. I didn't see this coming."

"Have you ever had an affair with him?"

Dani gave her a withering look. "I'm a lesbian. I don't fuck men."

"Some lesbians do, so I've heard."

"I don't."

"Does he know you're a lesbian?"

"Yes. As does everyone else who works here."

"And he accepts that?"

"He's known me for fifteen years. He even seemed to accept the other thing."

"What's the 'other thing'?" Dani hesitated. "Look, if I'm going to help you, I don't need any surprises."

Dani shrugged. "I'm into SM." She looked into Annette's eyes to check her reaction. She didn't flinch or look away. "I like to be beaten," she added.

"I see. And he knew this too."

"Yes." Dani told her about the incident the week before. "Of course, he may be having it off with his secretary, Maria. That would explain his overreaction."

"Or it could be money. You've just landed a big merchandising contract?"

"Yeah. With my ideas."

"So. I'll bet on the money over the sex any day." She looked up and smiled. Dani decided they would get on all right.

"Time to go. Don't want to keep the bastards waiting." Dani led the way to the boardroom.

Gordon was fiddling with his cufflinks, as usual. Dani nodded to Stephen Wetherby; they had met at their occasional official board meetings. She introduced Annette before sitting down.

"Look," Stephen said, "this is really very simple. It's like a divorce. You started this business together, so just split it down the middle."

"And what about the kids?" asked Annette.

"We would want an agreement that if Dani goes ahead with her own agency, she wouldn't take any MBE clients with her."

"I don't call that 'splitting it down the middle', Mr Wetherby."

"My client has worked hard to get these clients on board."

"And my client has provided the work to build the reputation of the agency."

"Could I point out," said Dani, "that when I leave, MBE no longer exists? So you'll just have ME."

Annette laughed but Stephen didn't crack a smile. "That's something else we have to discuss. You still have Saatchi and Saatchi, even though there's only one."

"We're hardly on the same scale. We dissolve the partnership. And I will take whoever wants to come with me."

Gordon spoke for the first time. "Do you really think Redmond will go with you?"

"Yes."

"Why?"

Dani smirked at him. "Because I'm sleeping with the financial director."

"Be serious, Dani."

"I am. Look, you're just a suit. You didn't come up with the creative ideas for the ad. You didn't draw the T-shirt designs. Face it, Mac, you're nothing without me. Suits can be hired on any street corner."

Gordon looked at Stephen. "I told you it would be a waste of time talking to her."

Annette spoke. "Actually, I don't think there is any basis for discussion. I've looked at your original agreement. You would have been well advised to go to a solicitor to do it properly back then. It's not worth the paper it's printed on. Dani's right. She can walk away now with half the profits and take whomever she wants with her. You don't have a leg to stand on. The best you can do is try to part amicably."

"Well, I...," Gordon spluttered. He looked at Stephen for support. "We were just kids, a couple of hippies."

"I was never a hippie," said Dani. "And while we're on the subject of halvesy/halvesy, I've asked Ms Harmon to have the books examined. I don't have to be an accountant to know you've spent a lot more of the profits over the years than I have. And the Inland Revenue will no doubt be very interested in some of your little tax dodges."

Gordon looked like he was going to explode. Stephen placed a hand on his arm. "I suggest we bring this meeting to a close. My client and I have a few things to discuss. We will talk again in a few days."

"Right," said Dani. "You know where to find me. I'll be at work in the studio." She walked out of the room with Annette following her closely.

"Well played, Dani," the solicitor said when they were out of earshot of the boardroom. "So I'm looking at the books, am I?"

"If you wouldn't mind. It just occurred to me, sitting there, that it's probably worth doing." She grinned. "He didn't expect that, did he?"

"No. And he didn't like the idea of the Inland Revenue taking a look at his activities, either. You do realise though, he may be having second thoughts now of breaking up the partnership. He would be better off leaving his wife."

"That thought had occurred to me."

†

When they arrived back in the studio, Dani asked Annette if she would like coffee. The solicitor refused, saying she couldn't stay long.

"Off the record, Dani, how did you and Gordon ever get together? You're like the proverbial chalk and cheese."

"It was at a folk-music gig in a pub. Nineteen seventy-eight. Gordon was playing guitar and singing some sappy song about parsley, sage, rosemary, and thyme."

"I wouldn't have put you down as a folkie."

"I'd produced a flyer for the event, and these two guys I knew persuaded me to go, just for a laugh, they said. Gordon and I got talking during an interval while I was waiting at the bar. I know it's hard to believe now, but he was a cool dude back in the day. At first I thought he was just another dope-head hippie, but he produced a business plan from his guitar case and asked if I wanted to join him setting up an agency. I was only twenty-one and had no idea what I was going to do to make a living, so I said I'd give it a try. The rest, as they say, is history."

"I would have thought with your talent that you would have had plenty of offers."

"Yeah. The two guys who invited me to the folk thing had asked me to join them, but they were computer geeks and their plans for world domination didn't really appeal."

"'Scarborough Fair'."

Dani looked at her. "What?"

"The name of the song with the herbs." Annette surprised Dani by singing the words. "'Are you going to Scarborough Fair? Parsley, sage, rosemary, and thyme. Remember me to the one who lives there. For once she was a true love of mine.'"

"That's the one."

Annette's next words surprised her further. "Are you really sleeping with Camila Callaghan?"

"Yes."

"I guess I could see her being a match for you."

"It's early days yet. I don't know if she's really into, you know, what I told you before."

"I can't say I know her well, but I think she could fit the role perfectly." Annette snapped her briefcase shut. "I need to go. If Gordon approaches you to discuss anything, just refer him to Wetherby or myself. We will take it from here."

Dani thanked her for her time and walked her out to Reception. As she made her way back to the studio, she pondered on their conversation. She hoped Annette was right. The middle-of-the-night phone call from Camila had ignited her fantasies. But there was every chance Camila had woken in the morning and dismissed the whole idea as a step too far, a bridge she wasn't prepared to cross.

†

Camila walked there and back past the dingy shopfront three times, screwing up the nerve to go in. It looked like nothing much from the outside, not what she expected. No lurid posters or flashing neon signs. As it was, she felt like there was a big sign on her back: *Camila Callaghan is going into a sex shop!*

When she did finally open the door and enter the darkened interior, she was relieved to see no one else there. She stared in awe at the rows of dildos—all shapes, sizes, colours—hanging on one wall. She had almost decided to leave quickly when a figure emerged from behind a beaded curtain at the far side of the room. "Can I help you?"

Camila looked at the speaker, hard to tell in the gloom, but probably the wrong side of fifty, wearing ordinary-looking clothes. No horns.

"Um, I don't know if you can help me. I'm looking for something a bit more…" She waved her arms around, indicating the merchandise on display. "…adventurous."

"Ah," said the woman, giving in to a momentary coughing spasm. "I guess you need to come through here." She held the beads apart.

Hoping she wasn't about to be overpowered and sold into the white slave trade, Camila followed the woman through the curtain and found herself in another world. Dani's world, she thought. The trawl through the SM bulletin boards during the night didn't quite prepare her for the reality. Having never been in a dungeon, she decided this would probably qualify as a model. Varieties of whips, chains, and masks adorned the walls. She shuddered. But she had come this far and she couldn't walk out now.

"Do you have any canes?" she asked the woman.

"Yes, of course, dear. We have a good selection here...ash, bamboo, birch, you name it."

Damn. She hadn't expected to have a choice. "May I?" she asked, indicating the nearest one. The woman nodded. Camila took the slim implement off the wall and flexed it. She swished it through the air; it sounded lethal. Was this really what Dani wanted?

"Good choice," said the woman, coughing again. "One of our bestsellers."

"Okay. I'll take two."

She arranged for the canes to be sent to her flat. Then she hurried out, back into the daylight, and her world, leaving the darkness behind her.

Chapter Thirteen

Dani had finished off another piece of work for a client's brochure. It was after seven and just time for her to get home before Camila landed. A knock on the door startled her. The face that appeared around it was a surprise. She hadn't seen her brother for months. "Brian! What are you doing here?"

"Thought I better check on you. Missed you last time you visited my place of work."

"I might have known. Did you know I was there all night?"

"Sure. Thought a night in a cell might do you some good. But when I heard they'd sent two goons to interview you, I thought I'd better get you out before you talked yourself into serious trouble."

"You're all heart, bro." Brian was an inspector in the Met.

He came over to her and surprised her further by giving her a quick hug. "I worry about you."

"Thanks, but I'm a big girl now."

"I know. What's this shit going on with you and Gordon?"

"How do you know about that?"

"People talk. So what's up?"

"Just a little disagreement over lifestyles."

"He's an idiot." He had wandered over to her drawing table. "You've got more talent in your little finger than he will ever have in his whole body."

"Thanks. But somehow I don't think you've come here to tell me that."

"No." He paused and looked at her. "It's me and June. She's finally decided she's had enough. The lot of a policeman's wife is not a happy one—"

"Hey, I'm sorry, but—"

"I know. You can say, 'I told you so'. But love is blind."

She knew he was upset when he talked in clichés. "What about the kids?" Her two nieces were very young, possibly still preschool age. Not that she would know them if she saw them. June hadn't wanted the girls to have anything to do with their "weird" aunt.

"They hardly know me as it is." He shoved his hands in his pockets.

"So is there someone else?"

"Yeah. Some smarmy git with a nine-to-five job."

Dani looked at her watch. She needed to make a move or Camila would be waiting on the doorstep. Brian caught the movement. "Got a date?"

"Yeah. I need to be going."

"I can give you a lift."

"Okay. Great." She had been thinking she would need to get a taxi.

During the drive he did most of the talking, telling her about a case he was working on. It wasn't until they were passing Hammersmith that Dani asked, "Where are you staying?"

"Dossing with a mate. Need to sell the house before I can afford to buy anything."

"I can sub you…if you need cash."

"It shouldn't come to that, but thanks."

Camila was indeed waiting on the doorstep when they arrived at the house. Before Dani could stop him, Brian jumped out of the car and approached her. "Hi, I'm Brian, Dani's brother."

"Camila."

"Pleased to meet you." He ignored the look Dani was giving him. "She's kept you a secret."

"Brian, thanks for the lift, but you can piss off now."

"Oh, I thought you were going to invite me in for a drink."

"No." She put the key in the door.

"Just one."

"Camila and I have some catching up to do. See you around." Ushering Camila inside, she shut the door firmly in her brother's face.

"Next time it will be two nights," he yelled through the letterbox.

"Sorry about that," said Dani, heading straight for the kitchen. "I was planning to get home earlier. He dropped by the office unexpectedly."

"What did he mean by that…two nights?"

"Oh, nothing. Just a family inside joke." They were in the kitchen now. Dani opened the fridge. "Oh damn. The maid hasn't done the shopping."

"The maid—" Camila suddenly started laughing.

"What's funny?"

"You are. I really thought you did have a maid."

Dani grinned at her. "You didn't?"

"I did." Camila was holding on to the table, doubled over with laughter.

Dani went over and hugged her. Then they were kissing with a desperate urgency, as if it had been much longer than two nights and days since they last made love. Camila's stomach rumbled loudly, causing Dani to stop her exploration of Camila's mouth with her tongue. "When did you last eat?"

"Must have been breakfast time. We worked through lunch and only had time for a mad dash for the plane."

"Right, so we can get a snack at the Lion or order a takeaway."

"Takeaway." Camila didn't seem to want Dani to let go of her.

"Chinese or Indian?"

"Indian."

Dani released her to find the menu. Camila went upstairs to shower and change while Dani rang the order through and prepared drinks, a gin and tonic for Camila and a beer for herself.

Later, having finished the last of the meal, licking the remnants of sauce off each other's fingers, Camila said, "Dani, I have to ask you something."

"Sounds serious."

"It's just a bit embarrassing."

"I don't think you could embarrass me."

"It's me who is embarrassed. I mean, I'm nearly forty years old and I feel like an inexperienced virgin in this regard."

"So are you going to tell me before you get much older?"

Camila looked down at the table and started tidying the cartons.

Dani stopped her, grasping her hands. "Come on, it's me. You can ask me anything."

"Promise not to laugh?"

"I'll try. Not promising though, as I don't know what it is."

Camila blushed. "Um, the thing is, I wondered, do you have a dildo?"

Dani bit her lip, trying not to burst out laughing. She looked at the ceiling to get herself under control before she could speak. "Yes, actually, one or two. Why?" she asked with feigned innocence.

"I just thought I might like to try it, if you're willing to, of course."

Dani took a deep breath. "I think I could force myself."

Camila studied her face. "Are you laughing at me?"

"Not at all. Come on, let's do it." She stood and pulled Camila up with her.

"What about the dishes?"

"Oh, we'll leave those for the maid."

†

Much later, lying in bed with Dani's arms wrapped around her, Camila sighed, a deeply contented sigh. It had been worth the trial of asking the question. She had never experienced such a high in lovemaking. But Dani had a skillful touch with the dildo; she had stimulated her, teased her, and when she was crying out with frustration, had penetrated her and used the implement to maximum effect, bringing her to orgasm again and again. She had heard of multiple orgasms but had never really believed they happened in real life.

They slept for a few hours. When Camila woke, the memory of the ecstasy of the night before flooded back and she started to feel aroused. Reaching for Dani, she realised she was still wearing the dildo, and this only excited her further. With her acute awareness of what Camila wanted, Dani started to rub against her clitoris. Soon, Camilla was lost in a state of all-consuming passion once more.

Getting up in the morning, preparing for work, was one of the hardest things she had ever done. Dani came into the kitchen while she was drinking a cup of coffee, waiting for her taxi to arrive. Only when Dani pressed herself against her did Camila know that her carefully constructed equilibrium was short-lived. Dani was wearing only a pair of black tight-fitting briefs and the dildo. Camila moaned softly, "Dani, I can't."

"You can. I know you can." With one swift motion, Dani had lifted her skirt and pulled her knickers aside. Resisting was useless; Dani had her pinned against the counter and it was all she could do not to cry out with her mounting desire. She pressed her nails into Dani's buttocks and was rewarded with extra movement inside her. Dani explored the inside of her left ear with her tongue. When Camila came in quick, shuddering gasps, she was aware that Dani had come as well. ◢

"You are in so much trouble," she breathed into Dani's ear.

"Good." The blast of a horn brought them both to their senses. "He'll wait."

"He better; it's on the company's account. Now let me go. I'll deal with you later."

†

Climbing into the taxi, Camila was aware of the wetness of her underwear and hoped the taxi driver wasn't overwhelmed by the eau de sex that now permeated the backseat of his otherwise immaculate cab. Taking the risk, she leaned forward to ask him to reroute to her apartment. She couldn't arrive at the office in this condition.

After a quick shower and change, she felt ready to pull on her finance director persona and terrorise the first hapless member of staff she encountered. The flashing light on her answerphone caught her eye as she stopped by the mirror in the hallway to check her hair. She was tempted to ignore it. If it was a message from Dani, she would need another shower and she didn't have time for that.

Still, it might be Eric, so she pushed the button to retrieve her messages. The first one was indeed from ER, reminding her that he needed her figures for the board meeting later. The next message was a long ramble from Chris ending with the suggestion that they meet for a drink. This she could ignore. The final one was more disturbing—her father's voice coming through loud and clear, informing her that they were landing at Heathrow at four o'clock and would be at her flat by five at the latest. Dinner was booked for eight at The Savoy and he had managed to get a riverside-view table.

Camila leant against the wall for support. An unexpected visit from her parents. Just what she didn't want right now. She wondered how long they were planning to stay. So much for her plans to give Dani what she so plainly desired that evening, or any time during the weekend.

†

Dani grinned to herself. The journey to work passed in a blur with the feel and scent of Camila all over her. She had fucked any number of women using a dildo, but the night with Camila, giving her so much pleasure, had been the ultimate turn-on. And what had Camila meant when she said she would deal with her later? It seemed Dani didn't know her at all.

She was still grinning as she walked through Reception and was only vaguely aware that Amanda had called her name. The receptionist called it again, louder this time.

Dani stopped and looked at her. "What? I'm not inappropriately dressed, am I?" Her jeans, although clean, did have a few rips in them, but she didn't think the Eagles Hotel California T-shirt could offend anyone.

"Message from Ms Callaghan. She asked if you could call her as soon as you get in."

"Oh, right, thanks."

"I asked her if she wanted to speak to Mr McKenzie, but she insisted it had to be you."

"That's fine." Dani smiled at her. "I'm sure I can deal with whatever she wants."

Certain that nothing could spoil her good mood, Dani continued through the building to her studio. Declan jumped to his feet as soon as she appeared and shot out the door.

"What's with him?" Dani looked over at Gary, who was staring intently at his computer screen.

"It's his mission in life to make sure you have a coffee on arrival. But we didn't know what time you would be in today."

"This mission doesn't have anything to do with the cute redhead in Accounts, by any chance."

"I wouldn't know about that," Gary said primly.

Dani continued through the outer office to her inner sanctum. There were several Post-it notes by her phone. She glanced through them. Nothing that couldn't wait. She dialled the Redmond number and asked for Camila. No hesitation from the receptionist this time, she put her straight through.

"Missing you already too," she said as soon as Camila picked up.

"Oh, Dani, I'm so sorry."

"You don't have anything to be sorry about."

"Yes, I do. My parents are arriving today and I'll be meeting them for dinner. They stay at my flat when they're here, so I won't be able to see you tonight."

"Oh." Dani felt the morning's high sliding out of her.

"I don't know how long they're staying, but if it's more than two nights, I will have to invent a business trip."

Dani bit back the disappointment taking over her mind. "Okay. I'll just have to be patient, I guess."

"Dani, believe me, I'm going to find this hard. Last night, this morning, I'm...oh, shit, I have an internal call waiting and I'm pretty sure it's Eric. I'll call you when I can."

Then she was gone and Declan arrived with the coffee to find Dani slumped in her chair, feeling as if all the air had drained from the room.

"Here you go, boss. This should give you a lift. I even scored a chocolate donut for you."

Dani gave him a weak smile. "Thanks, Declan. I'm sure that will help."

He bounced back out. After a few sips of coffee, Dani roused herself and made an attempt to organise her day.

†

Camila's day had been filled with one meeting after another. Now, on the ride home, she tried to gather her thoughts for the evening ahead with her parents. Knowing she wouldn't be able to leave the office until after six, she had alerted the concierge to their arrival so he could let them in and they would have time to freshen themselves up after their journey. Her father would no doubt have helped himself to some of her Bushmills whiskey. She didn't drink the stuff herself, but kept it in stock for these visits.

She had struggled to keep thoughts of Dani from intruding during the day. She would have liked to redirect the taxi to Chiswick and tell her parents she had to make an emergency trip to Amsterdam.

Her father was standing in the hallway when she opened the door to her apartment. He did, indeed, have a glass of whiskey in his hand. But the parcel he was inspecting was what caused her concern. She quelled her panic.

"Hi, Dad. Good trip?"

"Yes, no problem. We were in Paris and thought we would pop over to see you. What is this?"

"Oh, it's something I ordered for a friend's birthday. Just leave it there. I'll deal with it later." She dropped her briefcase and drew him into a hug. With all the willpower she could muster, she kept her eyes from the long, thin parcel and maneuvered her father into the living room, where her mother sat reading a magazine and sipping at a glass of sherry.

†

Dani couldn't face being in the house alone. The disappointment of not seeing Camila that evening was still raw. After the middle-of-the-night conversation on Sunday, actually Monday, she had been anticipating her lover's return with mounting excitement. Was Camila really thinking of playing the part Dani wanted? Or had she dreamt the whole scenario?

She walked into The Black Lion with the thought of drinking enough to dull her senses. Instead, she ate a lacklustre meal of eggs and chips washed down with a pint of beer. The evening was warm enough for sitting outside. She ordered another half when she finished eating and took it out to the patio. All the tables were occupied, so she perched on the wall nearest the river and watched the people passing by.

Couples holding hands, talking, laughing. A summer's evening and love was definitely in the air, for some anyway.

Dani finished her drink and took the glass back to the bar. Deciding it was a good time for a ride, she walked the short distance to her house to change into her leather gear. She had no messages on her answerphone and had to quell another surge of disappointment.

She retrieved the bike from her storage unit around the corner and headed off into the setting sun, towards Richmond. It was fully dark by the time she reached another pub, also by the river. A different clientele, no one she knew here. The barmaid serving her had a slash of black makeup across her eyes. She looked like the character, Pris, from *Blade Runner*. Glancing around the bar as she waited for her pint to be pulled, Dani could see she wouldn't be out of place here.

Accepting the full glass from the girl with a smile, Dani settled down on a bench seat near the door and hoped she could shake thoughts of Camila out of her head for a time. That hope was shattered when the next song to come out of the speakers above her head was "Sweet Dreams". While Annie Lennox's powerful voice belted out the words, she had a searing vision of Camila holding a cane, swishing it, testing its strength. By the end of the song, Dani was melting in her seat. She gulped down the rest of her beer and made a hasty exit, walking quickly back to her bike. The throbbing of the engine between her legs on the ride home only enhanced her need for instant relief.

†

The view along the river, London at night, was a sight she usually enjoyed. But as she sat at the table at The Savoy with her parents, Camila's eyes saw a different vision. It involved being in bed with Dani.

"Is your fish all right, dear? You haven't eaten much."

Camila looked down at her plate. "It's fine. I'm not very hungry."

"They work you too hard at that place. I'm sure you've lost even more weight since we last saw you. It's not healthy."

"It must be the string of secret lovers that keeps our girl so slim." Her father raised his glass to her.

"Is there someone special?"

Camila couldn't meet her mother's intense gaze. She shook her head.

"There must be something wrong with these Englishmen. Come to France and you'll be married within six months."

Her mother's aim in life was to see her blissfully wed with a child or two on the way. At one time she had even entertained the thought that Camila would marry Eric Redmond and give up work entirely. The first time her parents had come to her office, they had met Eric, and her mother hadn't stopped talking about him for days—"Such a handsome man, darling. You two are made for each other." Even her father had weighed in—"Can't go wrong there, love. Rich, good-looking, brains. Your children will be exceptional."

Now each time they talked on the phone, her mother would ask if Eric was still single.

Camila sighed and pushed the remains of her uneaten fish to one side of her plate. It was going to be a long night and she had the next two days to get through as well.

†

The smell of leftover curry assaulted her nostrils as soon as Dani opened her front door. She quickly cleared away the remains of the takeaway and washed the glasses.

Reminders of the previous night and early morning activities lay in wait for her in the bedroom. The tip of the dildo winked up at her from its nesting place in the black briefs on the bed.

She stripped off her riding gear and took the dildo to rinse off in the shower. As the cleaning fairy made an appearance as often as her non-existent maid, Dani gave in to the sudden urge to tidy the bedroom. After she had sorted out the clothes that needed to be washed or sent to the dry cleaners, she turned her attention to the bed. Much as she would have liked to spend the night breathing in Camila's scent, it was a torture she could do without. Wrestling with the duvet used most of her remaining energy, and after she dealt with putting the washing machine on, she collapsed into an armchair in the living room and wondered how she was going to get through the next few days.

Chapter Fourteen

After a mostly sleepless night, Dani gave in at four, dosed herself with a strong cup of coffee, and set off for the Tube station. The walk by the river was entrancing at that time of morning. No one else about, the birds twittering, the sun about to raise its head above the horizon.

The MBE building was deserted. With several hours of peace before anyone else arrived for work, Dani approached the monster in the corner of her studio. She had resisted the installation for as long as possible. The boys had a matching creature in their office, which they were both adept at using.

Dani turned the machine on. Good. Step one. The training hadn't been wasted. She had booked the three-day course for herself, Declan, and Gary six months earlier. After the first day she left them to it. She was the boss; no need to waste her time learning how to use something she wasn't ever going to need.

But she had noted Camila's ease with using her laptop. The technology was here to stay, and maybe it was time she stopped burying her head in the sand.

151

The machine finished the waking-up process and she was presented with a lit screen, a cheeky-looking logo of a partially eaten fruit in the middle of it.

What now? That first day on the course, they had spent an interminable amount of time learning how to use the controller. The mouse. Dani moved the thing across its pad and something moved on the screen. The pointer. It was coming back to her now. The instructor had written the word *WIMP* on his flip chart, making the boys giggle. After they'd settled down he explained that the letters stood for *windows, icons, mouse, pointer.*

When she moved the mouse, she could see the pointer. Place it on an icon and click. Yes! She could do this.

†

When Gary arrived in the office two hours later, she was immersed in the intricacies of finding her way around the drawing program's toolbox. She made shapes, coloured them in, moved them around.

"Shit. Am I out of a job?" He watched as she expertly manipulated some text onto a circle.

Dani looked at him and grinned. "Not yet. But I'm paying you too much. This is a doddle."

"Yeah, but you're just playing. That's not real work."

"Okay. I bow to your superiority. But not for long."

He humphed loudly and went back to his own desk. She could hear him telling Declan loudly, "The boss thinks she's a computer whizz now."

Declan came in as she was closing the program down. If he was thinking of making a smart remark, it didn't come out. He just smiled sweetly and asked if she wanted a coffee.

"Yes, thanks." She pulled a tenner out of her pocket. "Would you mind getting me a bacon sarnie? And whatever you and Gary want?"

"No problem."

"And tell Mr Wise Guy next door that he needs to give me an update on where we are with the toy store account."

He grinned. "Sure thing, boss."

Dani switched the computer off and returned to her drawing table. She knew that the storyboard for the furniture account needed tweaking. Before she could start, the phone rang.

"Ms Callaghan on line one, Dani."

"Thanks, Amanda." She took a deep breath and pressed the button to take the call.

"Hello." Camila's voice sounded distant.

"Hello, yourself. Business or pleasure?" Dani tried for a light tone.

"Mainly business, I'm afraid."

"How long?" It was no good; a measure of desperation was taking hold.

"They haven't said. I'm hoping it will be tomorrow."

"Lunch?"

Silence on the other end, but Dani could hear her breathing.

"I'm so sorry. I wish I could." More silence.

Declan arrived with her coffee and bacon sandwich. She nodded her thanks, keeping her hand over the mouthpiece.

"Dani, what time will you be home today?"

Hope leapt in her chest. She removed her hand to answer. "Um, probably about six thirty or seven."

"Expect a delivery. I'm sorry it can't be more, but consider it a promise."

Dani opened her mouth to ask what was being delivered, but Camila was gone.

†

Camila's foot brushed against the long thin box under her desk. She had managed to smuggle it out of the flat when she left for work. Her parents were still in bed. Leaving it there didn't seem safe. She was sure her father's curiosity would get the better of him at some point during the day.

Hearing Dani's voice, she had wanted to rush straight over to MBE's offices just to see her, to hold her. At dinner when her mother asked, yet again, whom she was seeing, she had dodged the question, yet again. Why was she acting like a teenager with something to hide? She was a grown woman. Her career choice had made her father proud; he had been a banker. Was she still trying to please him, worried her life choices would change how he viewed her?

There were so many times when she should have told her parents about the true nature of her relationship with Allison. That her lover had died without them knowing what she meant to her was something that haunted Camila still.

Although it had only been a few days, the connection she felt with Dani held all the intensity of the real thing. Camila promised herself that if it looked like more than just a passing fancy, she would take the plunge. Love shouldn't be hidden away. She didn't need to continue living a lie, keeping such a vital part of herself secreted.

†

Gordon put the receiver down without dialling and sat back in his chair. He closed his eyes. He really needed to do this, and it wouldn't help his cause if he kept chickening out.

154

Stephen had told him in no uncertain terms that if Dani were able to take the Redmond account with her, he was in big trouble.

Taking a deep breath, he opened his eyes, picked up the phone again and pushed the buttons for the number he knew so well.

He was in luck. The receptionist told him Mr Redmond was still there and would take his call.

Eric Redmond's voice came through loud and clear. "Gordon McKenzie. What can I do for you?"

Gordon swallowed and attempted an easy tone. "I was wondering if we're still good for the next phase of television ads."

"Ah. I thought we would be hearing from you. I've been informed that the MBE partnership is being dissolved."

"Yes, well, it's not finalised yet. We're still working out the details."

"Hm. It's always a painful business and I'm sorry, Gordon, but our inclination will be to go with Dani Barker after the split."

"Isn't that a conflict of interest?"

"In what way?"

"Dani told me she's sleeping with your financial director."

Gordon waited for the bombshell to hit home. The reaction, however, wasn't what he expected. There was a burst of laughter at the other end of the line, which turned rapidly into a coughing fit.

When he had recovered, Eric said, "Well, well. Our Camila is full of surprises. That makes the decision even easier. I've tried to poach Dani several times. For some strange reason, she stayed loyal to you."

Gordon gulped. "She would never fit into your organisation. You know she's totally off the wall."

Another laugh. "Oh, I know. Dani and I go back a long way."

"You're kidding. She's never said."

"Why do you think you got our account in the first place? It wasn't through your powers of persuasion. If Dani does go solo, we will find a way to work with her. Goodnight, McKenzie. And good luck."

Gordon sat back in his chair staring at his phone. Dani and Eric Redmond. He wouldn't have put them in the same room together, let alone being friends. How did he not know this? Perhaps Dani was right and he'd had his head up his own arse for too long. One thing was clear: he needed to talk to Dani. Somehow, he had to smooth things over. No way did he want to lose her to Redmond.

†

Dani ran the last few yards to her house. The Tube trains had been packed for the Friday night exodus from the city and she only had minutes to spare. The clock on her living room mantelpiece showed seven on the dot as she entered the room.

She stopped to catch her breath before going into the kitchen to open a can of beer. Deciding to be civilised for a change, she poured the liquid into a glass and took it into the hallway to wait by the door.

As she expected, knowing Camila's formidable organisational skills, the delivery came at exactly ten minutes past seven.

As she signed for the parcel, her eyes widened at the size and shape of it. Dani took it into the living room and tore the paper off. She paused to stroke the long contours of the fine mahogany case. It was a work of art in itself.

156

She took a deep breath before lifting the lid. Two beautifully crafted birch rods, approximately four foot in length, nestled in the felt-lined interior. Overcome with emotion, Dani sat and gazed at the canes in wonder. Camila's promise. This was beyond her expectations. Beyond even her wildest imaginings. She could now start to believe that Camila was indeed ready to take the next step in their relationship.

Chapter Fifteen

The only way Camila was going to get through the weekend was to stop thinking of Dani, but as she let the silky garment slip through her fingers, her mind was straying to their last night together.

"Well, dear, I can see there must be someone special in your life."

Her mother's voice brought her out of her daydream. Camila let go of the bright red camisole and turned around.

"You should buy it."

"Mother, really. I couldn't possibly wear anything like that."

"It doesn't hurt to be adventurous at times, especially in the bedroom department."

Camila had never had any kind of discussion with her mother about anything sex-related. Apart from brief instructions on what to do when she started having periods, they had never had intimate mother-daughter talks on the birds and the bees.

"What makes you think there's anyone special?" Camila moved away from the lingerie section.

"You've been distracted the whole time we have been here, looking like you would rather be somewhere else." Her mother patted her arm. "Don't worry. I've convinced your father to book the first flight back to Paris tomorrow. Then you can spend the rest of the weekend with your sweetheart."

The relief must have shown on her face as her mother added, "I knew that would please you. So when are we going to meet your mystery man?"

"It's all very new," Camila muttered, moving quickly towards the escalator.

"Does he at least have a name?"

"Dani."

Her mother closed the gap and stood on the moving step right behind her. "And what does he do?"

"Mum, please. I'm not having this conversation here."

When they reached the ground floor, Camila told her mother she had an errand to run and would see her at Foyles bookstore. They were meeting her father there, then going to a pub for a drink before dinner. She hurried off before her mother could protest.

As soon as she stepped inside the phone booth, she immediately regretted it; overwhelmed by the smell of piss and something unidentifiable. Shuddering, she put the money in the slot and dialled Dani's number. No answer. Camila stumbled out of the red box. Of course, it was pathetic to think Dani would be sitting around at home all weekend.

As she walked along the street towards the large bookstore, she passed another smaller one. Looking up at the sign, she remembered that Allison had sometimes bought books here. Silver Moon. She walked in and looked around. The shelves on this floor seemed to be mainstream fiction with some feminist offerings. She made her way down the

159

steps to the basement level and found herself in another world. Row upon row of lesbian books lined the shelves. Two other women were already browsing there. They didn't look around when she came in.

Camila told herself she would just have a quick look. It wouldn't do to keep her father from his pint. The only thing he missed about living in England, he said.

She opened a book and flicked through the pages. Allison had lapped this stuff up, but Camila couldn't see the point. She had tried reading one of the romances once, but it didn't grip her. She wondered what Allison's parents had made of their daughter's book collection, but then they'd probably thought they were Camila's. They would have thought it inconceivable that Allison would have any such subversive interests.

She was about to make a move towards the stairs, when a cover image on one of the lower shelves caught her eye. The rear view of a woman wearing a leather vest and chaps. Quickly reading the blurb on the back, Camila decided this was one she needed to read, for research purposes, of course.

After paying quickly, she placed her purchase in her large handbag, glad she had brought it out, and hurried up the street to meet her parents.

†

Dani checked the knot on her tie in the store window. Her hair was touching her collar. She'd need a haircut soon, but she was sure she could still pass. She carried on down the street threading her way through the crowds of theatre-goers and shoppers laden with bags and parcels.

Reaching her destination, she mounted the steps of the ornately pillared facade and showed her membership card to the doorman.

The dark panelling of the rooms always made her feel like she was walking onto a Jeeves and Wooster film set. Leather armchairs were grouped together in threes and fours, spaced out to give members privacy. She walked confidently to the back corner where she knew he would be sitting.

He lowered his newspaper as she sat in the chair opposite. "Good timing, Dani. The ice hasn't melted in your drink yet." He indicated the tumbler of whisky on the table in front of her. His own glass was looking in need of a refresher.

She didn't really like whisky, but it was part of the role she was playing.

"Thanks." She lifted the glass. "Cheers, Eric." Taking a sip, she managed not to pull a face. "Hm, that's not bad."

He tilted his own glass towards her. "I know you're a lightweight in the grown-up-drinks department. That's a lowland blend of Scotch. Mine's the real thing."

Dani could pick up the peaty scent from where she was sitting. "Laphroaig, I presume. Tastes like a goat's backside."

"And you would know what that's like!"

"Ha-ha! Is Carl joining us?"

"Later."

She sat back in her chair. "So you had a call from Gordon."

"Yes. He's a bit naïve, isn't he?"

"He's led a sheltered life."

Eric drained the rest of the smoky liquid in his glass and waved it in the air. A waiter appeared immediately and took it away for a refill.

"His little blackmail attempt was doomed to failure before he even opened his mouth."

"Blackmail? We are talking about my soon-to-be ex-business partner?"

"Yes, indeed. So how long has it been going on? No, wait, let me guess. You sent the roses. That got the rumour mill going with speculation on Camila's secret admirer. And you made a delivery to the conference. She certainly wasn't herself at breakfast the next morning."

Dani grinned. "Good to know."

Eric accepted his refilled glass of whisky and took a sip. "So now that you're free of that loser, are you going to join us?"

"Come on, Eric. I thought we would at least get to the main course before you popped the question."

"Come on, yourself. You can't seriously think you can make it on your own."

"I won't be on my own. There's a good team of people who would come with me."

When Eric phoned that afternoon, Dani had been sitting on her bed swishing one of the canes and enjoying a fantasy involving Camila wearing a tight-fitting leather outfit. She had known as soon as he mentioned that Gordon had called him that she was in for a discussion about her future plans. Still, she had agreed to have dinner with them as it gave her the excuse to dress in her favourite dark suit. Knowing they were meeting at Eric's club, she had chosen a discreet blue-and-grey-striped tie. Close enough to an old-school tie that would help create the right impression.

"Why don't you finish that bog water? I take it we're meeting Carl at the restaurant. I'll talk about my plans then."

Eric swallowed some more of his drink and smiled at her. "Okay. Change of subject. How on earth did you and

Camila connect? She's known as the ice queen in the company."

"Music to my ears."

"No really. I know she had a long-term relationship with someone but she was never open about it. Of course, I could hardly comment. When the woman died, we tried to persuade her to take time off, but she said she needed to work. And that's pretty much what she's done for the last three years. A week or two off at Christmas spent with her parents and that's it. I can't deny we haven't taken advantage of her work ethic. She's the best negotiator we've got, and with new markets opening up all the time, keeping her busy hasn't been a problem."

"So you never met this..." Dani searched her memory. "...Allison."

"Was that her name? No. Camila has always kept anything about her private life, well, private." He knocked back the rest of his whisky. "Come on, better shift or Carl will think we're not coming."

†

Camila could feel the book burning a hole in her bag. She wanted to be alone to savour the contents. She was sure her mother would have told her father the most important news of the day before she joined them in Foyles. Luckily, he was too focused on getting to the pub and making a choice from the selection of real ales to start on the third degree. She stood at the bar with him, ordering a gin and tonic for herself and a dry white wine for her mother.

"I don't know how she can drink that," he said. "Pubs never stock good wine."

"I guess you're a bit spoiled for choice living in France."

"Too right. Now, what do you think, Cammie? This Speckled Hen or the London Pride?"

Camila hated being called Cammie but she hadn't been able to break her father of the habit. She looked at the beer taps and remembered that Dani had London Pride in her fridge.

"Go for the Pride," she said.

"Is that what your new man drinks?"

Thanks, Mum, she thought glumly. "Mostly."

"She's bursting to know more."

"She will have to burst. Like I told her, it's all very new and I don't really want to talk about it."

"You're a strange one, Cammie. I've never met a woman who didn't want to talk about love."

"I think it's a bit early to be talking about love."

"Ah, it's like that, is it? Good for you, girl. It's time you had some fun in your life."

They took their drinks to the table, and Camila managed to steer the conversation to general topics.

†

Carl was effusive in his greeting, as always, air-kissing her on both cheeks.

The maître d' greeted the Redmonds enthusiastically and personally escorted them to their usual table.

"Nice suit, Dani," Carl said, taking the seat across from Eric.

"Thanks."

"You still go to Charles."

"Absolutely. Wouldn't dream of going anywhere else."

"Same here."

Two waiters arrived promptly, one carrying a bottle of champagne, the other with three glass flutes. Carl glanced at the label of the Veuve Clicquot held towards him and nodded. "Excellent, just pour."

"Can't beat the old widow." Eric gave Dani a sly wink.

"Indeed." She didn't rise to the bait and accepted the glass Carl handed to her. "I don't know how you put up with him."

"He has some redeeming features."

"Keep it clean, you two."

They studied their menus in silence for a few minutes. Eric put his down quickly.

"I know what I'm having."

"So do I," Carl commented acidly. "You always have the same thing. The chef's probably preparing it now."

†

They were finishing their main courses, deep in conversation about the royal family and whether or not toe-sucking would catch on as an erotic experience, when Eric suddenly said, "Don't turn around, Dani. But Camila and her parents have just arrived."

"You're shitting me!"

"No, I'm not. They're about three tables away. I don't think Camila's spotted us yet."

Dani put her knife and fork down carefully.

"Damn. David's seen me," Eric said.

"You know her parents?"

"We've met a few times." He smiled and waved. "Do you want me to introduce you?"

"No way. I'm not going to embarrass Camila here."

"Too late. He's coming over."

†

165

Her father had chosen the restaurant over her mother's protests that it was far too expensive.

"Money is no object where my two favourite ladies are concerned. And we have something extra to celebrate tonight." He gave Camila's arm an affectionate squeeze as they followed the waiter to their table.

"Dad, please."

He wasn't ready to let the subject go. The two pints of bitter he'd consumed in the pub had mellowed him considerably. When they were finally sitting down, he continued, "What's wrong with this Dani? Is he some sort of criminal? Is that why you don't want to talk about him?"

Camila glanced at her mother for support but she was looking at her expectantly as well.

"Oh my! This is a popular place. Your bosses are here." Her father smiled and waved. "I'll go over and say hello. If the wine waiter shows up, order a bottle of Fleurie."

Camila turned in her seat as he got up and walked past a few tables to where she could see Carl and Eric and the back of another man. Her heart lurched. Only it wasn't a man, was it? She knew the back of that head, and the profile when it turned to observe her father's approach was undeniably Dani's.

Eric stood to greet him and she watched as they shook hands and her father acknowledged Carl. Watching as Eric introduced Dani, Camila held her breath. Dani nodded and got up. Clearly she was being invited to come over to their table. Camila caught the look of concern on Carl's face as her father made his way back with Dani in tow. This was too much. How did Dani even know the Redmonds?

"Well, well. Seems we're in luck, Margaret. Let me introduce Dani, our girl's secret lover."

Dani smiled. "Pleased to meet you, Mrs Callaghan."

"Do you work for Redmond too?" her mother asked.

"No. I have an advertising agency. We recently did some television ads for them."

Camila saw her father's face transform with shock as something clicked for him. She stood abruptly. "I need to powder my nose."

She made her way out to the lobby not quite at a run.

†

Dani watched Camila's rapid exit with concern. Mrs Callaghan was looking puzzled but Mr Callaghan was obviously putting two and two together rapidly and reaching the right answer.

"Lovely to meet you both. I'll just go and make sure she's all right." Dani strode out of the room and thought she would find Camila in the ladies', although going in dressed as she was wouldn't do. Fortunately, she found her huddled by the telephone booth, shoulders heaving.

Words seemed inadequate, so she just embraced Camila and held her. When her breathing calmed, Camila pulled back and looked into her eyes.

"How do you know Carl and Eric?"

"Carl and I were at art college together, but after the first year, he got into computers and then he met Eric."

"What do you mean?" Camila's eyes darkened as the truth hit her. "They're not brothers," she stated in a flat tone.

"No." Dani held on to her, wanting so much to kiss her. "Look, it's not my story to tell. But it was a different time. Maybe in the early eighties they would have come out. Then the AIDS crisis hit and the business they'd so carefully built would have come crashing down if their influential backers knew."

"But neither of them has AIDS."

167

"Doesn't matter whether they do or not. In spite of the good work by Princess Diana, people still think all gay men are infected and you can catch it just by being in the same room."

"Things are changing."

"Yes, but slowly. Look at you. Afraid to come out to your parents. Although I think that cat is well and truly out of the bag now."

Camila's eyes were still brimming with tears. Dani brushed her hair away from her face and leaned down to kiss her. Their lips met and Dani lost herself in the softness of exploring her lover's mouth with her tongue. After a few minutes they broke apart, needing to breathe.

"Come home with me," Dani whispered. "You have a promise to deliver on."

"I can't. I'm going to have to talk to them. But they're leaving in the morning."

"Please don't keep me waiting too long."

Camila gave her a tentative smile. "I better get back. I'll see you tomorrow."

Dani released her and watched her go back into the restaurant. She turned and went into the gents' toilets. Checking her face in the mirror, she reluctantly wiped the traces of Camila's lipstick off her mouth.

†

Returning to the restaurant, Dani glanced at the Callaghans as she walked past their table. Camila was speaking in a low voice, holding her parents' attention.

Dani found Carl sitting alone, the debris of their main course cleared away.

"Where's Eric?"

"Phone call. He left a message at the club to say he could be contacted here."

"Doesn't he ever stop?"

"No." Carl twirled his dessert spoon around. "Is she okay?"

"I hope so. It didn't take Dad long to catch on."

"Are you serious about Camila, Dani? I don't want to see her get hurt."

Dani smiled at him. "I think that's the conversation I'll be having with her father at some point. But, yes, I am."

"Is she okay with...you know?" Carl made a swishing motion with his arm.

"Early days yet, but I think she's getting there."

Carl looked like he wanted to continue the conversation, but Eric returned before he could say anything else.

"How do you feel about a trip to Strasbourg?" he asked his partner as he sat down.

"Strasbourg?" Carl perked up like a retriever on a scent. "No way! They're interested?"

"Yep." Eric looked at Dani. "We may have cracked the European contract we've been after. I'm sorry, but it's going to impact on your love life. I'll need Camila to go with Carl. I'd go myself but I'm meeting the Americans on Monday."

"But she will have Sunday off, won't she?"

"Sorry, mate. The way the flights work, they'll have to travel tomorrow."

Dani slumped in her seat. "Why can't you go? She can meet the Americans." Even as she spoke the words, Dani knew she sounded pathetic.

"Camila's laid the groundwork. She knows the ins and outs of the project better than either of us. As I told you before, she's absolutely ace at negotiation."

"When are you going to tell her? It looks like she's having a serious chat with her parents."

"I've left a message on her answerphone. If you had plans for tomorrow, she's not going to like it any more than you, but there isn't any other option." Eric's tone was apologetic, but she could see the light of conquest dancing in his eyes. "So have you ordered dessert, Carl?"

"Of course. Crème brûlée for you and an irish coffee for Dani."

"What about you?"

"Watching my waistline. I'll have a spoonful of yours."

"Nothing wrong with your waistline." Eric eyed him flirtatiously.

"Give it a rest, guys, please." Dani glared at them. "Seeing as you've just put a spoke in my love life."

"Come on, Dani. It's only a few days. She will be all yours on Tuesday evening. If this deal comes off, I'll tell her to take some time off."

"Like that will work." Carl sniffed. "She hasn't had a proper holiday in three years."

Dani fought the urge to turn and look at Camila's table. The next half hour passed in excruciating slowness, as she felt malevolent eyes boring into the back of her head. When their desserts came, she drank the irish coffee as quickly as she could without burning her mouth and willed Eric and Carl not to linger over their crème brûlée.

Chapter Sixteen

The conversation with her parents during dinner had been uncomfortable. Her father kept looking over at the table where Dani sat with the Redmonds.

"I don't understand," had become her mother's refrain. "If you're going out with someone who looks like a man, why don't you go out with a real man?"

"I'm not attracted to men."

"But you're going out with someone who is dressed like a man."

"She doesn't dress like that all the time."

Camila had relaxed slightly once the other three had gone. Dani glanced back at the door and caught her eye. They shared a brief smile, although Dani's expression looked more like a grimace.

Thinking that she would see Dani the next day had sustained her throughout the meal and on the way home in the taxi. Only a few more hours and her parents would be headed back to France.

"You've got a message," her father said as soon as the door of the flat closed behind them. "Probably from your *boyfriend.*"

Camila ignored the sarcasm in his tone and shrugged out of her jacket. She set her bag on the floor and pressed the button to listen to the message. Her parents continued into the living room. Camila leant against the wall and closed her eyes. Eric's voice came through loud and clear. He sounded excited. But his words did nothing to excite her.

A week or two ago, going to Strasbourg to close out the deal would have brought a smile to her face. Now she could only think of Dani's disappointment and her own unfulfilled fantasies.

She told her parents she needed to prepare for the unexpected business trip and went into her bedroom, closing the door. After the evening's events, she craved her privacy more than ever.

Those few minutes of holding on to Dani had felt wonderful. In spite of the turmoil in her mind, her body had responded automatically to her lover's closeness. Their kiss had intensified that feeling and it had been a wrench to pull herself away, with the added difficulty of trying to explain to her parents that this was the best thing that had ever happened to her.

She picked out the clothes she would wear in the morning and repacked her travel bag, checking that her passport was there. Eric would look after providing the currency they needed although she had some French francs left over from her last trip to her parents' house at Christmas.

As she reached into her handbag to retrieve her purse, her hand met the unresisting contours of a paperback. She took it out and carefully removed it from the Silver Moon branded bag. The image on the front cover set her pulse racing again. Camila placed it face down on her bedside table.

From the sounds outside her room, she could tell that her parents had retired to their bedroom. She ventured out and went into the bathroom to retrieve the toiletries bag she stowed in the cupboard there for her frequent trips abroad. Satisfied that everything was ready for the next day's journey, she finished her own bedtime preparations and crawled under the duvet.

Camila opened the book and started to read.

†

Not wanting to go home, Dani had gone on to a club with Carl and Eric. They danced together while she fended off the attentions of several good-looking young men who tried to tempt her onto the dance floor. Having drunk more than she really wanted to by the time they left at two in the morning, she fell into bed with her clothes on and didn't wake until ten.

The shower helped to ease some of the hangover. She stuffed the suit into a bag to take to the dry cleaners on Monday and went downstairs to make a strong pot of coffee. The light blinking on her answerphone caught her eye, so she stopped in the hallway to listen to the message.

Camila sounded tired as she told Dani she would be back on Tuesday. Their plane was landing at five, so she would come straight to Dani's house. Dani caught her breath as the last words filtered into her mind: "I keep my promises."

She walked into the kitchen feeling more alive than two minutes earlier. Dani was still smiling when the doorbell rang before she had finished her first cup of coffee.

Opening the door to her brother, she was about to berate him in a few choice words about disturbing her at this hour on a Sunday morning, then saw he had company. Two little faces peered up at her from behind his legs.

"Morning, sis," he said cheerfully. "May we come in? It's a bit wet out here."

Dani hadn't noticed it was raining, but the umbrella he was holding should have been a clue.

"Sure." She stood aside as he collapsed the brolly and ushered the two little girls into the house.

"We were going to go to Kew Gardens, but the rain caught us out. You don't mind, do you?"

Considering she had never met her nieces and hadn't seen her brother for a long time prior to his arriving unexpectedly in her office the other night, she could only shrug.

"Why should I mind? Coffee's on if you want some. But I don't have anything suitable for these two, other than water."

"That's okay. We came prepared for a picnic." He slipped the heavily laden rucksack off his back. "So let me introduce you. The taller one is Lucy, and this little troublemaker is Holly. Meet your Auntie Dani."

Dani smiled at the two girls. Holly had one arm wrapped around Brian's leg and one small fist shoved in her mouth. Dani wasn't good with children's ages but she guessed Lucy was about six and Holly maybe four. Lucy was giving her a puzzled look.

"Mummy says you're a peevert."

"Really." She waved off Brian's shushing to his daughter. "And what do you think that means?"

"That you pee a lot."

"Hm. No more than most people, I think. Anyway, there's a bathroom just there, if you need to pee." She looked at Holly. "Do you want to pee?" The little girl shook her head. "Okay, so if there is no peeing to be done at the moment, let's all go into the living room."

The girls sat side by side on the sofa, looking around wide-eyed. Brian followed Dani into the kitchen. "Sorry about that."

"What are you really doing here? I'm not buying the Kew story." She refilled her mug and poured one for Brian. "There's milk in the fridge."

"I thought it was time the girls met their aunt."

"Even though I'm a 'peevert'?" She took two glasses out of the cupboard. "Here. I'm guessing you've brought some juice for them."

"Yes, thanks. Is your girlfriend not here?"

"Ah. That's the real reason, isn't it? Perving after my girlfriend."

"She did look rather nice. Too good for you, anyway."

"She's away on business, so you're out of luck."

They returned to the living room to find the two girls sitting quietly where they had left them. Dani wondered what else they'd been told about her. They looked like they were afraid to move. Brian pulled a bottle of lemonade out of his rucksack and poured a glass for each of them.

"Can we have a biscuit, Daddy?" Lucy was obviously the more outgoing of the two, or maybe she just had the innate confidence of the firstborn.

Brian smiled at her, reached into the bag, and brought out a pack of custard creams. Lucy shook her head at him. He reached in again and this time came up with a packet of Penguins.

"Yes!" She ripped it open and spread the selection out on the coffee table, a row of vibrant-coloured bars. Lucy put her hand on the blue one, then seemed to remember she was

175

in a strange house. She smiled at Dani. "Do you want a Penguin, Auntie Dani?"

"I like the red ones. And just call me Dani, please." She accepted the red-wrapped biscuit Lucy handed her. She gave a yellow one to her sister, a green one to Brian, and scooped up the blue one for herself.

They all munched their chocolate-covered biscuits and sipped their drinks.

"Do you like drawing?" Dani asked as it looked like it was her job to start a conversation. Both girls nodded.

Dani walked through to the back of the house and retrieved some paper and colouring pencils. She placed them on the floor in front of the coffee table and sat on the floor herself.

"Come on. Let's see what you can do."

†

An hour later, Brian was stretched out on the sofa asleep. Holly had lost her earlier inhibition and crawled onto Dani's lap, watching as she sketched a picture.

"That's me," she said, clearly delighted.

"It is. Shall I do one of Daddy?"

"Yes, please, Dani."

When she had opened the door to Brian and the girls, Dani hadn't been happy to see them. But now she was glad. The unplanned visit was an ideal way to spend a Sunday morning and helped to keep thoughts of Camila at bay.

The two girls had settled down to drawing quickly, but Holly got bored first. From what Dani could see, Lucy seemed to be creating a fairly complex picture. Holly's effort was standard fare. An outline of a house and a blob at the top that was likely meant to be a sun.

Dani bent her head and concentrated on bringing Brian's features to life on the page. Drawn from memory, as she didn't think he would thank her for depicting his face as he lay with his mouth open, letting out the occasional snuffle. She had joined in with the girls, giggling at the sight when he first fell asleep.

Lucy looked up from her drawing. "I like being a peevert," she announced.

"I don't think you should tell your mother that."

"Why not?"

"She doesn't approve of peeverts."

"Oh." Lucy's brow furrowed in the way it did when she was thinking. "Why can't Daddy live with us anymore?"

"I don't know. Sometimes things just don't work out."

"I wish he would come home."

"Why?" Dani watched her niece's face closely.

"He smells funny."

Dani thought all men smelt funny but she wasn't going to tell Lucy that. "Who smells funny? Your dad?"

"No. Mummy's friend. He stays at our house some nights. I don't like it when he kisses me."

Those words sent a shiver through Dani. "When does he kiss you?"

"At bedtime. I don't want him to kiss me."

"Have you told your mother that?"

"She says it's nice, that it shows he cares. She says Daddy never cared."

"Well, she's wrong. He cares for you, very much."

Holly squirmed and said quietly, "I need to pee now."

"Okay. Can you go on your own?"

"Yes." Holly gave her an indignant look. "I'm a big girl."

"You are. Off you go."

Brian woke after Holly left the room.

"Sorry. Have I been out long?" He stretched his arms over his head.

"Long enough. I think Lucy's created a masterpiece while you've been sleeping."

†

The rain had eased off and it looked like the afternoon would be sunny. Brian joined Dani at the window looking out at the river while the girls gathered up the pencils and paper in the living room.

"Thanks, Dani. They've really enjoyed themselves."

"Good. Listen, what do you know about June's boyfriend?"

"Nothing much."

"I think you should check him out. Lucy's afraid of him. Personally, I'd be suspicious of a guy who takes an interest in a woman with two small girls."

"What has she told you?"

"He kisses her goodnight. Sounds innocent enough, but from the way she said it, I think there is more to it. Sounds creepy to me."

Brian sighed heavily. "Thanks, I'll look into it. I've only met him once and can't say I took to him either. But I should have picked up on this." He surprised Dani by pulling her into a hug.

"Can we have hugs too, Daddy?"

After a round of hugs—aunt, nieces, brother, sisters, daughters—Dani watched from her doorstep as the three walked slowly down the street to Brian's car, each of the girls holding one of his hands.

Chapter Seventeen

Once she started, Camila couldn't stop reading. It was after three in the morning before she finished the book, and she lay awake for another hour or so, tossing and turning, trying without success to calm her thoughts and the reactions in her body.

Camila woke later than she had planned, and when she stumbled out into her kitchen, she soon realised her parents had breakfasted and gone. They'd left a brief note on the counter saying they would call later in the week when she got back from her business trip.

Relieved that she wouldn't have to face them, she refilled the kettle and switched it on. Only as she was spooning coffee grounds into the cafetière did she notice the time. She had less than forty minutes before the taxi was due to take them to the airport. Carl wouldn't be amused if she kept him waiting.

At least the preparations she had made the night before meant she only needed a quick shower to wake herself up. Drying her hair took twenty minutes. A light application of

179

eye shadow and lipstick and her face looked less like a death mask than it had when she first awoke.

She rechecked her bag for passport, money, hairbrush, and other minor essentials, picked up her case, and left the apartment. The taxi pulled in to the kerb just as she stepped outside the building.

Carl greeted her with a smile when she settled herself in the seat next to him. "Perfect timing as expected, Ms Callaghan."

She gave him a brief smile in return. "Of course."

"You won't mind if I doze off on the way. Bit of a late night."

"Not at all."

He was asleep before they reached the end of the road. Camila closed her eyes and was surprised when she jerked awake and saw they were turning into the Heathrow complex. She turned to Carl, who was observing her with an amused grin.

"Wild night with Mr and Mrs C?"

"No, just stayed up reading."

†

Their check-in didn't take long. They were both frequent flyers, and they made their way to the business-class lounge to wait for their flight to be called. Camila sat down with the complimentary *Financial Times* while Carl went to the counter and collected two coffees. The headlines swam in front of her eyes. She was going to need a strong injection of caffeine and perhaps another hour of sleep on the plane if she could manage it.

Hiding behind the newspaper wasn't an option when Carl sat down and said, "So how did it go with your parents after they met Dani?"

Camila would have told anyone else to mind their own business, but she had always had a good relationship with Carl. "Not well. I think it will take them some time to get used to the idea."

"It's serious, then?"

"Who knows? It feels like it could be. We've only known each other a few weeks." Camila sipped her coffee, pleased to find it was stronger than she'd expected. "You, on the other hand, have known Dani for much longer. I think you and Eric have some explaining to do."

Carl examined the contents of his own coffee cup intently before answering. "Yes, I suppose we do."

"Dani told me you were at art college together. I have a hard time imagining you as friends."

"We had a few things in common. Both outsiders, for a start. Nineteen seventy-five. She perfected the grunge look before it became fashionable. And I was annoying my parents by imitating David Bowie in his Ziggy Stardust phase. Only for me it wasn't just a fashion statement. I knew I was gay."

"I still don't see how you and Dani would connect."

"She was, is, so talented. I struggled. I mean, I was only there because I was rebelling against my father's plans for me to follow in his footsteps and do a degree in engineering. Dani helped me out with my projects and we just hit it off. I suppose that's the clue, isn't it? We also have a certain obsession, shall we say, in common."

Carl was watching her face for a reaction, and Camila knew that she failed to conceal her shock at this last statement.

"You and Eric...?" she whispered.

"Hey, it works for us. If you love someone, you put your trust in them, and whatever anyone else may think, it's the most wonderful, freeing experience you'll ever have."

Trust. That word had cropped up frequently in the book she read during the night. Trust and feeling safe. Safe words.

An announcement broke into her thoughts.

"Time to go," Carl said. "That's our flight."

†

Gordon wondered how he had let his wife talk him into buying the monstrosity of a house they were now living in. He would need another ten years to make even a sizeable dent in the mortgage repayments.

Although he knew it wasn't fair to put all the blame on Melissa. He had fallen in love with the size of the garden, the fully grown weeping willow at the far end reminding him of his childhood home. Summer days spent playing games under the branches, hidden from adult view.

Theo and Tessa were out there now. He could hear their high-pitched voices and laughter. He wanted his children to embrace outdoor activities as much as possible. Sometime soon, though, he was sure he would be losing at least one of them to the lure of constant computer games, most likely Theo. Boys did seem to get addicted more quickly than girls. Tessa's day would come, when she turned from being their sweet eight-year-old to a surly sixteen. Possibly before, the way kids grew up so fast these days.

"Are you listening to me, Gordon?"

He sighed and turned from the window to face his wife. "What?"

"Either she goes or I go. And if I go, I'm taking the children."

Could his nightmare week really get any worse? It seemed it could. Not only did Melissa know about his affair with Maria, she was threatening to leave him. Her parents would be only too happy to have their daughter and grandchildren living with them. They had never approved of him.

"I keep telling you, it's all over with Maria and has been for a while."

"I don't care. She sees you every day."

"Look, it's not a problem. I'll get rid of her. Tomorrow." It really wouldn't be any hardship. He should have done it before now anyway. Maria was no great shakes as a secretary and he had tired of their liaisons some time ago.

"Good. And once you're free of that Dani creature, we will all be able to move forward."

Gordon wasn't sure how she expected that to work out. Without the Redmond account, he would have difficulty maintaining their extravagant lifestyle. And Dani's threat to have her solicitor look into his finances would destroy his chances of getting back in business anytime soon.

His first priority on Monday morning, after firing Maria of course, was to talk to Dani again. See if they couldn't come to an amicable agreement.

†

Dani was at work early on Monday, getting in before everyone else. Her Sunday afternoon and evening had been quiet. The freshness of the air after the morning rain drew her out into the garden. She sketched for a while, an image of Camila's body arching under her touch. The drawing was so realistic that she had to hide it under some other drawings and retire to her bedroom for some much-needed hand relief.

Afterwards she showered and changed and went out for a walk by the river. But the sight of so many couples arm in arm, enjoying the sunshine and each other, was too much to bear.

She kept reminding herself that she only had to get through another two days. Hardly any time at all in the grand scheme of things.

Engrossed in her work, she wasn't aware of other people arriving in the building until Declan came in with her coffee and a chocolate éclair.

"Thanks, Declan."

He hovered in the doorway until she looked at him again.

"Yes?"

"Um, just thought you would want to know, Maria's gone."

"About time. She was fucking useless."

"The thing is, people are talking. Wondering who might be next."

"I see. Okay. Thanks for letting me know."

Dani sucked the chocolate off the top of the éclair and thought about the situation. She should have a chat with Gordon but didn't have the energy for a full-on confrontation now. He wouldn't be in the best of moods if he had just fired his mistress. Melissa was obviously still pulling his strings.

Her phone rang. Amanda's voice was brisk and professional, "Ms Callaghan on line one."

Gordon certainly had the staff rattled.

"Hello. How are things in Euro-land?"

"Boring. We will be in meetings all day, so I thought I'd try to reach you now."

"I thought you enjoyed meetings."

"Usually I do. But right now all I can think about is what I'm going to do with you when I see you."

Dani shifted in her chair. "Have you considered starting a sex-chat line?"

Camila's soft voice purred in her ear. "I don't want to waste time talking about it. I hope you'll be ready for me."

"I'm ready now."

"Damn! Carl is waving at me. Time to go and switch into meeting mode."

Dani didn't miss the suggestive inflection Camila put on the word *switch*. Well that was her early morning concentration shot.

She spent some time talking to Declan and Gary about their workloads. On the way out for a change of scene, she stopped by the reception desk.

"Amanda."

The woman looked at her, and Dani could see the fear on her face. She leaned forward. "You have absolutely nothing to worry about."

Amanda gave her a tentative smile.

†

After a pint of London Pride and a chat with one of the other Rising Sun regulars about whether or not having a tunnel link to France was a good idea, Dani returned to the office determined to get some productive work done.

Amanda stopped her as she walked through Reception, looking concerned.

"What is it? I thought I told you not to worry."

"Gordon's waiting for you, in the studio."

"Oh. By himself?"

"Yes."

"Right. Thanks for the heads-up."

Gordon was standing by the window. He turned and took a step back when he saw her. "Jesus! You scared me."

"What do you want?"

"Look, maybe this isn't a good time...."

185

"Any time is a good time for you to be leaving."

He took a deep breath. Dani had walked over to her table and started to arrange her drawing materials. "Look, Dani. Maybe I was a bit hasty. This split…it isn't really what either of us wants, is it?"

"Oh, isn't it?"

"You don't really want to go it alone, do you?"

"I won't be alone. I'll just be without you." She had started doodling on a pad.

"Dani, we can't just throw away fifteen years of working together."

"You already have."

"I just don't think we should go down this route."

"Oh, get a grip, Gordon. This is what married couples do, isn't it? Stay together for the sake of the kids. It doesn't always work. You can't fix something once it's broken. We need to let it go, move on."

"I don't know if I can."

"Well, that's your problem now. And I'd appreciate it if you spoke to my solicitor in future instead of me." She stalked over to the door and held it open for him.

†

The meetings weren't as boring as she had indicated to Dani. Camila did enjoy watching the male members of the panel squirm when they realised she was on top of her game and knew more about the legislative processes than they did.

By the end of the long day, she and Carl had something to celebrate. They met in the hotel bar.

"Eric didn't think we would pull it off. He's ecstatic."

"It's certainly a relief to get this one done and dusted."

The waiter approached their table with the champagne Carl had ordered. After the first swallow of the delicate bubbles, Camila asked the question that had been nagging at her all day.

"The mocked-up packaging designs you showed the panel...who did the artwork?"

"Oh, just this small outfit we subcontract to."

Camila had seen the name on the back of one of the display boards. "DBS."

Carl cocked his head, and his smile confirmed what she had suspected.

"Let me guess, Dani Barker Services."

"Got it in one, Ms Callaghan."

She had seen the DBS name on the financial reports that crossed her desk, but until now hadn't connected it with Dani.

"How long has that cosy little arrangement been going on?"

"Not long after I started in the business. Eric was complaining about the poor-quality design work on one of the products and I suggested Dani."

"I'm guessing Gordon McKenzie knows nothing about this."

"No, and I think Dani would like to keep it that way."

"I wondered how she could afford a house that backs onto the river."

Carl finished his drink. "Come on. Better make a move or they will give our table away."

They walked across the square to the small family-run restaurant that Carl assured her had the best Italian food outside Italy.

†

Later, Camila blamed it on the combination of the adrenaline high from their success and the amount of red wine they drank. After they'd finished the main course and declined an enticing array of desserts in favour of sharing a cheese board and another glass of red, she leaned towards her dining companion and asked quietly, "Are there any sex shops here?" Camila had always thought of Strasbourg as a rather conservative place.

Carl laughed long and hard before answering. "Are you kidding? All these Euro MPs on expenses, living away from home…what exactly are you looking for?"

When she told him, he smiled and said he knew just the place, not far from the hotel.

"We can go there in the morning." They had a few hours to kill before heading to the airport.

"I wish we could have got an earlier flight." Camila placed a slice of blue cheese on a cracker.

"Fran tried, but there was no chance. The other flights were fully booked."

"I'll be glad when the tunnel is finally open. Next year, isn't it?"

Carl seemed happy with the change of subject. "Yes, I'm looking forward to popping over to Paris on day trips. We've talked about having a presence there."

Back at the hotel they parted in Reception to go to their respective rooms. Carl kissed her lightly on the cheek and whispered, "Sweet dreams. See you at breakfast."

†

Monday had been unproductive. After another restless night, Dani arrived at the office on Tuesday morning determined to work on the creative concepts for a new brand of toothpaste. The deadline was on Friday and it was a job she had been putting off.

The phone call from Annette Harmon destroyed that early impetus. Dani hadn't heard from the solicitor since the meeting the week before and was surprised by the frosty tone Annette greeted her with. She thought they had parted on good terms.

"Full disclosure, Ms Barker?"

"I told you everything."

"DBS slipped your mind, did it?"

"Ah. Yes, I guess it did."

"I take it Mr McKenzie is unaware of your sideline."

"Yes."

"If this goes to court…."

She left the sentence hanging, not needing to spell it out.

Unable to get her mind back on the toothpaste after the call, Dani spent the morning on the computer. Getting to grips with the drawing-program features wasn't as daunting as she had thought. She tried out more of the options and discovered she liked the ease with which she could manipulate shapes and change colour combinations.

†

Deborah carried the two bags of groceries into the house. If Chris were home, she would enlist her help to bring in the bottles from the car. These were the supplies for her birthday barbecue, after all. Ever since her examination of their recent phone bill had revealed numerous calls to Camila's home number, Deborah's resentment about holding this party had been growing. Another number she didn't know had appeared several times as well. With a quick check in the Yellow Pages, she found it belonged to Redmond, Camila's employer.

Chris put the phone down as Deborah reached the hallway.

"Who was that?"

"No one."

Deborah knew she'd caught her out in a lie from the way Chris's eyes shifted away from the phone. Controlling the turmoil in her chest, she said calmly, "Good. Could you bring the drinks in from the car?"

As she started to unpack the bags in the kitchen, her anger rose to the surface. What did she have to lose, after all, by asking the question?

Chris placed the box of beer on the table and turned to go back out.

"What's going on, Chris?"

"What do you mean?" Chris's face was red and Deborah knew it wasn't from the exertion of carrying a heavy box from the car.

"I think, as I pay the phone bill, I have a right to know why you've been making so many calls to Camila. Is she your latest squeeze?" Deborah decided to keep up the pretense of not knowing about their earlier fling. Something to have in reserve.

"I...no, of course not."

"So why all the calls? You'll be seeing her on Friday."

"Well, I just wanted to know who she was bringing. She didn't say, did she?"

"No, she didn't." Deborah busied herself, sorting out the items that needed to go in the fridge from the ones she would store in the cupboard. She didn't want Chris to see she was wound up. "Anyway, it's about time she found someone else." Plastering on a fake smile, she turned away from the sink to face her lover. "I'm pleased for her, aren't you?"

"Yeah, I am. Um, do you want the beer in the fridge now?"

"I'll sort it. But you could check to make sure we have enough charcoal for the barbecue. If we need more, I'll pick some up after work tomorrow."

Chris nodded and hurried out of the room. Deborah let out the breath she hadn't realised she'd been holding and released her grip on the package of buns, now squashed out of shape. She could get through the next few days. But after the party, they would talk properly. Something had to give in their relationship. And so far she was the one doing all the giving.

Why hadn't she said something when she first figured out Chris had slept with Camila? Chris had told her it was someone she'd met at a bar, but Deborah recognised Camila's brand of perfume lingering in Chris's hair when she arrived home late that evening. She'd agreed to go along with an open relationship in the beginning, and the only rules she insisted on were very simple: no threesomes, no men, and no friends. No doubt Chris would wriggle out of that last one by saying Allison had been more of a friend, as Camila always faded into the background at dinner parties.

Deborah had soon discovered that the life of a swinger wasn't for her. Flirting with other women was fine, but she always balked at taking it any further. Was her own insecurity what kept her from telling Chris she wasn't happy with the way things were? She had willingly believed Chris's insistence that she loved her. That whatever she had with anyone else was only sex.

She swiped away at her tears with a dishtowel. No point crying about it. Camila was bringing someone to the party. That would put an end to Chris's obsession with the woman.

†

Camila was glad Carl was with her when they visited the shop. She would never have been able to make the purchase without his help.

Settling back in her seat as the plane taxied out to the runway, she closed her eyes, thinking of the look on Dani's face when she'd unveil this outfit.

"Doesn't take much imagination to know what you're thinking." Carl interrupted her vision.

"Doesn't it?"

"Just remember, you need to have the attitude to go with it."

During the ride to the airport, Carl had outlined various scenes he and Eric played out. "Take a firm line with her," he advised. "She will love it."

Now she turned to him and said, "How did I not know about you and Eric? Being gay, I mean. Not the other thing."

"We have had years of practice playing the part."

"Yes. I always thought you were involved with that woman you've brought to a few functions. What's her name, Lisa, isn't it?" Camila recalled a small woman with delicate features.

"Ah, yes. Lisa. She has provided cover for me on occasion."

"I didn't think she was your type when I met her."

"Oh, she's my type all right. Sometimes does me favours of another kind when Eric's away for any length of time. Something else Dani and I have in common."

Camila stared at him, absorbing the information. She recalled the cut on Dani's cheek. What was it she had told her? A woman had hit her because she was thinking of Camila and wouldn't do what she wanted the woman to do.

"This Lisa…" She lowered her voice. "She's a…?" Camila couldn't bring herself to say the word.

Carl smiled at her, the conspiratorial smile she was getting to know. "A Miss Whiplash, yes. But she generally only does women," he said calmly.

The cabin crew had returned to their seats, and the plane started its acceleration along the runway. As the wheels left the ground, Camila rested her head against the back of the seat and wondered at the revelations of the last few days. Her well-ordered life seemed like a distant memory.

Chapter Eighteen

Dani had managed to do some grocery shopping on her way home, stocking up on bread and milk. They could at least have coffee and toast in the morning. She also bought eggs in case Camila wanted something more substantial. Jan had also made the delivery she'd asked for earlier in the day. So she was fully stocked up with beer as well as tonics for Camila's favourite drink.

It was a beautiful sunlit evening; she considered taking her bike out for a run down to Kew and back, but she wasn't sure when Camila would be arriving. As it was, she didn't have long to wait. She was only on her first beer when the doorbell went.

She smiled at the vision from her dreams who looked to be wearing just a mid-thigh Burberry coat and black stockings. A strange combination for a summer's evening. Camila's greeting knocked her back mentally, but it was the push on her chest that propelled her into the hallway.

"You have a lot of explaining to do."

"Um, well…."

"I've learned a lot over the weekend. About you and Carl and Eric...and Lisa." She placed extra emphasis on the last name. "You are in a lot of trouble," Camila continued, the stern look unwavering. "I want you to go to your room, remove your clothes, and lie face down on the bed."

Hardly daring to believe her dreams were coming true, Dani gulped and said, "Yes, ma'am." She raced up the stairs, taking two at a time.

†

Taking in a few deep breaths, Camila dropped her overnight bag on the floor, removed her coat, and studied herself in the hall mirror. She certainly looked the part. With Carl's help, she had found the perfect outfit with a tight-fitting bodice, laced at the front. She hadn't worn a suspender belt since her late teens when her mother introduced her to wearing stockings. Getting into the costume had taken a bit of time as she tried to remember how it had looked on the mannequin in the shop. She had to think of it as a costume. Carl had told her this was role play. For it to work she had to be convincing.

She had a few drinks on the plane and another stiff gin and tonic when she got home. Camila was trying hard to convince herself she could play this part.

Dani was lying on the bed as instructed and had laid a cane by her side. Camila's resolve faltered as she gazed at her lover's long legs, leading to her perfect buttocks. Carl's final words of advice came back to her. *"You know what she wants, but think about what you want."*

For Dani this was the ultimate turn-on. But was it going to do anything for her? There was only one way to find out.

Picking up the cane, she marvelled at how thin it was. It flexed easily when she moved it through the air. Dani's body twitched with the sound it made.

Camila looked down at her again, at her tensed shoulders, arms wrapped around her pillow. "Is this what you really want?"

"Yes, yes, please." Dani's voice was muffled by the pillow but there was no mistaking the raw need in her tone.

Camila raised the cane to shoulder height and brought it down gently, laying a soft stroke across Dani's butt. A slight twitch and a moan came from the bed.

"Harder, please!"

Camila took a deep breath. She could do this. If she couldn't, Dani would go running back to that Lisa woman. But Dani wanted her to do this. Hadn't she said she was thinking of Camila when Lisa was beating her? She raised the cane again and brought it down harder this time. She managed two more strokes before dropping to her knees by the bed. The cane slid out of her hand.

"God, Dani. I can't bear to hurt you like this."

Dani rolled onto her side and gazed at Camila. Tears were running down her face, but she looked stunning. Hard to believe this was the same prim woman she had first seen in a boardroom setting only a few weeks ago.

"That was brilliant! Come here." Dani scooted over to make room.

Camila climbed onto the bed and lay down awkwardly next to her. Dani held her for a few minutes, feeling her breathing calm before saying, "Put your hand between my legs?" She smiled as her lover complied.

"You're so wet!"

"I told you it turns me on. I was wet before you came upstairs. That outfit is amazing, by the way." She kissed Camila softly on the lips, salty-tasting from the tears. "I'm so thrilled. You did this for me. Now, what can I do for you?" She kissed her again, with more forceful intent this time.

After fumbling unsuccessfully with the laces on the front of the bodice, Dani gave up. "How do you get out of this thing?"

Camila laughed. "With great difficulty. It took me twenty minutes to get it fastened properly."

"Roll onto your back." Camila complied and Dani straddled her, sitting back to study the lacing. "Okay, I think I've got it."

With Camila's torso finally free of the constraints of the garment, Dani bent down and took one of her breasts in her mouth, teasing the nipple with her tongue. She knew Camila loved this. The other nipple peaked to hardness under her probing fingers.

†

Dani watched Camila's sleeping form as the first light of dawn crept into the room. Their lovemaking had reached another level of intensity, and a surge of happiness flooded through her with the memory of the caning. The strokes burned across her buttocks, and her body responded to the warmth of the woman's breath on her shoulder.

Camila's eyes fluttered open and she grabbed hold of Dani's arm.

"I need you, inside me, now!"

Dani quickly moved her hand between Camila's legs. She was soaking wet.

"Not just your fingers, something more."

197

"Okay. Don't move." Dani leapt off the bed and groped around in the top drawer of her dresser. She quickly strapped on the dildo and positioned herself between Camila's legs. Guiding the tip of the dildo into the welcoming opening, Dani relished the pain rippling across her backside and gave herself to giving her lover what she so plainly desired.

†

As they showered together, Camila realised what she had done.

"Dani! I'm so sorry, I didn't think...."

"What?"

"The straps on the harness. That must have hurt even more."

"It did. And I loved it." Dani pressed her against the wall and kissed her, letting the water cascade over her head and shoulders. "By the way, didn't Eric say you could have the day off?"

"Yes, but I've got too much to do."

"You could do it here. Set up your laptop."

"You don't have a modem for an Internet connection, plus you would be too much of a distraction."

"Am I just a distraction?"

"You're a whole lot more, and you know it. Now I think you promised me breakfast."

†

"Do you still want to go to the barbecue on Friday? I can cancel," Camila said, watching Dani as she stood by the kitchen counter eating toast.

"Yes, of course I want to go."

198

"I just thought you might be, you know…a bit sore."

"It will wear off. And at the moment it feels good."

"Does it really feel good?"

Dani put her toast down. "Yes, I'm high as a kite. It's better than any drug."

Camila came closer and gripped Dani's waist firmly. "I don't know if I can do that for you again."

"It doesn't matter. What you did last night was amazing." Dani put her arms around her and breathed in the intoxicating smell of her hair.

"I've got to go." Camila pulled back. "I'll see you this evening. Unless you have other plans."

"No plans. Just you."

†

After Camila left, Dani returned to the bedroom to get ready for work. She would be walking and taking the Tube. Sitting down for any length of time wasn't really an option.

She found a faded Pet Shop Boys T-shirt that smelt clean although she hadn't worn it for some time. As it was shaping up to be a hot day, she located a pair of cutoffs that were long enough not to be too disreputable, although Gordon wouldn't approve of them. But it didn't matter what Gordon thought anymore, did it?

Or did it? He wouldn't be happy if he knew about her DBS work. What had started out as doing a few favours for a mate, turned into a lucrative little earner. Initially she figured what he didn't know wouldn't hurt him. But if she came clean now, he would be more than a little upset.

When she reached the street near the office, she decided to surprise the boys with coffee and bacon sandwiches. Declan was sitting at his desk when she arrived, but Gary's chair was vacant.

"Wow, thanks, boss." Declan wrapped an eager hand around his sandwich.

"You haven't already had a full English?"

"Nope. Only thing left this morning was a manky Weetabix that could be used as roadfill." He shared a flat with two other young men, and their catering skills were about on a level with Dani's.

"So where is Gary?"

Declan smirked. "Sniffing around Mr McKenzie's new PA, I think."

"What? He's hired another bimbo already?"

"No. I mean, yes. He's hired someone. But not a girl."

"Not a girl." Dani leaned against the wall by Gary's desk and took the lid off her coffee container. "So what is it?"

"It's a boy."

"Don't make me smack you."

"Seriously. His name is Jeremy and he has a beard. Well, a goatee really, sort of. A bit of fuzz on his chin."

"Don't take up copywriting, Declan."

"Oh, yeah, speaking of copywriting, Penny wants to see you."

"Fine, tell her to come along whenever she's ready."

†

Penny sighed inwardly when she saw Dani, knowing any audible sign of disapproval would only annoy her. But how could she disapprove? Dani was glowing, radiating happiness. There were the remains of a bacon roll on her desk and she was humming to herself standing at her drawing board, sketching what looked like a large dildo. As she closed the gap between them, she realised it was a tube of toothpaste.

"You know what that looks like, don't you?"

Dani turned towards her, beaming. "Good morning to you too." She glanced back down at the board. "Yes, I see what you mean. Subliminal message."

"I don't think anyone finds toothpaste remotely erotic."

"Why not? You put it in your mouth…."

"And then you spit it out."

"Hey, catchy. That could work for your jingle."

"I'm not writing that!"

"So what's this? Social call?"

Penny moved over to the window. Dani had the same view as she did from her office. Uninspiring.

"Not really. There are a lot of rumours flying around. After Maria's sudden exit on Monday, everyone's on tenterhooks. But now Gordon's hired someone else. And people just want to know what is happening."

"Maria had it coming. She was the worst PA I've ever seen. And everyone knows why she lasted this long."

"Dani! A straight answer would be nice."

"You want a straight answer from me?" Her teasing tone matched her sunny mood. Dressed in a grungy old T-shirt and faded cutoffs, Dani exuded sheer sexiness. It looked like something had happened with the mystery woman.

"Yes." Penny waited while Dani rearranged the pencils on the board.

"The answer is nothing."

"Nothing?"

"Nothing I can tell you. It's in the hands of the solicitors at the moment."

"That's not going to satisfy people who are going on holiday now. They will wonder if they have jobs to come back to."

"Are you the union rep?"

"No, I'm only letting you know what they're saying."

"Nothing is likely to happen for a few weeks yet. Solicitors work at their own pace and there will be a lot of legal shit to wade through. So tell them not to sweat it."

Penny left the studio none the wiser. Other than knowing that Dani was evidently seeing someone who was giving her satisfaction.

Declan called out as she passed his desk. "Hey, Pen. Want a bacon sarnie? Dani brought them in for us and Gary's is getting cold."

"No thanks. You have it." She thought Declan looked like he could do with putting weight on.

Walking down the hall back to her office, she was struck by a sudden thought. Dani's daft comment about the toothpaste jingle had sparked an idea. She needed to capture it before it disappeared. She had been struggling for a week to find any creative ideas for the toothpaste copy.

†

Camila had made a sizeable dent in the pile of reports that required her immediate attention and was sitting back with a fresh cup of coffee when her phone rang. She hoped it wasn't another call from Chris. She'd binned the six message slips that had awaited her that morning. However, the receptionist, Kylie or Kelly, she could never remember, told her Mr Callaghan was on line two.

She had expected a call but not quite this early.

"Hi, Dad. How was Paris?"

"Expensive and full of French people."

Camila laughed. It was what he always said after a visit to the city.

"We will need to move to a bigger house. Your mother's filled all the wardrobes in this one."

Another regular statement. When Camilla spoke to her mother, she made the same remarks only about needing a bigger wine cellar.

"How was Strasbourg?"

"The same as Paris, only on a smaller scale."

"Your mother and I have been thinking..."

Here it comes.

"You know we only want you to be happy. Do you really think this Dani person can make you happy?"

An image of Dani in the shower flashed through her mind. "Yes. She already does, Dad."

"We thought you might eventually want a family."

Meaning you want grandchildren. Well, tough. "But that was never part of my thinking."

"A career isn't everything."

She had to give him credit for trying.

"Your mother thinks this is a passing phase."

"Dad, I'm thirty-nine."

"Exactly. You need to think about starting a family before it's too late."

The Internal Call light on her phone was flashing. *Saved by the light.* "Sorry, Dad. I have an incoming call. Love to you both."

†

Minutes later she was sitting in Eric's office in one of the easy chairs arranged in the alcove by the window. The room bore more resemblance to a hotel suite than a place of business. The only thing missing was a bed.

Eric sat opposite, legs crossed, Carl in his familiar pose, standing by the window. Now she knew why. She didn't think Dani would be sitting down today either.

"Congratulations to you both. It's a bit early for champagne, so we will have to make do with tea. Carl, would you be mother?"

Camila waited while Carl poured tea into china cups. She only drank tea when she was with the Redmonds, but she knew it was a morning ritual for them.

"Carl says the panel was impressed with the thoroughness of our report. They couldn't pick any holes in it. And I believe that's down to your hard work." He raised his teacup in a mock salute.

After discussing the way forward for their newly approved product, assigning a brand manager, and looking at extra staffing requirements, Dani's name came up.

"So there won't be any problem with Dani working on the packaging spec?" Eric looked over at Carl for confirmation.

Camila crossed her legs, aware of a gathering warmth.

"I shouldn't think so. Whatever happens with MBE, she will carry on doing work for us."

"Shame we couldn't persuade her to come on board."

Carl winked at Camila. "Somehow I don't think that's really on the cards now."

She smiled weakly.

Eric turned his gaze on her. "Ah, yes. So how did it go last night?"

Camila looked from one to the other. A week ago she wouldn't have dreamt of sharing details of her sex life with either of them. Now, though…who else could she talk to?

"It was harder than I thought it would be. I don't think I was as domineering as she would have liked."

Eric grinned at her. "Takes practice."

"Fine. Do I need to go on a dominatrix-training course?"

Carl joined in. "Another business opportunity we've overlooked."

After their laughter died down, he added, "But seriously, Camila. You just have to do what feels right for you. It will come." He smiled at their expressions. "Sorry, poor choice of word."

"Is it, perhaps, the words that bother you, Camila?" Eric leaned forward, resting his elbows on his knees, hands clasped. She recognised this as his "closing the deal" pose, which she had seen him use on many prospective clients. "*Dominance, submission, erotic pain...*they can sound intimidating to a novice. Personally, I like to think of SM as sensuality and mutuality. It's a prearranged agreement, a contract, if you like. You're our expert on negotiating contracts." He leaned back in his chair and smiled. "I'm sure you and Dani will be able to agree to personal terms satisfactory to both parties."

Camila looked from one to the other, as both gave her reassuring looks. She was grateful for their support, but unless they changed the subject, she was going to need to go home for a change of underwear, at the very least. She smiled back. "Speaking of contracts, I would like to recheck the numbers on the American one."

They both grinned as if she had said something funny. Eric switched back into business mode first and said, "Yes, of course."

She escaped back to the sanctity of her office and closed the door. Leaning against it, she took a few deep breaths in an attempt to calm her body's reactions to the images swirling around in her mind. Camila felt she had slipped down a rabbit hole like Alice. In Strasbourg, buoyed by the success of their mission, talking to Carl about intimate things hadn't seemed strange. Here in the office, the place where she was in control, it was too unsettling. Shaking her head, she sat at her desk and immersed herself in the first spreadsheet she could find.

†

Several times during the day, Dani thought about going to see Gordon. She even set off towards his office midmorning with the intention of talking to him—if he wasn't there, she could at least check out the new version of Maria—but got no farther than the door of the studio before the phone rang again.

It was Annette Harmon's secretary wanting to set up an appointment. Dani put her off, saying she would call back later.

She overheard Gary enthusing about Gordon's new PA's attributes when he returned. Penny had left the door open, so she clearly heard him say, "He is so cute. The smallest mouth I've ever seen—"

"You can stop there. I don't want to know where you're going with that," had been Declan's caustic response.

Dani smiled to herself, gently closing the door so she could return to her own work undisturbed. She saw what Penny meant about the toothpaste drawing. It needed some modification to look less like a sex toy.

By the end of the day, she still hadn't seen Gordon, but with each hour that passed all concerns faded into the background as she anticipated the evening ahead with Camila. She hadn't phoned, but Dani guessed she would have a lot of number crunching to keep her busy after the Strasbourg visit.

She walked back along the river and resisted the temptation to visit any of the pubs en route. The crowds of after-work drinkers enjoying the sunshine made it difficult to walk past, though. But she found herself smiling as she walked. Everything today just seemed brighter; she felt more alive.

†

At home she checked the state of the bedroom first. It was as they'd left it that morning, a mess. Dani picked up Camila's discarded bodice and stockings, wondering what to do with them. Eventually she decided to lay them out on the bed in the spare room opposite. She replaced the cane Camila had used next to its twin in the box and laid that reverentially next to them.

Turning her attention to the bed, she thought changing the sheets would be a good idea. They would probably need changing again by morning, but Camila would appreciate the effort. She had just finished struggling with the duvet when the doorbell rang. Smoothing the cover over the top, she ran down the stairs to open the door.

Dani caught her breath at the sight of Camila's loveliness, highlighted by the sun's rays reaching down from the end of the street. She was holding a suit bag in one hand and her briefcase in the other. Dani stood aside to let her in.

Swallowing hard, Dani asked, "Are you going away again?"

"No. We're meeting some of our American suppliers tomorrow."

Dani took the suit bag from her and hung it on the coat rack. Camila put her briefcase down and pulled Dani into a hug.

"I've missed you," she whispered, her hands reaching around to cup Dani's backside. "Are you still sore?"

"Yes, but it feels so good." Dani kissed her and moaned as Camila's tongue sought out hers while her hands increased their pressure. This was ecstasy, and her clit throbbed as a pulsating desire built throughout her body.

They lay on the floor in the living room as the sky darkened towards night. In the fading light, Dani suddenly laughed. "I changed the sheets. I think I might need a new carpet now."

Camila stroked her arm. "I'm sorry. I just couldn't wait."

A rumbling noise startled them and they both laughed. "Guess that's another hunger that needs satisfying." Dani sighed. "Sorry, it's either toast or takeaway. Oh, but there are eggs."

"Eggs will be fine."

"You'll need to cook them. I can only do toast."

"My cooking skills aren't up to much either, but I think I can manage eggs."

†

Camila woke with the light streaming through the window. Dani never closed her curtains, but her bedroom overlooked the river, so unless a low-flying plane was going past, no one could see in.

She looked at Dani's sleeping form. Her long legs were tangled in the sheets. The welts from the cane were clearly defined. Not quite sure why she felt compelled to do it, Camila moved down the bed and placed her tongue on one of the cuts. She licked the length of it and was greeted with a stifled moan from her lover. Starting on the second one, she placed her hand between Dani's thighs and found a warm liquid trickling across her fingers.

Dani's moans turned into loud cries and she screamed Camila's name as the orgasm shook her whole body and the bed.

Camila drew herself up to meet Dani's gaze when Dani turned over.

"Where did you learn to do that? I've never experienced anything like it before."

"It just felt right."

"It felt more than right. Oh, my God." Dani's body convulsed again.

Camila held her until her breathing calmed. They kissed, and when Dani had recovered, she made love to Camila tenderly, but with a passion that had Camila on the edge of losing her mind completely before she came.

†

Parting from Dani that morning was hard. Made harder still telling her she couldn't see her that night. They were entertaining the Americans and Camila needed to be on top of her game.

"See you at the barbecue tomorrow. You have the address, don't you?"

"Yes."

The arrival of her taxi stopped her from pulling Dani into another embrace. Willing herself not to look back, she climbed into the vehicle and kept her eyes on the road ahead.

Chapter Nineteen

Dani rang the doorbell and waited. The fine summer weather was holding; it was a lovely evening for a barbecue. She had been able to smell the cooking hamburgers as she approached the house, which she had been relieved to find was within a half-hour walk from home. In fact, when she'd checked the address in the London A–Z map book, she saw it was only a few streets away from where Eric and Carl lived. She had asked what Camila's friends did for a living to be able to afford a house there. Not surprisingly, one of the women, Deborah, had inherited it from her parents. She didn't have a full-time job, just volunteered a few days a week at a tourist office.

A small woman, with long dark hair draped loosely around her bare shoulders, opened the door.

"Hi, I'm Dani."

The woman looked her up and down as though she suspected her of selling something.

"Is Camila here yet?"

"No." Her expression softened. "Oh, you're her guest."

"Yeah. She said she might be a bit late."

"Come in, then. I'm Deborah." She led the way down a short hallway.

"Deborah. That's a nice name."

The woman turned and looked at her again. "My friends call me Debs."

Dani grinned at her, "Okay, Debs. This bottle is for you." She handed her the wine she had bought at the off-licence on the way, still wrapped in green tissue paper.

"How long have you known Camila?" Deborah asked, taking the bottle.

"A few months, I guess."

"Yes, but how long have you known her?" She placed the emphasis on *known* and winked.

"Two weeks, on and off."

"Hm. That's interesting."

"Why interesting?" They were in the kitchen now. Deborah had unwrapped the bottle and seemed duly impressed by the label.

"We knew she had met someone through work, but knowing Camila, it didn't seem likely she would pursue it."

"Why's that?"

"She's not really been interested in anyone since Allison. Nothing serious, anyway. No one who could compete with a dead person." Deborah gave her another appraising look. "Seeing you, though, I can see how she's managed to overcome her reticence."

"How am I supposed to take that?"

"However you want. What would you like to drink?"

"Beer, if you've got it."

"There's some London Pride in the fridge."

Dani reached past her and opened the fridge door. There were several rows of cans; she selected one and popped the tab.

"Glass?"

"Nah. I wouldn't want to ruin my image."

Deborah laughed. "Come on, you might as well start to mingle."

Deborah introduced her to some other women who were in the living room. The television was on with the sound off but no one was watching it. More guests were outside, some hovering by the barbecue, others sitting round tables—drinking, chatting—in the fragrant-looking sunlit garden.

The doorbell sounded and Deborah went off to answer it.

Camila appeared by her side and slipped an arm around her waist. "Sorry, the meeting went on a bit."

Dani kissed her lightly. "Not a problem. I just got here."

"So, Camila, is she any good…as a graphic designer, I mean?" asked one of the women in the group. They had just got through basic introductions and finding out what the newcomer did for a living.

"The best," said Camila easily as Deborah appeared at her elbow with a gin and tonic.

†

Dani wasn't at all what Deborah had expected. When she opened the door to the stranger, a tall, slim figure wearing a white T-shirt, black vest, tight black jeans, and studded belt, her first thought had been that the woman had the wrong house.

Watching Dani as she interacted with some of the other guests, Deborah could see the attraction though. She drew people to her with her stunning looks and confident stance. Hard to believe Camila had met her through work.

She was in the wrong job—she didn't have anyone like that coming through the door of the tourist office in Kingston.

Deborah was checking Chris's movements as well. She kept asking when Camila would be there and each time the answer was "later", she poured herself another glass from the potent punch on the sideboard. With only a few weeks until the end of term, her partner seemed to be treating this as a start of the summer holiday party. She was definitely demob-happy.

When Camila did finally arrive, full of apologies for being late, Deborah thought she must have gone home to change first. Her office attire surely didn't consist of a strapless summer dress that clung to every curve on her body. Chris couldn't keep her eyes off her—the soppy infatuated look on her face made Deborah want to slap her.

She didn't intend to make a scene now. Not in front of their guests. She should have made the change a long time ago. This was her house, the legacy from her parents along with their substantial fortune. She paid all the bills. And Chris was treating it like a hotel with all amenities to hand, including her. Deborah sucked in a deep breath. A new life was most certainly going to begin at forty for Chris…and for her.

†

The evening progressed with the eating of charred food interspersed with salads, bread rolls, and more drinks. Camila stayed close to Dani throughout. Neither of them drank or ate much. At some point they all sang a raucous, out-of-tune "Happy Birthday" to Chris, and Deborah brought out a cake with four large candles on it—one for each decade. By this time, Dani was in a high state of longing; she just wanted to go home with Camila and make love.

"Do you think we could go now?" she asked while the cake cutting was going on.

"Yes. I'm just going to the loo. Then we can slip away." The look on Camila's face told Dani her desire was reciprocated.

"Right, don't be long." Dani gave her a lingering kiss on the lips.

Camila patted her butt suggestively. "No fear."

Dani watched her go thinking of the night ahead. A hand gripped her shoulder forcefully and she turned to find an angry-looking woman glaring at her—the birthday girl, she thought.

"You keep your filthy hands off her!" the woman screamed and punched her hard in the face, followed by another hard blow to the stomach. Dani doubled over with the pain. "Fucking pervert."

†

Camila arrived back in the room to see Dani on the floor with Chris kicking her in the ribs. Deborah was trying ineffectively to stop her. Everyone else was just standing, looking on like kids in a playground. Although they weren't cheering or shouting, "Fight, fight," they were mostly stunned into inaction.

"Chris," she said quietly. Chris looked up at her and Camila hit her with full force on the nose. She heard the crack and was satisfied to see the shock in Chris's eyes as she clutched at her face. Then she crouched over her lover. "Dani! Look at me. Can you stand?"

Dani nodded, as though not trusting herself to speak. With Deborah's help, Camila was able to support Dani and walk with her to the front door.

"I'll drive you," Deborah said.

"Thanks. It's not far."

None of them said anything on the drive over to Dani's house. Camila crouched next to Dani, who was laid across the backseat.

In the living room, Camila carefully removed Dani's vest and lifted her T-shirt. Bruises were already forming on her torso, and she had the beginning of a black eye.

Deborah had found the kitchen and came back with ice wrapped in a dishtowel. She handed the package to Camila, who helped Dani to apply it and let her hold it against her face.

Deborah pointed to her hand. "You'll need some ice on those." Camila looked at her hand as if seeing it for the first time. The knuckles looked red and slightly swollen. "Did I hurt her?"

"Too right. Broke her nose by the sound of it."

"Good." Then she realised how that sounded. "Oh my God! I'm sorry, Deborah."

"Don't be. I would have hit her myself if I could have."

"Look, would you mind staying with Dani while I go home and get some things?"

"Sure, take my car." Deborah handed her the keys.

†

When Camila had gone, Deborah went into the kitchen and found a bottle of whisky and glasses. She poured two generous measures and took them back to the living room.

Dani squinted at her with her good eye. "Sorry about the party," she mumbled.

215

"It will be the talk of the town for a few weeks at least."

"I didn't even have any cake."

Deborah laughed. "Come on, drink some of this," she said, handing her a glass. "How are the ribs feeling?"

"A bit sore, but I've had worse. Bad move on Chris's part, wanting to hurt a masochist. Any more abuse and I'd be asking her to marry me. What was it all about anyway?"

"Oh, I guess you wouldn't know. And they both think I don't know. Chris slept with Camila a few times. It wasn't long after Allison's death, so maybe Camila just wanted some comfort. I've always thought Camila was a bit of a cold fish, but I can see she cares about you."

"You think?"

"Yes, I think. She really clocked one on Chris. You'll need to make sure she takes care of her knuckles; they'll be hurting. I don't suppose she has any experience with fighting."

"You never know."

"No, you don't." Deborah knocked back her whisky. "Could I use your phone?"

"Yeah. It's in the hall."

Deborah rang her house; it was only twenty minutes since she had left and she guessed people would still be there, revelling in having something exciting to talk about. Nothing like seeing someone get a good kicking to cause a stir.

Someone voiced a tentative hello.

"It's Debs. Is that Niki?"

"Yes. How is she?"

"She'll be okay. Some heavy bruising on her ribs. She says she's had worse."

"So we've heard."

"Oh?"

"Yeah. It seems Sandy goes to some of the same clubs. She's seen Dani a few times."

"I didn't know Sandy was into that kind of thing."

"Come on! She's a PE teacher. They're all sadists in my book."

"So I guess she passed this info on to Chris."

"Yeah. Oh, could you remind Dani I gave her my card? She said she would call Monday about a brochure we want a quote for."

"Great. I'm sure she's really concerned about work right now."

"Anyway, since you haven't asked, Chris has gone to A and E. Sandy took her. A few of us are staying on to clear things away. Are you coming back?"

"In a bit. And thanks."

"Hey, great party, by the way."

"Don't mention it."

†

Dani took the tea towel away from her face as Deborah returned. "I think the ice has all melted."

"Looks like you'll have quite a shiner."

"Great. Just the thing for a Monday morning."

"Do you know a PE teacher called Sandy?"

"Tall, dark-haired, loud mouth?"

"That sounds like her."

"I know of her. She's not my type and I've heard she can be a bit heavy-handed. Not my scene at all."

"It seems she decided to let Chris know where she had seen you."

"Figures. Has she cheated on you before?"

"Yes, all the time."

217

"Jeez, call me a masochist! Why do you stay with her?"

"Habit, I guess."

"Come on, Debs. You're an attractive woman. You don't have to put up with shit like that. Has she ever hit you?"

"No."

"Look, it's none of my business. I've only just met you, but I'd say you could do a lot better."

"Thanks."

Peering at Deborah with her one good eye, Dani couldn't make out her expression, but the slump of her shoulders was an indication she wasn't in a happy place. "It'll take Camila a while to get to Battersea and back. Why don't you put some music on? Get back in the party mood."

"Sure. Any requests?"

"Nah. You choose."

Dani watched the other woman as she leafed through the record selection on the shelf near her drawing table. She made some appreciative noises before finally holding out an album. "This fits the bill, I think."

"I can't see it from here."

"Lou Reed, *Transformer*." Deborah took the record out of the sleeve and placed it on the turntable. "Let's take a 'Walk on the Wild Side'. Seems appropriate for this evening."

†

They listened to the music, mainly in silence, absorbing the hypnotic tone of Reed's voice and the seductively suggestive lyrics. When the last notes died away, Deborah got up and replaced the record in its cover. She glanced down at the artwork on the drawing table. The top page looked like a rather boring furniture advert. Moving the paper aside, she gasped.

Underneath was a drawing of Camila as she had never seen her, but Dani obviously had. Her head was arched back at an almost impossible angle, and her body arched to meet the disembodied hand cupping her pubes.

"Wow! Has she seen this?" Deborah asked, holding the page so Dani could see it.

"No! Please put it back where you found it."

"Sorry. I guess you're right. There's a lot I don't know about Camila." She slid the page back under the pad.

They heard the front door open and moments later Camila came in and handed Deborah her keys. "Thanks. How is the patient?"

"Doing fine. Have you done anything with your hand?"

"I ran it under cold water."

"You really should ice it for a while."

"Okay. Is there any left?"

"Another tray. I'd better be going. See how the cleanup crew is doing. Oh, and Dani, apparently you promised to ring Niki about a brochure quote on Monday. She said she gave you a card." She waved at her and headed out to the hall.

Camila followed her. "How's Chris?"

"At A and E with Sandy. So she will be gone for most of the night. And after that she'll be looking for somewhere else to live."

"Oh, Deborah. I'm sure she will be sorry...."

"Sorry doesn't cut it. What she did was unforgivable. Dani hadn't done anything to provoke her, other than being with you. You see, it's taken me a while to figure this out. None of the others really mattered. But you did. It was okay while you were unattached, but then she sees you with Sex-on-Legs in there and realises what she thought she had with you was nothing...."

"But I never let her think there was anything…and we didn't think you knew," Camila finished lamely.

"Yes, I knew. You were the only one she didn't tell me about, so I should have known you were the only one who meant anything to her."

"I really didn't think it meant anything."

"Didn't all those phone calls these last two weeks tell you anything?"

"I ignored those. I've been rather busy."

"Anyway, all it took was Sandy telling her about where she had seen Dani before, and seeing the two of you loved up gave her the excuse to attack her."

"Sandy? Oh, the PE teacher…I saw her talking to Chris."

Dani appeared in the doorway. "Hey, Debs, thanks for everything." She stood behind Camila and wrapped her arms around her. "Next time you want a party wrecking…."

"Sure, I'll call you." She smiled at Dani and went out the door.

†

Camila leaned back into her. "I'm sorry, Dani."

"What for?" Dani held her hand, raising it to her face to kiss the swollen knuckles. "You have one hell of a right hook by all accounts."

"Dani?" Camila turned to face her. "Do you feel up to, you know…?"

"Yeah. I don't suppose you want to hit me…?"

Camila stroked her cheek gently. "Not tonight. I think you need a bit of tender loving care. Will you let me do that for you?"

Dani nodded. The events of the evening crashed into her senses, harder than the kicking she'd taken and she slumped against the wall.

"Come on, tiger. Upstairs, now."

†

Camila lay next to the sleeping form of her lover. Getting her fully undressed had taken some time, but Dani hadn't been much help, flopping onto the bed as limp as a rag doll. Once Camila was satisfied Dani was as comfortable as she could be and had fallen asleep, she went down to the kitchen. The application of ice on her swollen knuckles had offered some relief, but when she returned to the bedroom, lying down next to Dani and closing her eyes, sleep wouldn't come.

Was she to blame for Chris's extreme reaction to seeing her with another woman? Deborah's revelation that she'd known all along that she and Chris had slept together was a surprise but it did explain her coolness towards her. The fact Chris had read more into their brief liaisons than she had was also a surprise. It seemed she really was clueless when it came to knowing people. The easiness of her relationship with Allison had sheltered her from the need to interact with others.

She had the feeling being with Dani was never going to be easy. But did that matter? In their short time together, she felt a connection that was stronger than anything she had experienced with anyone else, even Allison. A pang of guilt shot through her and tears erupted from her eyes.

Dani was different. Remembering the night Dani had walked out of her flat, Camila knew that Dani's perceptions had been correct. She wasn't likely to fit in with her lifestyle.

But she wasn't alone. The talks with Carl during their time in Strasbourg and seeing both him and Eric in a new light had freed something in her. She would be forty next year. So a new life was beginning for her, if she had the courage to embrace it.

She was here, with Dani. She knew in her heart it was where she wanted to be. It seemed like her mind had some catching up to do.

Dani moaned in her sleep. Camila shuffled closer and laid a protective arm softly across her belly.

Chapter Twenty

Saturday afternoon was clear and bright. Dani watched the rowers passing by on the river, enjoying the breeze on her face as she stood on the patio enjoying the scene. Her ribs were still sore, but they didn't hurt as much as the last time.

Camila had gone back to her flat to do some work. When the doorbell rang she hurried to answer it, not expecting her lover back so soon. She opened the door with a wide smile, but her sunny mood was deflated by the sight of her brother waiting on the step.

"Fuck, what happened to you?"

"Good to see you too." She looked down at his feet. "No munchkins with you today?"

"No. I only have them every other weekend. Can I come in?"

"Oh, yeah, sure."

He followed her through the house to the patio at the back.

"So who beat you up this time? Give me a name and I'll have them arrested."

"No need for that. It was just a misunderstanding." She grinned at him. "Drink?"

"Thanks. A beer if you've got one."

"Of course."

When Dani returned with two cans, he accepted his gratefully and seemed to swallow half of it before she had even taken a sip. She leant against the doorframe and watched his face.

"So to what do I owe the pleasure of your company this time?"

"Can't I just enjoy the company of my favourite sister?"

"Your only sister, and I've now seen more of you in two weeks than in the last two years. So what gives?"

Brian sighed and drank some more beer. He put the can on the table between them and looked across the river.

Dani waited. She could play the cop-interview game as well. Finally he looked up at her. "That bloke June's seeing. I checked him out like you suggested."

"And?" She didn't need to be a detective to know this wasn't going to be good news.

"He has a record. And he's lied to her about his job. Told her he's a stockbroker and has to make regular trips to New York. However, he hasn't left the country since getting out of prison in 1990."

"Another woman somewhere?"

"Yeah. I had him followed. He spent three days this week at a house in Ruislip. And, this is the worst part." He paused and drained the rest of his beer. "The woman has a daughter. Looks to be the same age as Lucy."

"Shit, Brian. What will you do?"

"I don't know. If I just go and tell June she's being duped and that I think Lucy's in danger, she will think I'm making it up to have a chance of getting back with her."

"But if you have proof…?"

"What do the photos prove? He could say the woman's his sister or something."

"But they could be married. You could find that out."

They sat in silence for a while, both looking out over the river. Another scull passed, the four rowers moving in perfect union.

"This thing with Lucy." Brian sounded hesitant. "Is that what happened with you and Dad?"

It was Dani's turn to stay silent, drinking some more of her beer. Brian's relationship with their father had been so different to hers. He was the treasured son. They went to football matches together, bonded with kickabouts in the garden. She was the awkward daughter who wouldn't behave like a girl.

"Look, you need to sort this guy out. Lucy's afraid of him."

"You said that before, but how does that relate to why you left home at sixteen? Why Dad destroyed any evidence of you ever having existed?"

There was no way to make it sound anything other than what it was. Dani looked at him, seeing something in his features of the sweet boy he had been. The innocent boy who couldn't understand why his sister was always in trouble. "Because I didn't conform to how a girl should behave. When I was little he was able to control me, make me wear dresses, help Mum in the kitchen when I wanted to play out, but by the time I was eight or nine, I knew this wasn't what I wanted. I fought him at every turn from then on. It became a battle of wills. He gave in on certain things, like me wearing trousers around the house. But later, when it became clear I wasn't interested in boys as he thought any girl of fifteen should be, he decided to show me what I was missing. I had to try to avoid him if we were alone in the house. The casual groping was bad enough. This escalated fairly quickly to pressing my hand against the front of his trousers so I could feel his hard-on, whispering, 'This is what you want, my girl.' On that last day he told me he was going to make me a woman. He was going to fuck me, Brian."

"No!" Brian stood suddenly, upsetting the table. His empty beer can rolled onto the path. "No way!"

"See, it's not easy, is it? Are you going to believe your little girl when she tells you this man is touching her inappropriately? At the age she is now, she won't know what's happening really. But she will know it feels wrong. How far are you going to let it go?"

Tears had started in his eyes. He walked away from her, towards the river. The doorbell rang and Dani watched her brother for a moment before going to answer it.

†

Camila noticed it as soon as Dani opened the door. The bruising around her eye wasn't as angry-looking as the night before, but there was a look in her eyes she couldn't decipher.

"Are you okay?" she asked, pulling back from their kiss.

"My brother's here. He's just had some bad news."

"Oh. I brought some sandwiches for us. Do you think he will want to stay for lunch?"

"No. Maybe some other time."

Camila followed Dani through to the garden. Brian was walking back from the river's edge, head down. He looked up when he reached them.

"Oh, hi." He gave Camila a bleak smile. "Sorry, I can't stay."

He set the table back on its legs and placed the empty can on it. "I'll see myself out," he said as he passed Dani without looking at her.

"What happened?" Camila could see that Dani was upset by his abrupt departure.

"Oh, just some home truths he will find hard to accept. I think he knows it's true, but he's closed his eyes to it for a long time."

"What kind of home truths?"

Dani looked away from her and Camila wondered if she would answer.

"Please, Dani. I don't want us to have any secrets from each other."

"My father abused me, but Brian idolised him. And now I've told him why I ran away from home, because I think his daughter is being groomed by his wife's new boyfriend."

"Oh, Dani." Camila moved closer and held on to her.

After a time, Dani pulled back and walked slowly down the path to the river. Camila kept pace with her. At the end there was a bench. When Dani sat, Camila joined her and reached for her hand.

"Can you tell me about it?" she asked softly, rubbing her fingers lightly over her arm.

Dani sighed and gazed at the river. Two single sculls passed by quickly. The rowers looked like they were engaged in a race. Her eyes still fixed on the scene in front of her, Dani finally started to speak.

"I think I told you I left home at sixteen. My father wasn't happy with my lack of interest in boys. After months of innuendos, groping me whenever he got the chance, he finally decided the time had come to show me what I needed.

I don't know why he thought I would just let him fuck me. He was grinning as he unzipped his trousers, no doubt expecting me to be thrilled at the sight of his erect dick. I kicked him as hard as I could in the groin, and while he was doubled over, I grabbed his wallet and my backpack and legged it. When I was a good distance from the house, I removed the cash and chucked the wallet over a hedge. Luckily it was a payday and he hadn't stopped in the pub before coming home."

Camila squeezed her knee.

"Why did I take my backpack?" Dani was still gazing into the far distance. "It contained the only thing worth having from that house. My sketchpad and pencils. Anyway, I used some of Dad's money to buy a train ticket to London. And the streets weren't paved with gold as in the fairytale. But I met my Puss in Boots, if you like. My third night wandering, looking for a place to bed down where I wouldn't be disturbed, Mistress Bea found me huddled on the steps outside her apartment building. I'd run out of money by then and hadn't eaten for a day or two."

Dani looked at Camila then and gave a small smile. "I never knew her real name. She took me in. Gave me room and board, paid for my college tuition fees."

"What did she want in return?" Camila wasn't sure she wanted to hear the answer.

"Not a lot. Hard to believe, I know. Sounds like a real fairy story, the tart with a heart. Mainly she wanted an escort, someone who wasn't one of her punters. I got my hair cut short and wore men's suits and passed well enough for her to introduce me as her son. We went to see all the latest plays in the West End. We ate in the best restaurants where she educated me on which wines to order. I had really landed on my feet.

"One day she found me in what she referred to as her playroom—I really do know what a tart's boudoir looks like—swishing one of the canes she had hanging on the wall. She sat me down and we had 'the talk'. You know, the one mothers are supposed to have with their daughters. My mother hadn't told me anything. I had to find out from a school friend what to do when my first period started. Anyway, Mistress Bea managed to discover what my preferences were, something I had never voiced to anyone before."

"Did she...?" Camila couldn't say the words. She didn't want to visualise this older woman taking advantage of a vulnerable youngster.

Dani picked up Camila's hand and kissed her palm. "No, she didn't. As I said, she really was like a mother to me. After my confession, she said if that's what I wanted, she could introduce me to a young woman who was just starting out in the business."

"And that would be Lisa?"

Dani stared into her eyes. "Carl told you about her, didn't he?"

"Yes, he said she was something you had in common. Are you in love with her?"

"No! It's an arrangement. We grew up together, if you like. Grew into our respective roles. It's a mutual thing, but it's not love."

Camila looked away from Dani's pleading gaze. She recalled Eric's words from the meeting in his office after the return from Strasbourg; *"I like to think of SM as sensuality and mutuality."* She could understand the sensuality part; her senses were on fire whenever she was with Dani. The mutuality was still evading her.

"Do you keep in touch with the woman who took you in, this Mistress Bea?"

"Up until she died, yes." Dani took Camila's hand in hers. "You have to understand, living with Bea was the best thing that could have happened to me."

"But you've had no contact with your family since you left home, apart from your brother."

"No, and we only reconnected by accident. I took part in a student demo and got hauled off to the cop shop along with some others. He recognised me and pulled me out before my name could go on the charge sheet." Dani gave her a tentative smile. "All this talking has made me thirsty."

"Me too. And I brought lunch."

†

They walked back up to the house in silence. Dani hoped she hadn't said too much. But so far, Camila hadn't pushed her away. Somehow it hadn't been as hard as she'd thought it would be. She'd never felt secure enough with any of her other lovers to talk about her past. But everything felt different with Camila.

While Camila went into the kitchen to get the drinks and the sandwiches she had brought, Dani fetched the two cushioned loungers out of her storage area and placed them on the patio.

She wasn't unduly worried about Brian's reaction to her revelation. His cop's instincts would kick in when he calmed down. She wouldn't have been able to forgive herself if anything happened to her nieces because she had been afraid to tell him what kind of man their father really was. Brian would do whatever was necessary to protect his daughters, she was sure of that.

Camila arrived with the sandwiches on plates, a cool-looking glass of gin and tonic for herself, and another can of beer for Dani. She set them on the low table Dani had placed between the loungers.

They ate in silence, and when Dani looked across at Camila, she was lying back with her eyes closed.

"Camila, seeing as we're not having any secrets, tell me about Allison."

Her lover's eyes snapped open and she turned to look at her.

"What do you want to know?"

"How did she die?" Dani lay on her side, head propped on one hand.

"She was killed at work, stabbed by a patient. I didn't know about it until two police officers knocked on my door." She swallowed, hard.

Dani nodded. Brian had told her of times as a junior officer when he had to deliver death notices.

"I hardly had time to take in what they were telling me before her parents turned up at the flat demanding access to her things. They knew we lived together, but it was only when they looked around our living space that they realised we were more than just friends. One bedroom, one bed. They cut me off after that. Didn't want me at the funeral."

Dani absorbed this information. Camila wasn't looking at her, but she could see the sadness in her face.

"They took her ashes. I have no idea what they did with them. I think that was the hardest thing to bear, not having a place to mourn, a graveside to visit. That, and not having the chance to say goodbye."

Camila took a large gulp of her drink and stared at the river. Dani drank some of her beer and let the peace of the garden wash over them.

After a time, she asked the other question that had been bothering her. "And Chris is the only woman you've been with since?"

"Yes, but it wasn't something I really wanted. Just looking for comfort, I guess."

"It obviously meant a bit more to Chris."

Camila sighed and turned towards her. "Can we talk about something more cheerful? How about you tell me how you've managed to hide your DBS activity from Gordon."

"You find that a cheerful topic?"

"Yes, of course. If it involves numbers. I find accounting uplifting."

Dani grinned at her. "You're weird, you know that?"

"Each to their own. So come on. Spill the beans."

"Easy. It would never occur to Gordon that I could do anything other than draw pretty pictures."

"Are you going to enlighten him?"

"Depends. If he is serious about wanting to stay together. He's taken a step in the right direction by getting rid of his bit of fluff on the side, Maria."

"Bit of fluff? Is that what I am, Dani?"

Dani stood and offered her hand to help Camila to her feet. "You are not a bit of fluff. Come on, I think we need to take this inside."

"Take what inside?"

"What I'm going to do to you to hear you scream out my name."

Camila readily followed her into the house and up the stairs to the bedroom.

Chapter Twenty-one

Monday had come round too soon, as far as Dani was concerned. It had been another intense weekend of lovemaking. Camila had gone back to her flat for a few hours on Sunday morning to do some work; she said she couldn't concentrate with Dani anywhere in the vicinity. She had a fax waiting for her and several phone messages from Eric telling her she had to go to Madrid on a Monday afternoon flight. So the rest of Sunday had passed in a blur. But at least Dani had remembered to place the order for a special delivery while Camila was out. She smiled at the thought of how the unsuspecting recipient might receive it.

The events of Friday's party receded into the background. Camila had made a joke of wanting to meet some of Dani's friends to see if she could do similar damage to anyone's relationship. Dani reminded her that most of the people she knew would just enjoy a good fight.

They'd had a more in-depth discussion on Sunday morning about whether or not she and Gordon were going to separate or stay together. Camila suggested that if they

233

decided on the latter, they needed to get Annette to draw up a proper business agreement.

Dani said she would think about it. Now, in the office and facing four days of withdrawal from Camila, she did do some deeper thinking. Tempting as it was to try to go it alone, she didn't really want the hassle of managing the marketing and business side of things. She rang Gordon and asked him to meet her in the pub across the road.

He was already there when she arrived; he had bought her a drink. "So what is this, no lawyers?"

Dani sat and took a sip of the beer before replying. "I think we've scored our points. My heart's not really in it."

He smiled. "Is it business as usual, then?"

"Sort of," she said. He raised an eyebrow. "I mean, how long will it last if you're going to jump every time Melissa pulls your chain?"

"That's not going to happen."

"You don't mind working with a 'fucking pervert'?"

"No. I'm used to you."

"There's something else you need to know."

"Dani, I'm not that interested in your private life, although it was a bit of a shock to find out you really are seeing Redmond's financial director. Hell, I'll never be able to look Ms Callaghan in the eye again! On top of that I discover you're good mates with Eric and Carl Redmond. You haven't seriously considered joining them, have you?"

"No, although Eric has made me a number of offers. You see, I've actually been doing work for them for a long time. They subcontract to me sometimes. I have a business under another name, DBS."

Gordon looked like he had swallowed a piece of glass. "Shit, Dani! I can't believe it! And you were threatening me with looking into my finances?"

"Yeah, well. I was just rattling your cage."

"Jeez! It worked."

Dani sipped her beer and watched his face as he absorbed this shock. Setting her glass back down, she said, "Okay, here's the deal. I wind up the DBS business. We have our solicitors do a proper agreement and we get on with doing what we're good at, together."

"Right." He breathed out a huge sigh of relief. "I've been thinking too. I'm going to sell the yacht and the timeshare in Portugal. I want to put the money towards upgrading our computer system. Since you're such good buddies, do you think Carl Redmond would work up a spec for us?"

Dani smiled. "I'm sure he would." She raised her glass. "To our partnership."

They clinked their glasses together and drank.

"Better go and tell the troops," he said, not bothering to disguise his relief.

"Yeah. Oh, and we've got a new client to meet this afternoon. Quoting for a brochure, but it sounds like they could do with some point of sale as well."

"Excellent." He finished his beer. "Are you going to tell me how you got that shiner?"

"No, but our new client might. She was there when it happened."

"Oh. She's not...you know...into things, like you?"

"Not that I know of." She winked at him with her good eye. "But looks can be deceiving."

†

Camila finished putting the documents she needed into her briefcase. She had already checked and double-checked she had her passport. Eric handed her a walletful of pesetas. She knew he had a range of European currencies in his office safe. He was looking forward to the day when there would be a single currency throughout Europe, but she privately thought that was a long way off and she hoped the UK would stay out of it. She had welcomed the Black Wednesday of the year before when the government was forced to withdraw the pound out of the European Exchange Rate Mechanism. To her mind, it demonstrated the weakness of the whole idea.

She walked through to Reception to collect her case. The taxi was already waiting. Someone was shouting at the beleaguered-looking receptionist who was holding her hands in front of herself in a defensive pose. With a shock, Camila saw that the person causing the girl distress was Chris.

"What's going on?" she asked, keeping her voice level.

Chris turned. "Oh good. I asked to see you and she said it wasn't possible."

"I'm on my way to the airport, so she's absolutely right." Camila smiled at the girl who promptly wheeled her suitcase out from behind the desk. "Let's take this outside."

She walked out through the main doors of the building.

"What do you think you're playing at? Haven't you caused enough trouble?" Outside, in the clear light of day, Camila could see the bruising around Chris's taped-up nose.

"Oh, and I suppose none of it's your fault. You did this to me." Chris pointed to her face. "And now Debs has kicked me out."

"About time too, I should think."

"Don't come all high and mighty with me. You were a willing partner."

"I think it was exactly twice and more than two years ago." Camila moved towards the taxi waiting at the kerb. "Why are you here, Chris?"

"I thought you could put me up at your flat. I know you've got an extra bedroom."

"I heard you were staying at that other woman's place. The PE teacher."

"It's little more than a bedsit. I can't stay there for long."

"I guess you'll have to go the YWCA or something."

"You really are a hard-hearted bitch, aren't you?"

"So I'm told."

"Okay." Chris raised her voice again. "I'll just go back in there and tell your boss you're shacked up with that piece of shit, Dani What's-her-name."

Camila smiled as she opened the taxi door. "You do that. I'm sure he'll be happy to have you bad-mouthing one of his friends. Goodbye, Chris." She climbed into the back of the cab and didn't look back as it pulled out into the traffic. Her heartbeat slowly returned to normal as the taxi turned the corner. She checked her watch and thought there was just time. Leaning forward, she asked the driver to make a detour to the MBE offices.

†

Dani had refused to tell Gordon where they were going and he'd given up trying to guess by the time the taxi was crossing Blackfriars Bridge.

"I had lunch somewhere around here once. The Tall House, that was the name. It looked like those houses you see in Amsterdam along the canals. Squeezed like a tube of toothpaste. Speaking of toothpaste, I'm not sure the client's going to like what you've done. Still, I guess you know what's best."

He knew he was babbling. But the knowledge that their partnership was intact had lifted a weight off his chest. With that and the fact Dani's solicitor would no longer be probing into his financial dealings, he felt quite light-headed.

237

The taxi stopped on an unfamiliar side street and they climbed out. The fare would go on their account, but Gordon passed the driver some coins for a tip. When the taxi had driven off, he looked at the sign on the building. VidScreen, suppliers of video walls for corporate events, concerts, multimedia of all descriptions.

"Damn, Dani. You are a sly one. I've tried to get something out of this lot for years."

"Yeah, so don't blow it. Leave the talking to me for a change."

Gordon agreed and followed her inside. Only minutes later they were shown into the sales manager's office. Niki Preston stood to greet them, and after Dani introduced Gordon, they settled into chairs at the round conference-style table in the middle of the room.

"Hey, Dani, you're looking better than the last time I saw you."

"Thanks."

They talked through the briefing notes Niki presented them with, and Gordon only intervened when the discussion veered into the budget area.

On their way back to MBE, he could hardly contain his excitement. "VidScreen! This is great, Dani. Think of the contacts Niki has with the work they do for multinationals, television, roadshows."

"Calm down, Gordon. It's only a brochure."

"Yeah, but who gets the brochure, that's the thing. They're looking to expand their markets into other countries, so this could go global."

†

The young man she had seen with Dani before showed her into the studio and said his boss was on her way back from a client meeting. Camila thanked him and dropped her briefcase on the chair in front of the desk. If Dani didn't turn up within the next ten minutes, she would have to leave without seeing her.

She wandered over to the drawing table near the window. The incomplete storyboard images caught her eye. The angle of the tube of toothpaste was rather suggestive. Perhaps Dani was aiming for a subliminal message. Not something she would associate with brushing her teeth, though. Moving the board aside, she was startled to see her own eyes staring back at her.

"Hey. Is that your taxi waiting outside?" Dani kicked the door shut and covered the distance between them in three quick strides.

"Yes. I just have a few minutes." Camila looked down at the drawing. "This is really good."

"Do you like it?"

"I love it."

"But that's not why you're here, is it?"

Camila reached out and pulled her close. "Chris ambushed me at the office just now. Seems she thinks I owe her something. Like letting her stay in my apartment."

"Shit. I'm so sorry."

"I think she's really lost touch with reality. She even threatened to tell Eric about our relationship."

Dani snorted. "Hardly news now."

"Until the other night, I didn't realise she had such strong feelings for me."

"She might be an arsehole, but she has good taste."

"I'm worried she'll make more trouble for Deborah."

"Oh, I don't think you need to worry about Debs. She'll be okay."

Dani's arms enfolded her, and Camila gave herself to the kiss as their lips met. After a few minutes, she broke the contact reluctantly. "I really have to go now." She lowered her arms to grasp Dani's butt cheeks. "And don't you forget, I'll be back to take care of this."

"Damn. Is it really going to take five days?"

Dani's tremulous smile tugged at her heartstrings. If she could cancel the trip, she would.

"Yes. Unfortunately. The Spanish don't rush anything. Dealing with the Germans is much more straightforward. But I can look forward to excellent food and wine in Madrid."

With one last lingering kiss, Camila finally broke away and rushed out the door before she could be tempted to stay longer. She was cutting it fine to make her flight as it was.

†

Deborah opened the door cautiously. Although Chris had stopped phoning every hour since Sunday morning when Sandy had come round to collect the belongings Deborah had left in black plastic bags on the driveway, she didn't want a face-to-face confrontation with her now ex-lover. The messages had been escalating into full-on threats.

A young woman wearing leather biker gear, helmet tucked under one arm, stood on the step holding out a very expensive-looking bouquet. If this was an attempt by Chris to win her over, she wasn't going to accept them.

"Deborah Grant?"

"Yes."

"I've been asked to make sure you get these personally."

"Well, you go back and tell Chris to shove them up her arse." Deborah prepared to shut the door.

"No, wait, please. I don't know who Chris is or what she's done to deserve that treatment. Perhaps you should read the card first."

The courier handed her an envelope. Her first name was written in an elaborate script on the front. Deborah pulled the card out and read the message. For the first time in days, she felt a smile tugging at her lips.

"I guess you'd better come in..." She checked the name on the card. "...Jan."

†

The cupboards and the fridge were bare. There wasn't even any beer left. Dani sighed and wondered how she was going to get through the week. Camila wouldn't be back until late on Friday.

She was just thinking of walking across to the Lion when her doorbell chimed. Deborah was standing on the step holding a casserole dish.

"What's this? No one's died, have they?"

"Just my way of saying thank you for the flower delivery."

"Good timing. I was heading over to the pub for some nosh." Dani led the way into the kitchen. "I can't offer you a beer right now. But I can pop over the road and get some."

"No need. All part of the service."

The doorbell chimed again. Dani looked at Deborah with a raised eyebrow.

"Go on. Answer it."

"I do love a bossy woman, you know that, don't you?"

Deborah flicked a tea towel at her. "Go and answer the door."

Jan stood there, holding two six-packs of London Pride. Dani smiled at her. "Come on in."

"You were right." Jan gave her a wide grin and whispered, "She's hot."

"Did she like the flowers?"

"Aye, and the rest."

When they reached the kitchen, Deborah had set the table and ladled a wonderfully aromatic curry onto three plates.

Dani put glasses out for her two guests while Jan put three cans of beer on the table. "I don't want to seem ungrateful, but I didn't expect all this. A simple thank you for the flowers would have done."

"I don't think thank you would have covered it." Deborah gave Jan a quick smile. "The flowers are lovely, but the bonus delivery was delightful."

"I thought you might need some protection. Turns out I was right. Chris made a scene at Camila's office this afternoon."

"Fuck's sake. What did she want?"

"I think she thought Camila would let her stay at her place. Obviously not going to happen and Camila's in Madrid for the rest of the week."

"Good thing we're here then, making sure you're fed and watered."

They all sat at the table, and for a few minutes the only sounds were ones of appreciation muffled through mouthfuls of vegetable curry.

Dani leaned back and patted her stomach. "That was wonderful. Better than any takeaway."

"Yes. While the cat's away, so to speak, I'm going to teach you how to cook."

"Ah, come on, Debs. That's not necessary. I can get anything I want by picking up the phone or walking across to the pub."

"That hardly makes for a healthy lifestyle. One day it will catch up with you."

Dani looked at Jan for support, but she was just watching Debs and grinning like the Cheshire cat.

"Camila's just as bad. When she's not eating at fancy restaurants, she exists on toast and jam. Allison was the cook."

Grasping at the chance to change the subject, Dani asked, "Did you know Allison well?"

"We weren't particularly close, meeting up at other friends' parties a few times a year. Allison was very easygoing, definitely the more dynamic of the two. She was fun to have around, telling amusing stories about the people she met in her job, not naming anyone, of course. I never really got a handle on Camila. She seemed content to sit back and let her partner do the talking. Even now, she'll just watch and rarely join in the conversation."

"If she's that boring as a guest, why did you keep inviting her after Allison was gone?"

"We felt sorry for her. Chris said we should try to get her to come out of her shell. I guess Chris took that a bit further than the occasional dinner party."

Jan reached out and put a hand on Deborah's arm. "She's an idiot."

Deborah smiled at her. "Agreed. But Dani, what do you two talk about? You couldn't be more different from Camila."

Dani took a sip of her beer and set the can back on the table before answering. "Um, so far we've covered all the Russian authors and agreed that *Anna Karenina* was a better read than *War and Peace*. Tolstoy really could have done with a good editor for that one. I was surprised to learn that she prefers the Brontë sisters over Jane Austen."

Jan made a choking noise and looked like she was having difficulty swallowing.

"We've agreed not to talk about football. I mean, really, I don't know how she can support Chelsea…."

This time, Jan failed to hold it in and started to laugh uncontrollably. Deborah glared at Dani. "It was a serious question."

"I know. Sorry, I couldn't resist. Anyway, we just talk. Maybe being different helps. And even when we don't talk, it doesn't feel uncomfortable. I lose myself in drawing and she communes with her spreadsheets."

"Sounds perfect." Jan raised her glass to her. "She doesn't really support Chelsea, though, does she?"

"We haven't actually discussed it. Something we do have in common, neither of us follows sport of any kind. If she did, I would think she would be a cricket fan."

Deborah nodded. "Yes, I can see that. I guess my idea of matchmaking was bound to fail. She wasn't going to be interested in a rugby-obsessed PE teacher."

"You don't mean in-your-face Sandy?"

"Yeah. My mistake. I invited her to the dinner party we had on Chris's birthday, her actual birthday, not the barbeque." Deborah caught the look of disgust on Dani's face. "I thought it was worth a try. I knew Chris was still interested in Camila. After that party, Chris told me Camila had met someone through work. I was relieved and it seemed Chris had encouraged her to go for it. So I thought maybe she was finally over that particular obsession. How wrong could I be?"

"Hey, don't worry about it. People at work are used to seeing me come in on Monday mornings with a black eye or two." She stood and collected the plates. "Why don't I clean this lot? Jan, you know where everything is. Put a record on and you two put your feet up."

A few minutes later the sound of Fleetwood Mac's "Monday Morning" filtered through the open doorway. Dani grinned. This evening was turning out to be better than she'd expected. The only thing missing was the person she would have liked to share it with.

†

Madrid was one of her favourite European cities, but Camila wasn't enjoying it as much as on previous visits. Her hosts were charming but they couldn't be rushed into making business decisions and she couldn't let her frustration show.

She was happy to return to her room for the post-lunch siesta. Taking a nap wasn't on her mind, but spending a few hours with the book Carl had secreted in her case was. The note he'd placed as a bookmark in the middle of chapter ten, said he hoped she would find this useful.

"A bit too academic for my taste, but some exquisite descriptions and anecdotes make up for that."

The author, Lillian Faderman, was indeed a professor who had written several award-winning books. Looking at the image of the two women on the front and the title, *Odd Girls and Twilight Lovers*, Camila wondered what had made Carl buy this book in the first place. As she delved into the portions of text he had helpfully highlighted, she realised he viewed it as a training manual. It certainly did clarify the terminology she had been struggling with and explained the roles for the kind of relationship Dani was clearly hoping to have with her.

Camila had never thought it necessary to give her sexuality a label and she didn't think she needed one now. Could she really be comfortable with the description of herself as a "femme top" to Dani's "butch bottom"?

The memory of Dani's naked body on the bed twitching with anticipation as she gripped the cane, wondering if she could make that first stroke—Camila replayed that scene in her mind. The sound of the cane as it moved through the air, and the angry-looking stripe it left on Dani's skin were vividly etched in her senses. Her hand moved down her body. The book fell to the floor as she touched herself, the wave of arousal catching her unawares.

As each stroke landed, her fingers delved deeper. "Oh, God, Dani!" Her lover's name tore out of her throat as she came. Never, in any of the times she masturbated, had she experienced such intensity. Only as she withdrew her fingers, did she wonder if anyone was staying in the room next door, and if she might have disturbed their peaceful slumber.

Glancing at her watch, she realised she only had time for a quick shower and change of clothes before her next meeting. She picked the book off the floor and shoved it into the closet. "Damn you, Carl." But she smiled as she walked out of the room ten minutes later, whispering, "And, damn you, Dani, but you are in so much trouble when I get back."

Chapter Twenty-two

The drafted VidScreen brochure was ready by Tuesday afternoon, and when Dani called to make an appointment, Niki said she was happy to stop by MBE to look at it the following morning on her way to her office.

Dani arrived in time to make good on her promise to supply coffee and bacon butties.

"That smells heavenly," Niki exclaimed when she came into the studio. "I don't know what your brochure design looks like, but I'm sure I'll love it."

"So breakfast or brochure first?"

"Brochure. I don't want to put sticky fingers all over your artwork."

"Okay." Dani led the way across to her drawing table, where she had the mock-up board on display.

Niki took a few minutes to look at each section. Dani had used some "lorem ipsum" wording as Penny was still working on the copy that would be used in the final version.

"Wow. I love the colours. We can, of course, provide the product images."

"Yes, that's not a problem. If you're happy with the overall layout, we'll work it up on the computer and add your pics. Once our copywriter's got the wording ready, I'll fax it over to you."

"Wonderful. I'm impressed. But I had heard good things about your work."

"Thanks. Shall we hit the food, before it gets cold?"

They soon finished the sandwiches. Niki sighed with contentment. "Those are great. I'll have to stop in here more often."

"Do you want another coffee?"

"No, thanks. I'll need to head off." She stood and picked up her briefcase. "By the way, Suzanna and I are having a dinner party next week. Would you and Camila be able to join us?"

"Are you sure? You've seen what happens when I'm around other people."

"It shouldn't be a problem this time. It's just us and another couple. One is a systems analyst for a bank, so she and Camila might have some rapport, and her partner's a police officer."

"Oh dear. I'm on non-speaking terms with a number of WPCs."

"They're not all bad. She's been a good friend for years. I'll tell her to leave the handcuffs at home."

Dani grinned. "Damn. There goes another of my fantasies."

"Hey, behave. You don't want to get on the wrong side of Camila." She caught Dani's mischievous look. "Okay. Forget I said that. Anyway, it's next Friday, eight o'clock."

"Right. I'll check with Camila when she gets back from Madrid. And thanks."

"For what?"

"For not writing me off as a nutter."

Niki shrugged. "You're a nice one, anyway."

The phone on Dani's desk rang, an outside line. "I better get that. Can you find your way out?"

"Sure. And thanks again for breakfast."

Dani waited until she'd closed the door before picking up the call.

†

Camila paced her room, willing the phone to ring. She had placed the call ten minutes earlier and the receptionist said she would pass the message on. It was only eight o'clock, but she knew someone would be there.

Another five minutes passed and Camila started to panic. This wasn't like her. When the phone finally rang, she pounced on it.

"Eric. Thanks for calling back." She hoped her voice didn't sound overwrought.

"Fine. What's the problem?"

"They're not taking me seriously. I haven't experienced it with the Spanish before, but their new CEO, this Sergio Mendez, seems to take offence at discussing business with a woman. I wouldn't normally ask, but could you or Carl come over? I know it's short notice—"

"Okay. Leave it with me. I'll make the arrangements and let you know our ETA."

He rang off before she could thank him. Fifteen minutes later the call came through. This time it was Carl to let her know Eric was on his way to the airport and expected to be with her early afternoon. Her siesta time would be given over to bringing him up to speed…relief of a different kind.

"How's the reading going?"

Camila gulped. "It's…um…interesting."

249

Carl laughed. "I'll bet. I hope Dani benefits from your research."

"I've no doubt she will."

"Good. Oh, and don't let Eric drag you into any clubs."

"This is business, Carl."

"Of course it is. But he might be thinking of expanding your education further."

"I'm happy to stick with book-related research."

"Excellent. I don't want you two getting into trouble with any sexy señors or señoritas over there."

"Don't worry. I'll keep him on the straight and narrow."

"Somehow I don't find that very reassuring. Anyway, good luck with your meetings."

With her worries about the outcome of the negotiations eased, Camila gathered her notes together and ventured out of the room to enjoy breakfast sitting in the sun.

†

Eric met her in the lobby of the hotel. He had already checked in and was counting on her to find a suitable venue for lunch.

Camila led him down a narrow alleyway. "It doesn't look like much from the outside, but the food is excellent," she reassured him.

Once they were settled at their table with a bottle of Rioja from the Tempranillo region and had placed their orders for six tapas dishes, Eric moved into business mode.

"So tell me about this Mendez character."

"What's to say? He's a misogynist pig. As soon as I told him my partner would be here for this afternoon's meeting, he lightened up. And started talking about fashionable dress shops in the city that I might like to visit

250

while I'm here. I think he expects you to take over completely while the little woman, *moi*, goes shopping. He even recommended his wife's hairdresser to me."

"Okay. I think it's best if we play along."

"I am not going shopping, or having my hair done."

Eric held his hands in the air in mock surrender. "No, no, I didn't mean that. Do you think you could pretend we're a couple? Let him think we're more than business partners."

Camila smiled. "Yes, I think I could do that." She sipped her wine. "Especially after a few glasses of this."

"You're a cheap date. Carl would have held out for champagne."

"Maybe later. Once they've signed on the dotted line."

Eric held up his glass to toast her. "I like your thinking."

†

Dani worked through the lunch period, sustained by the bacon sandwich and several more cups of coffee after Niki left. Penny came in with the VidScreen copy during the morning, and after tweaking it slightly, Dani asked Amanda to fax it through.

By midafternoon she'd had enough but it was too early to go home. She was thinking of Camila when her phone rang and she snatched at it eagerly. Then slumped back in her chair when she heard who it was.

"Hi, Carl."

"So the cats are away, do you want to play?"

"What do you mean?"

"Eric's hopped over to Madrid to help Camila out with her research, I mean, business. We could find out if Lisa's free. If not, there's always Freddie's."

Dani felt a fluttering in her stomach. "I don't know." She had been to Freddie's once before but didn't feel comfortable in the mixed venue. Too much testosterone in the air.

"Come on. You don't want to be moping around at home all evening. They won't be back until Friday."

"I can't. I've got plans for tonight."

"So change them."

She decided the ache in her gut was from having skipped lunch. Carl would die laughing if she told him Debs was giving her a cooking lesson. Either that or he would think it was a euphemism for some weird sex act he'd not heard of.

"Sorry, mate. I'm just not up for it right now."

"Okay. It was worth a try. Stay safe."

"You too."

She placed the receiver carefully back on its cradle. *Stay safe* had been their watchword for so many years. She wondered if he would call Lisa or go to the other club. Camila hadn't called from Madrid. She must be experiencing problems if Eric had gone there on short notice. Dani put her head in her hands. She would give anything just to hear Camila's voice right now.

†

"They're really making us work for this, aren't they?" Camila leaned into Eric to whisper in his ear.

He turned to her with a sickly-sweet smile plastered on his face and said loudly, "Just another hour, sweetheart, then we can retire for the night."

Sergio clapped his hands together. "*Bello!* We leave now. *Hasta mañana, amigos.*"

252

After a brief haggle about who would pay the bill, which Eric won, Sergio and his wife left the restaurant, and Camila breathed out, moving her chair slightly to give Eric his space back.

"Well that was hard work. I'm not sure you're paying me enough for this."

Eric laughed and poured the rest of the wine in the bottle into their glasses. "So, do you think they bought it?"

"Sergio, yes. His missus, I'm not so sure. You looked like you were going to throw up when she said we would have beautiful children."

"Yes, unfortunately, my rudimentary understanding of Spanish caught that."

"What could be worse? Actually being married to me, or the idea of having children?" With the change in their relationship over the last few days, Camila had no qualms now about teasing her boss.

"Oh, marriage to you, definitely." He grinned. "Carl and I have talked about adopting. But adoption agencies won't even look at us as prospective parents."

"Well you've had me fooled all this time. I've always thought that was your wife in the photo you keep on your desk."

"My sister. And, yes, that helps to promote a normal family image for clients."

"You actually have a sister."

"I guess I deserved that." Eric gave her a wry smile. "Yes, she's real. I don't see her often. She married an investment banker and lives in New York."

They finished their wine. Eric paid the bill with his credit card but left a generous cash tip on the table for their waiter. Camila had caught him watching the young man whenever he approached and particularly when he walked away. She refrained from commenting.

The evening air was cool enough to make an evening stroll a pleasurable experience. Eric took her arm to guide her down the street.

"You can drop the act now."

"I know. But someone around here probably knows Sergio or some of his crew."

They turned left into a narrow passageway.

"This isn't the way to the hotel."

"No. It's part of my evil plan to lead you astray."

"Really, I don't think I can drink anything else."

"Trust me. You'll enjoy this. I know Carl gave you a book, but it wouldn't hurt to have some hands-on research."

†

Camila's eyes adjusted slowly to the dim lighting in the cellar. She was aware of Eric's quickened breathing next to her. The doorman hadn't hesitated to let them in; Camila suspected Eric had slipped money into his hand.

Eric guided her to a bench by the wall. The combined smells of leather and sweating bodies permeated the air. She sat next to him and took in the room's décor. At first glance it could have passed for a school gymnasium combined with a hospital birthing room. The sight of the leather-covered vaulting box reminded her of the PE classes she'd tried hard to avoid at school. The pull-up bars in the gym hadn't had a naked man dangling from them though, his toes just touching the ground, his wrists firmly attached to the rings at either end of the pole. He was being whipped by another man dressed in leather from head to toe, including a face mask that wouldn't have looked out of place in a horror film. Another man was laughing as he attached nipple clamps onto his partner. Two others were in a corner trying out various whips and flails. One of them swished a cane, and Camila knew she had to get out of there before she started hyperventilating.

She touched Eric's arm. "I don't think I can stay."

He nodded and led her out again.

†

"I'm sorry. I just felt weird watching. Like some kind of pervy voyeur."

"No, I'm sorry. I should have warned you. I did think it was a mixed venue, but maybe they have separate ladies' nights."

Camila took a sip of her brandy and gazed at the passers-by on the street. The city was just starting to come alive with late diners and buskers crowding the outdoor cafés.

"Does Dani like being restrained?"

"Yes." Eric smiled at her. "Believe it or not, it enhances the whole experience. Complete submission. And it's a rush for the dominant partner too. The absolute trust you're given. You need a safe word that she can use if she wants you to stop, though."

Another sip of the brandy sent liquid fire straight to her belly. Camila saw Dani handcuffed to the bedposts, stretched out, naked...waiting. She turned to Eric, who was focused on her through the haze of smoke from his cigarette. "A safe word, huh?"

He nodded and tried to wave some of the smoke in another direction.

"I can do this."

"I know you can."

The warmth of the brandy spreading throughout her torso matched the heat now coursing through her pelvis, melting her core and with the imminent danger of a rush of molten lava spilling out between her thighs.

"I think I need to go back to my room now."

The smirk on his face told her that he was only too aware of the images running riot through her thoughts.

†

"Honestly, Dani, it's not rocket science. Have you never beaten an egg before?"

"I've never wanted to. It's not done anything to harm me."

"Now you're just being silly."

"Are you sure you wouldn't rather go to the pub?"

Deborah put her hands on her hips and glared at her. "You're not leaving this house until you've succeeded in making an omelette."

"Could be here for some time."

It really wasn't that hard. Sitting back in her chair with a stomach full of the cheese and mushroom omelette she'd managed to produce with Deborah's tuition, Dani felt a sense of accomplishment.

"Shame Jan had to miss out on this fine meal."

"I think she said something like she would rather starve than eat something you cooked."

"The ungrateful little toerag. After all I've done for her." Dani's smile took the sting out of her words.

"From what she's told me, you've done a lot for her." Deborah's voice was serious.

Dani fiddled with the fork on her plate. "I do what I can. Someone gave me a chance when I arrived in London, naïve, clueless, homeless. She's a good kid."

"I hope you don't mind. I put her in touch with a courier company in Kingston. She has an interview on Monday."

"That's great. Tell her to let me know if she needs a written reference."

Deborah smiled at her. "Who would have guessed you're such a big softie? What's with all the leather gear? Some kind of armour?"

"You could say that." Dani hadn't thought of it that way before, but in a way she could see it made sense.

Jan returned after they had finished washing the dishes, with the reek of fish and chips clinging to her. Dani declined the offer of coffee as the looks exchanged by the other two women made her feel like the proverbial gooseberry.

†

When she got home, she pinned the recipe Deborah had printed out onto her refrigerator door with an MBE fridge magnet. Sometime before Camila's return, she would go grocery shopping to acquire the ingredients so she could show off her new skill.

Deborah had also given her a list of the kitchen equipment she needed. Dani had just located a heavy-duty skillet in the back of one of the cupboards when the phone rang. She banged her head in her haste to reach it. She quickly forgot the pain as Camila's voice reached her.

"How's it going? Carl told me Eric had to fly out today."

"Fine, now. The client just needed to know there was a man in charge."

"Oh, that sucks. This is 1993, not the middle ages."

"Different culture, I guess. Anyway, I think we're on track now. So what have you been doing? I tried to ring earlier before we went for dinner."

"I was with Debs. She's teaching me to cook."

"Debs? Deborah Grant?"

"Yes. Don't sound so surprised. We get on really well."

"Not too well, I hope."

"No, not like that. And she's got Jan to keep her company."

"Who's Jan? Another girlfriend already?"

"Jan does odd jobs for me. So I'm paying her to give Debs some protection in case Chris causes any trouble."

"Is that really necessary?"

"I don't know. But I kind of feel responsible for what happened."

"Why? Chris attacked you."

"I just want her to be safe. Chris seems a bit unstable, especially as she turned up at Redmond's to confront you. Anyway, I shouldn't think I will be paying for Jan's services much longer. She and Debs seem to be attracted to each other."

There was silence at the other end of the line, and Dani wondered if Camila was upset. The next question caught her completely unawares.

"Do you have any handcuffs?" Camila's voice had taken on a huskier tone.

"Um, yes."

"Good. I'll see you on Friday. Oh, and our safe word is T-shirts." The line went dead, leaving Dani wondering if she could possibly have misheard.

She put the receiver down and licked her lips. Kitchen implements forgotten, she ran upstairs to locate the cuffs. They were tucked away in the back of her bedroom closet.

She took them out and walked across the hall to the guest room and laid them down carefully next to the box holding the canes. The next two days and nights were going to be the longest of her life.

Chapter Twenty-three

Thursday evening, Dani persuaded Penny to accompany her to a bar. It was nine o'clock and early for the serious punters, so Penny had agreed, but only because Astrid was working a late shift and wouldn't be home until midnight.

After Penny called it a night and went home at eleven thirty, Dani carried on to the club. She really only wanted to stave off the longing she was feeling for Camila. However, a few minutes in the room and she knew she didn't want to be there. She was moving towards the door when she heard her name, and turned to find Lisa right behind her.

"Hey, stranger. I hear you're hooked up now."

Dani swallowed, "Yeah, well…."

"I thought we had something."

"We did, I guess."

"So, where is she, this wonder woman?"

"Working."

Lisa ran an exploratory hand over Dani's butt and squeezed a cheek. "I could give you what you need."

Dani's mouth had gone dry. She shifted uncomfortably. "I know you could. But it's not what I want."

Lisa backed off and shook her head sadly. "That's too bad. When you're back in circulation, give me a ring."

Dani stumbled out of the door needing to walk to clear her head. It was a beautiful night, and the sight of Hammersmith Bridge when she reached it cheered her. Each step she took on the Upper Mall felt lighter. The pubs were all closed; not even a dog walker in sight. She had just opened her front door when the phone rang.

"Dani!" Camila's tone sounded irritated.

"Hey, great to hear from you. It's late, though."

"I know. I've tried calling a few times. Where have you been?"

"Walking along the river."

"And?"

"Went for a drink after work." Dani leaned against the wall and closed her eyes.

"It's late for a drink."

This was it. She wanted this woman so badly. But she couldn't lie to her. Their relationship had to be built on trust. Her next words could either make or break the foundation of their fledgling partnership.

She took a deep breath. "If you really want to know, I went to a club." Silence. "And I saw Lisa." The silence on the other end seemed to deepen. "But, you know what, I blew her off. Because, Camila, the only touch I want now is yours."

Camila found her voice and asked her, huskily, "Will you be home tomorrow evening?"

"Yes."

"We're wrapping things up here in the morning. I'll see you later, and, Dani…?"

"Yes?"

"You better be ready for me." The line went dead, signalling Camila's complete control once more.

Dani stood in her hallway, holding the phone and feeling weak at the knees. How could Camila do this to her with just a few words? A few weeks earlier she wouldn't have believed she would be feeling this way about one woman. A woman who could turn her insides to jelly with a look and a light touch.

Sleep was out of the question now. She walked through the house to open the doors onto the patio. The river was moving swiftly on the tide's turn. She leaned against the doorjamb and took in several deep breaths. The wait would be long, but she knew now it would be worth it.

†

Camila settled back into her seat on the plane. When the steward asked what she wanted to drink, she told him gin and tonic. "Make it a double."

Eric glanced up from his newspaper. "What's that for? Dutch courage?"

"Of course not. Just relaxing from one of the toughest, and longest, contract negotiations ever. Who does Sergio Mendez think he is, Bill fucking Gates?"

"Well, it's done now." Eric accepted his own drink from the steward, a whisky and a soda. "Anyway, you're avoiding the subject."

"What subject?" Camila knew what he was referring to but studiously continued to mix her drink, making sure it contained more gin than tonic.

"I could tell you what I'm going to do with Carl as soon as I get in the door, if that would help."

"It would not. You're still my bosses."

"So what is worrying you?"

"Who says I'm worried?"

"That." Eric pointed to the now half-empty glass in her hand.

"Oh." Even with the friendship developing between them, Camila hated to show any signs of weakness. She put the glass down on the seat tray. "It's just that, I don't know if I can satisfy Dani. She doesn't really need me. She's got this Lisa woman she can go back to at any time."

Eric shifted in his seat to look at her. "I've known Dani a long time. Paying someone for services rendered isn't the same as being part of a loving relationship." He patted her arm. "I know you've only just taken the first steps, coming out to me and Carl. This is another coming out, a different closet. But you can do it. And, believe me, it is exactly what Dani needs."

For the rest of the trip, Eric immersed himself in reading the paper, while Camila lay back with her eyes closed. The conversation with Dani the night before came back to her, and Dani's words reverberated through her mind: *"...the only touch I want now is yours."*

†

The waiting was almost over. Dani positioned the cuffs on her bedstead, leaving them open. She had checked and rechecked that everything Camila would need was laid out in the guest room. By the time she heard the taxi draw up outside the house, she was in a state of nervous excitement she hadn't experienced since the very first time Lisa had caned her.

Camila didn't make eye contact as she handed Dani her suitcase and jacket. The stern look she did eventually give her brushed aside the momentary worry that Camila wasn't going to carry through on the suggestive promise of the night before.

"Go upstairs and wait for me."

Dani needed no further instruction. She raced up the stairs, placing the case and the jacket in the guest room. In the bedroom, she stripped and lay face down on the bed. Camila came in and without saying anything, snapped the cuffs shut around her wrists.

She heard the shower running and then waited in what felt like the longest ten minutes of her life

Lying as she was, she couldn't see Camila in full view when she heard the unmistakable sound of high heels approaching the bed, but was aware that she was wearing the tight black lace bodice and stockings as before. The cane swished through the air, and Dani trembled in anticipation. Camila stroked it lightly across her buttocks, then placed her hand between her legs; Dani was already dripping wet with desire.

"You want this now, don't you?" asked Camila in a husky voice.

Dani nodded vigorously.

"I can't hear you."

Dani turned her head. "Yes, I want it now."

The first stroke landed with precision across her butt and she chewed on the pillow to stop herself from crying out. With the skill of a practiced dominatrix, Camila paced the strokes to have Dani primed to a high level of anxiety waiting for the next blow. After six she stopped.

Camila reached above her head and released her wrists from the cuffs. Dani heard her moving about and felt something land on the bed beside her. "Put these on and meet me downstairs. Don't keep me waiting."

Dani waited until she heard her going down the stairs. Taking a few deep breaths, relishing the hot, stabbing pain on her backside, she got off the bed and stood slowly. Then she looked to see what Camila wanted her to wear. Another pleasant surprise: a new dildo, somewhat larger than the one she'd used before, a white T-shirt, her leather vest, and a pair of black jeans, a carbon copy of the outfit she had worn to Deborah's party. It took her some time to adjust the strap-on and pack it in the tightly fitting jeans.

She negotiated the trip downstairs with difficulty, each step increasing the pressure of the base of the dildo on her clit. Camila was waiting for her in the living room. Her outfit really did look like it had come from Miss Whiplash's wardrobe, and she carried it off well. Dani couldn't quite believe what she was seeing. This wasn't the woman she'd had lunch with only a few short weeks ago.

"Come here and fuck me," the apparition in lace and silk said.

Dani went to her and held her close. They kissed deeply, and as if in a trance, Dani found herself in another place entirely as she made love to Camila, the hot sensations rippling across her buttocks matched only with the internal fire. The intensity of their orgasms startled them both, and then they started again.

†

From the sounds of the birds outside the window, Dani knew, without looking at the bedside clock, it was the hour just before dawn. Camila's head was on the pillow next to hers and she was snuffling softly, deeply asleep. Dani couldn't recall when they'd finally made it back to the bedroom, but she remembered helping Camila out of the bodice, and the image of kissing each plump breast as it was released from confinement flashed through her memory bank.

265

Dani stepped quietly out of the room, stopping only to grab her shorts and T-shirt from the floor. As she pulled on her shorts, each of the strokes from the night before made themselves known. She breathed out slowly as a rush of joy surged through her.

Downstairs, she opened the patio doors and stood watching the red streaks flaming across the horizon. Turning back inside, she went to her drawing board and slid out the picture Deborah had found the week before: the image of Camila in the throes of ecstasy. She couldn't have imagined that from their first tentative meetings. And now…she opened the pad to a clean page and sucked on the end of a pencil…now she didn't require any imagination at all as she started a new sketch.

†

Camila awoke and stretched lazily as sunlight spread across the bed. A languorous feeling of well-being pervaded every part of her body. Last night, giving pleasure and receiving it, she finally understood the mutuality of their shared experience. When people said, "Life begins at forty", she didn't think they meant something like this. Something she hadn't known she wanted.

The space next to her was empty and cold. Rising up to look around the room, she saw the evidence of their activities was spread around: discarded clothing—her bodice a tangled heap on top of Dani's jeans, the tip of the dildo poking out from the midst of the pile.

Desire swept through her and she gasped at the intensity that gripped her core. "Oh God, Dani! What have you done to me? I need you now!"

†

Unaware of the passing of time, Dani was startled by the feel of an arm snaking around her waist.

"What are you doing? You're not working, are you?"

"Good morning to you too." Dani turned her body so Camila could see the drawing. The full daylight now streaming into the room showed the picture clearly.

"Do I really look like that?"

"Yes, better in person, though." Dani reached around Camila's shoulders to draw her closer. Their kisses became more insistent. Dani gasped when Camila's hands moved down and grasped her buttocks.

"You're hot here," she whispered.

Dani grinned down at her. "I'm hot all over for you."

"Good. Because I want you upstairs, in bed, now."

"You're the boss."

"Yes, I am. And I don't intend to let you forget it."

Taking her hand, Camila led the way up the stairs to the bedroom. With each step, Dani felt a lightness take over her being. Happiness engulfed her as she followed the woman she loved back to their bed.

Epilogue

Six months later
Christmas Day, 1993

The aroma of roasting turkey filled the house. Standing back to survey the large fir tree blocking the view of the street in the living room's window, Dani wondered how this had happened. Hosting a Christmas Day lunch for the disparate group of people she called friends and family. The only person missing was the one she most wanted to spend the day with...Camila.

Although Eric had explained it to her that the week spent in Brittany over Christmas and New Year with her parents was the only holiday time Camila took, Dani wished it could have been different this year.

The only positive side to Camila's departure to France two days ago was the delicious sensation of pain rippling across her backside with every move she made. She could have worn a looser pair of jeans, but she craved the reminder of her lover's touch.

Before she could lose herself further in that memory of their last night together, the doorbell rang. She was expecting the visitors, so she had left the door unlocked and she moved into the hallway to greet them.

Jan marched past carrying a large box. "The vegetables have arrived," she announced.

"Oh, Carl and Eric are here, then."

"I heard that." Carl put down the box he was carrying and pulled her into a hug. Eric was following closely behind with another box.

"What's all this?" Dani asked when Carl released her.

"A few more bottles of champagne, red and white wine, plus beer for the plebs."

Dani didn't rise to the insult that she knew was aimed at her and Jan. "You didn't need to bring anything. I've got enough here to stock a small bar. You'll all have to walk home if you get through that lot."

"We came in one car. Debs isn't drinking."

They had reached the kitchen and put their boxes down. Deborah was bringing up the rear and placed two plastic bags on the counter. "What?" She looked around at three grinning faces and a stunned one. "Have I missed a joke?"

"Looks like the joke's on me," Dani said. "When were you going to give me the news?"

"Now obviously. Although I thought we would be sitting down with a drink first." She gave Carl a mock angry glare. "Okay, big mouth. Open the champagne."

He reached into a box.

"Not one of those unless you want to spray it around the room. I'm sure Dani has a bottle or two in the fridge." Debs glanced between Carl and Eric. "Did I pick the wrong one? I thought he had brains."

"Only the geeky kind." Eric opened the fridge and removed a bottle. Jan had already set out five glasses.

"So when is it due?"

"July."

After they had raised their glasses, four filled with the bubbly drink and one with orange juice, toasting the parents-to-be, Deborah shooed them out of the kitchen so she could make a start on preparing the veg.

"Nice tree," Eric commented, taking a seat on the sofa.

"I've never had a tree before. Brian chose it, and my nieces helped with the decoration."

"Are they coming today?"

"No. They're having their own family Christmas. He's hoping for a complete reconciliation, and being there for important occasions like birthdays and holidays is a step forward. June seems more open to the idea. But it's taken her some time to get over the revelations about her boyfriend."

"Brian couldn't get him put away?"

"Apart from being a two-timing creep, he wasn't committing a crime. If he'd married June, then they could have got him on bigamy." Dani stood by the fireplace and picked up a card that had fallen over on the mantelpiece. She looked over at Carl and Jan. "Do you guys think you're up for this parenting lark?"

They both beamed back at her. "Of course. And you'll be a super godparent." Carl sat next to Eric, knees touching.

Jan walked over to the record collection and started sifting through albums. "When are you going to start buying CDs? Some of these are scratched to hell."

"Yeah, Dani. Time you caught up with technology. Compact discs are the future. You don't even have a TV."

Dani gave Carl a withering look. "This is my house and I don't need to clutter it up with your newfangled gadgets."

"Televisions are hardly new."

Before they could continue bickering, Jan found the record she wanted and put it on the turntable. It was one of Dani's newer albums. She left them listening to k.d. lang's mellow voice and went into the kitchen to see how Deborah was getting on. She was sitting at the table peeling sprouts.

"You know no one will eat those. Why don't we just have peas?"

"It's not a Christmas dinner without brussels sprouts." Debs carried on calmly, deftly removing the outer leaves before cutting a cross in the base of each tiny cabbage-looking vegetable.

Dani bent down to look in the oven. "Does it need basting again? I put it in at eight like you said."

"In a bit. I'll add the bacon strips on top then."

"Talking of turkey basting, when did you actually find out you're pregnant?"

"Two weeks ago. But I didn't tell the others until today."

When Debs told her she wanted to have a child before her fortieth birthday, Dani hadn't reacted too favourably.

"What do you want kids for? Get a dog if you want unconditional love," she'd said.

"That's what Chris said when I first mentioned it a few years ago. I'm glad I waited. Jan's thrilled with the idea. You'll be a godparent, won't you?"

Dani had laughed at the idea and asked her what the opposite was, a demonparent, perhaps? She had jokingly suggested Eric or Carl as possible sperm donors, thinking they would never agree. How wrong she had been. This arrangement fulfilled their desire to have a child without having to suffer rejection from adoption agencies. After they met Deborah and found out they lived in the same neighbourhood, the three of them immediately started making plans for shared childcare and setting up an education trust fund.

Deborah was an attractive woman but now, only two months into her pregnancy, she was positively glowing. "I'm glad it's worked out with you and Jan. Although I honestly wasn't matchmaking when I sent her to you. I just thought you might need a bodyguard for a while."

"She guards my body very well, thank you." Debs finished with the last sprout and grinned up at her. "Chris did come to my workplace once. She was waiting outside when I left for the day. Jan turned up on her bike before things could get nasty, though. That was the last I saw of her."

"She tried that with Camila, confronting her at the Redmond building. Waste of time. From what Camila told me, I almost felt sorry for Chris."

"Well, I don't. And you don't need to feel guilty for what happened either. I should have kicked her out long before. Now, go and do something useful. See if the others need refills."

Dani took the hint and grabbed the open bottle that had been left on the table. When she returned to the living room, Eric had disappeared and Jan was patiently explaining the offside rule to Carl. She had never known him to show an interest in football, but he didn't even look up when she topped up their glasses.

She wandered into the hall, feeling like a guest in her own home. Eric was putting the receiver back in its cradle and looked up guiltily.

"I didn't hear the phone ring."

"No. I just needed to make a quick call. Business doesn't stop for Christmas. There's a loo here, isn't there?"

Dani pointed to the door next to the coat rack. After Eric had gone in, she returned to the living room. She located her champagne glass where she'd left it on the mantelpiece and took a quick slug. Two framed colour prints now adorned the mantel—one of Brian with Lucy and Holly, and a photo of herself with Camila taken on a weekend away in Devon. They both looked windblown and happy by the seaside. Glancing around the room, decorated for Christmas with her friends, she thought it was looking more like a home, rather than an extension of her studio at work. She just hoped filling the house with food and drink and laughter on this day would keep her from thinking too much about what it would be like to share it with Camila.

"What's not to like about football?" Jan was saying. "I thought you would be all over it. Fit young men running about in shorts."

Carl shrugged. "Nah. Doesn't do anything for me. Now American football, that's another matter."

"Oh, come on. That's not a proper game. They're all padded up and hardly move three feet before play's stopped."

"Yeah, but those tight-fitting uniforms, when they bend over...."

"I bet you like baseball too."

"I've never really got into that. Cricket's okay, though."

"Ugh...like watching paint dry. Right, Dani?"

"Don't drag me into this. I'll leave you two jocks to it."

Dani walked out and crossed the hall to the dining room. She'd set the table for five earlier but she hadn't put the Christmas crackers out. Eric was doing just that when she went in.

"Thanks. I was going to see to those."

"No problem. All done."

Dani narrowed her eyes. "Why are there now eight place settings?"

"Oh, well that's what Debs told me to set up for." Eric straightened the last cracker on the placemat at the far end of the table.

"Is there something you're not telling me? Who are the mystery guests? Penny and Astrid are off skiing somewhere in the Alps, Niki and her partner are with her parents. I asked Gordon as he's on his own now, but he's gone to Barcelona with his guitar in search of his lost youth. I would have invited Lisa, but Carl told me that was a bad idea. So, come on, give."

He opened his mouth and closed it again. The doorbell rang and he blew out a relieved breath. "You better answer that."

Dani gave him her best I'll-kill-you-later glare and stalked out of the room. She yanked open the front door and nearly fell backwards into the hall. Camila was standing there with the two people Dani would least have expected to see on her doorstep, Mr and Mrs Callaghan.

"Merry Christmas, sweetheart. May we come in?"

"Yes…I…." Dani was saved from saying anything more as Eric appeared and greeted Camila's parents effusively.

With the flurried exchange of "Merry Christmas" and "how lovely to see you again", and the removal of coats and scarves, Dani managed to pull Camila into the dining room.

"I thought you were in France."

"Change of plan this year. They didn't take much persuading. Mum loves the bright lights of Oxford Street and will be first in line for the Boxing Day sales tomorrow while Dad indulges himself with a few pints and binge-watching football."

"Why didn't you tell me?"

"I need to keep you on your toes. I don't want you taking me for granted."

"I would never do that."

"No?" Camila reached around and placed both hands on Dani's buttocks, pulling her close. "Would you have waited two weeks for more of this?"

"I would." Dani gasped as Camila increased the pressure.

"Well, I wouldn't. Couldn't. So you're stuck with me."

Their lips met and Dani savoured the taste of her lover's mouth as their tongues danced around each other, her senses inflamed by the movements of Camila's hands, fire spreading through her belly to her groin.

Camila broke their kiss and whispered, "Do you think they'll miss us if we go upstairs?"

"No. They're probably already immersed in baby talk. And dinner won't be ready for another hour."

The door opened before they could move apart.

"This is the dining room," Carl announced, following Mrs Callaghan into the room. "Ah, there you are, Dani. Hope you don't mind. Just giving Margaret the tour. Has your maid been in this week?"

"Um, yes. Thorough job in preparation for today." Dani caught his wink and managed not to laugh. She felt a tremor running through Camila's body.

"It's a lovely house, Dani. From what I've seen so far."

"Thank you, um, Margaret. Carry on, Carl. I'm going to see if Debs needs a hand with the turkey."

She left the room with Camila close on her heels. Deborah wasn't in the kitchen, so Dani turned to embrace her lover again.

"I would have preferred the bedroom. But this will do. I have fond memories of doing it here."

"I don't think it's going to happen now. Too many people around. Anyway, how did you get your parents to come here? I thought they didn't approve of me."

275

"I told them I wasn't hiding anymore. I love you and want to spend my holiday with you."

Tears prickled behind Dani's eyes. This was the first time Camila had uttered the *L* word. "I love you too." The words felt right, and seeing the smile taking over Camila's features, she knew that this time it meant something. All it took was a change in perspective.

About the Author

Jen Silver

Jen lives in West Yorkshire with her long-term partner, whom she married in December 2014. Reading, writing, golf, archery, and taking part in archaeological digs all form part of Jen's everyday life. Her novels, published by Affinity Rainbow Publications, include the Starling Hill Trilogy: *Starting Over*, *Arc Over Time*, and *Carved in Stone*. *The Circle Dance*, *Christmas at Winterbourne,* and *Running From Love* are standalone books.

For the characters in Jen's stories, life definitely begins at forty, and older, as they continue to discover and enjoy their appetites for adventure and romance.

Other Affinity Rainbow Books

<u>Death is Only the Beginning</u> by JM Dragon
What would you do if you were in a fatal accident with a stranger and ended up in heaven with them? Only to find out it wasn't an accident, it was murder. Follow the ghostly adventures of these two acrimonious strangers, who help two women find love and find closure for their predicament.

<u>Shotgun Rider</u> by Ali Spooner
Kim and Laney, sweethearts for fifty years go on a road trip to their childhood home state of North Carolina. They follow trails they made as younger women, and relive cherished memories of their lives together. A haunting story, of romance, and lifelong friendship.

<u>For the Love of a Woman</u> by S. Anne Gardner
In a world where oil is supreme, passion rules reason and there is always the threat of civil war. In this jungle of power Raisa Andieta resides as one of its masters. Her only desire is to rule it alone. Carolyn Stenbeck is just trying to keep her marriage together. Her only desire is to be able to escape and never look back. When Raisa and Carolyn meet, it is like fuel

and fire...A storm is brewing. Civil War is in the air, and passion like the coming storm begins to erupt.

<u>Dress Blues</u> by Dannie Marsden
Lucinda (Luce) Velazquez had it all; a job she loved, a woman she loved, and a bright future ahead of her. In a flash of light surrounded by the sound of twisting metal, her life changes dramatically. Her inability to share her deepest thoughts and fears threaten all that she holds dear. Can she allow her lover and others in or will she lose it all?

<u>The Bee Charmer</u> by Ali Spooner
After the death of her father, Nat St. Croix needs to decide on which direction her life should take. Does she continue her life alone, as a trapper and trader, or does she start over and try to fit into a town surrounded by strangers? Will the call of the wild and all that is familiar or, will the call of love capture Nat's heart?

<u>We're Not in Kansas Anymore</u> by Annette Mori
Silver Lining, a successful lesbian romance writer, is just starting to come out of the dark tunnel after her wife's untimely death when she has the crazy idea to sponsor a contest. Silver has more than an unwelcome stalker to overcome as she struggles with the guilt over her attraction to Jasmine and the lingering memories of her dead wife. In this prequel to, The Review, learn where it all started.

<u>The Organization</u> by Annette Mori & Erin O'Reilly
The feisty, fiery women from Asset Management are back for another heart-stopping adventure! This time, their sites are set on a new mob boss Leonid Petrov. Val is tagged as the go-to member to infiltrate Leonid's inner circle. Tasked with keeping Leonid's impossible new wife, Gina, safe, Val

encounters more problems than solutions. Will wild card Gina be Val's Achilles heel and lead to her demise, or will it fill her with a strength she didn't know she had?

Jeager's by JM Dragon
When your world turns upside down and all your safe secure yearnings are thrown to the wind what happens? What would you do? University lecturer Dr.. Kirsten Van De Pelt shortly due to retire early from her academic life is about to find the answers to those questions when Corley Anders, a TV star, enters her life. Will Kirsten take an opportunity of a lifetime or simply settle for the safety net that has been her life.

Running From Love by Jen Silver
Sam Wade returns home from a business trip to discover her wife, Beth left her for another woman, Lydia. To take her mind off the breakup, Sam accepts an assignment to learn to play golf at the newly opened Temperley Cliffs Golf Resort in Cornwall not knowing that is where Beth and Lydia plan to go too. There is more than one way to run from love; from never having to make a commitment and say those magical three words, "I love you." Find out what happens when they find themselves together—sport, betrayal, jealousy, and love form an unforgettable fusion of emotions.

Specter of Fear by Erin O'Reilly
Anne and Bailey are in love and planning a future together. Only the letters that Anne keeps getting are filling her with fear and doubt. Could the love they share really be a sham? Or is there something more behind the letters? Is the sender of the letters after Anne, Bailey or both women? Find out in this suspenseful tale…or is it a real story?

Back in the Saddle by Ali Spooner

The crew from <u>*Cowgirl Up*</u> are back in the saddle for more fun. In their new adventure, Coal, Stormy, and Gene get the chance to be part of something they have always dreamed of—a cattle drive. Even without the gang being at the MC2 ranch, there's still plenty of action going on with a new addition, Doc Bo, brings a hint of jealousy and maybe the start of a new romance. Pull on your boots and hats, and hold on tight as you ride along with the crew of the MC2.

<u>Faith in Rayne</u> by Dannie Marsden
Welcome back Rayne and Lisbet from <u>*Rayne Comes to Town*</u> and <u>*Rayne's New Beginnings*</u>. Their life has flourished since meeting. Rayne ventures to Telluride, Colorado, where both adventure and trouble land at her feet. Lisbet heads to Telluride to reunite with Rayne, her head filled with dreams of their future only to have her dreams come crashing down. Can she find the strength to fight for Rayne, allowing her faith to guide them back to their love?

E-Books, Print, Free e-books

Visit our website for more publications available online.

www.affinityebooks.com

Published by Affinity E-Book Press NZ LTD
Canterbury, New Zealand

Registered Company 2517228

Printed in Great Britain
by Amazon